This novel is a work of fiction. Any resemblance to actual persons, living or dead, is coincidental.

Published by Olivia Gardner
Printed by CreateSpace, An Amazon.com Company

ISBN-13: 978-1515229131
ISBN-10: 1515229130

The Library of Souls

A novel by Olivia Gardner

CONTENTS

For Max,

who listened to my stories even

before I knew how to tell them.

ONE
Once upon a time

There once was a wizard.

The words rang through his head as he dragged himself up the last flight of stairs, each breath more ragged than the last.

There once was a wizard who swore to loyally serve the kingdom.

He tripped and fell to his knees on the landing before the great clock face, the last rays of sunset glowing through the opaque glass.

To advise the rulers justly.

Footsteps thundered up the narrow wooden staircase behind him, faster and louder, nearer and nearer.

To protect the innocent.

Trembling, he drew the crumpled paper out of his pocket.

Until he breathed his last.

Pounding, pounding, pounding, the footsteps drew nearer. Pounding, pounding, pounding, the end only a breath away.

But one day, the wizard broke his promise.

Now or never. Now, or all would be lost. He picked himself up, dragged himself towards the opaque glass of the clock face, that glowing beacon, that magical portal.

He slew the queen and tried to take the kingdom for his own.

But how would they know? His children, his wife, how would they know? He stuffed the page in his pocket and tossed the jacket into the corner with a prayer for the one who finds it, a prayer that help would come.

So the king rode out to meet the wizard in battle.

He pushed his weight against the clock face. The clock face creaked and swung out, out of this world and into a new one, into a room with bookshelves far as the eye could see. Golden rivers flowed between the shelves, shimmering in the blinding light from above. Pages formed from the waters and fluttered through the air until they found the books they called home. For some, it was the last page and others the first. The Library of Souls. He staggered inside.

But where the wizard once stood, there remained only shadow and ash.

He slammed the circular door shut, but it was too late. The books began to crumble. A black cloud formed overhead, blocking out the light. Just a moment too late, the gears in the clock face whirred, the door locked, sealed shut until a champion proved worthy to defend the Library against an evil that was already inside. The black cloud sped towards him. He braced himself, closed his eyes. He hadn't even said goodbye.

And the kingdom was covered in darkness.

~ ~ ~

The door opened with a shrill cry from its hinges. A cloud of dust filled Maya's lungs. As a cough escaped her lips, she glanced over her shoulder, back down the length of the empty school library. The long hall was almost perfectly symmetrical. There were twelve tables on the left and twelve tables on the right with sturdy bookshelves dividing them, twelve on the left and twelve on the right, and above them extended tall windows that reached the ceiling high above, twelve on the left and twelve on the right. The warm afternoon sun stretched across the wooden floors like stripes on a tiger. Just behind Maya, the librarian's desk stood abandoned for the night.

No one could have known of the two intruders standing at the threshold of the book stacks.

Which was a good thing since students were not allowed to enter the back room behind the librarian's desk under any circumstances, despite the fact that most of the useful books were housed there. No one knew why the room was off limits, but no one dared question it either. The book stacks were creepy, and the last three people who had tried to sneak into them had been expelled.

The floorboards moaned beneath Maya's feet as she flipped the light switch in the book stacks. The dim flickering lamps revealed a vast expanse of bookshelves placed haphazardly at best. Here, shrouded in shadows and darkness, forgotten tomes gathered dust, and secrets lay in wait. Rumors were born, and truth faded into distant legend. The labyrinth beckoned, calling only the truly bold to enter, to lose themselves in new worlds, to surrender to the sweet scent of musty pages and the stillness of a thousand and one stories bound and silenced until willing ears lent them voice.

"We shouldn't be here." Felix's voice was low and hushed. Indeed, his small, quiet voice did not do justice to his size, which was towering at best and terrifying at worst – terrifying to everyone but Maya. To her, he was simply her "little" brother. A little brother who was already a foot taller than her, despite being a year younger. In his football pads, he looked even bigger. The black jersey barely stretched across his massive frame. Felix pinned his arms over the golden number 88 on his chest and shivered. There was a sacredness to the quiet that condemned all those who dared disturb that hushed anticipation. Every molecule in the room knew: this place was forbidden.

Her hands trembling, Maya skimmed the wrinkled onion-skin page for the thousand and first time. Sometimes, she could swear she still smelled their father's scent on that precious page—charcoal fires on a summer evening, ocean spray at the crack of dawn, dusty books, fresh squeezed lime—everything she missed most wrapped up in one nostalgic whiff from the past. That page was the last trace he had left behind, a crumpled page in the pocket of his coat, a page torn from its proper place. The page spoke of a "Library of Souls" and a "Wizard" and a "guardian of the Library," but Maya had no context to understand those things. Worse yet, she did not know how the tale ended. She stuffed the page back into a pocket hidden inside her red zip-up hoodie, right where she always kept it, right above her heart.

"Maya, I'm going to be late." Felix tugged at his shoulder pads nervously. The game was about to start. But they both knew that they would never have a chance like this again. All the faculty had been asked to attend the season opener, and in her haste, the librarian had left the library unlocked. This was their one chance to enter the book stacks without the risk of discovery.

"It won't take long."

"Isn't there another library, somewhere, we haven't looked through?"

Maya simply shook her head. They had searched them all. Every single library in the county. They had searched them all, and all had been in vain. Hardly a surprise. Their father would not have gotten that page anywhere else. It could only be here, here on the very shelves he used to stock. Felix pressed on, "Even Dad never let us in here while he was the librarian, and this is the same man who let us play with fireworks as kids."

"It's been six months, Felix," she said, more to herself than to him. "I think it's time we got some answers." If it could somehow bring her father back, Maya would go to great lengths to finish that story tucked over her heart. And so, taking a deep breath, Maya plunged into the forbidden book stacks.

There was next to no order in the book stacks. The path turned at odd angles and twisted around itself until they could no longer remember where the door was. The books were just as disorienting. History books lay next to cookbooks, and medical journals lay next to the Greek myths. And the library seemed to go on forever. Maya climbed a shelf and peaked across the vast expanse, but the borders of the library extended like the horizon, always out of reach. Felix brushed cobwebs out of the way and held his breath. The place seemed benign for now, but danger could have been lurking around any corner. Why else would the book stacks be so forbidden? Weaving from shelf to shelf, they passed beneath flickering lights and through shadows, to dead ends and abandoned desks and—

"Maya, is that a bear trap?" Felix skidded to a stop, filled with an appropriate level of alarm. He searched the area for his sister, "Maya?"

Maya had already wandered off in a new direction, towards a round clearing in the bookshelves. At the center of the clearing stood a marble podium in a spotlight of its own, and on top of it sat an old leather-bound volume, full to bursting with yellowed pages. In the marble were inscribed the words, "To the champion."

A draft made Felix's short hair stand on edge. In the pit of his gut, he knew that book was trouble. After all, it was too enticing to come without a price. And goodness only knew who was intended as "the champion." As he saw Maya approach the podium with a reckless and inquisitive glint in her eye, he warned, "We should leave."

But Maya did not hear. Every step she took towards the book reverberated through her core with exhilaration, anticipation, terror, but the book drew her still, like the ebb of the tide, the tug of the current, pulling her, pulling her, pulling her until she saw the words etched into the cover. Her heart leapt, and soon she was running. For six months, she had scoured the collections of every library in Los Angeles for even a mention of the Library of Souls. For six months, she had made a fool of herself, asking anyone who might have a clue, trying to solve the riddle, failing at every turn. For six months, she had searched for something, anything that might help her understand. And now the answer lay before her in this, "The First Book of the Library of Souls."

"Maya, don't—"

Maya picked up the book. As soon as she laid a hand on it, the bookshelves began to shift. They scraped across the wooden floor and closed around the siblings with a thud, encircling them in a paperbound prison. The shelves towered, ten feet tall, immovable fixtures burdened by the weight of the human experience. At the edges of the library, the lights flickered out. A wave of darkness rushed towards them. Books flung themselves at the intruders like birds pecking at a new threat. Maya slammed the book back into place, but to no avail. The bombardment did not let up.

A roar shook the room. Felix and Maya glanced at each other, the blood draining from their faces. The shadow loomed over the bookshelves, great and beastly, claws and teeth in sharp relief, casting the siblings into darkness. The twelve-foot tall Grizzly bellowed once more and smashed a row of bookshelves with a single swipe of his paw. Then, it rushed forward.

Felix shoved his shoulder into the bookshelves like he was pushing through enemy lines on the football field. The bear was already making gains. Maya swept up the First Book of the Library of Souls and sprinted for Felix's breach between the bookshelves just as the bookshelves began to close off the exit again. With a mighty roar, the bear crashed through the shelves on the other side of the clearing. The floor shook. Clouds of dust billowed all around. Gripping the thick, leather-bound book firmly against her chest, Maya had only one thought in her mind. "RUN!"

~ ~ ~

Zizi Harris skipped down the hall with a giddy bounce in her step, a thousand strands of colored yarn flowing behind her as her knitting needles worked the streams into a masterpiece. The sea of gold and black-clad students drifted in exactly the opposite direction Zizi wanted to go, but it proved to be a delight. There were so many things Zizi got to see this way and so many more she wanted to. She had always been homeschooled before, but now—so many new people, so many new experiences. And she was about to go to her first football game ever. But only after she'd read up on the rules, of course. It wouldn't be fun if she did not understand what was happening.

At long last, Zizi broke free from the crowd surging down the hall towards the football stadium and stepped into the empty library. Letting the warm beams of afternoon sun wash over her in the stillness of that long study hall, Zizi breathed in the smell of books and felt that stillness penetrate her being. Crowds could be exciting, classes stimulating, but nothing compared to the serenity of a library.

Her eyes popped open again and, with renewed vigor, Zizi skipped through the bookshelves until she found what she was looking for, tucked away in the back corner.

~ ~ ~

The tunnel was closing in. The light was fading. That sun-filled rectangle, their only escape, was just out of reach, and Maya could definitely feel the bear's hot breath on her neck. Of all the enchanted libraries in all the world, she had to find the one with a bear. Typical.

Just a few more steps.

Maya slammed the door behind her only a fraction of a second before a large mass careened into it, cracking the wall over the doorframe. Gasping for breath, her skin tender from the onslaught of books—whoever said reading wasn't dangerous?—Maya stared wide-eyed at the empty hall, the leather-bound volume clutched firmly against her chest. At least now she knew why students were forbidden from entering the book stacks. "That was weird. Was that weird? That was weird."

"We were attacked. By bookshelves. Bookshelves," Felix gasped. Then, he turned on Maya with a stink eye and muttered, "And you just *had* to pick up the fancy book on the pedestal."

Maya gripped the tome tighter to herself. "It's not my fault the books started attacking us. And the filing cabinets started chasing us. And we unleashed an angry Grizzly bear." A roar echoed through the library.

"I told you we shouldn't go in there. But did you listen to me? Noooo. Instead, you almost got us killed by inanimate objects!"

Maya pushed a particularly unruly bit of hair out of her face as she examined the book, hundreds of yellowed pages wrapped in brown leather. Most of her bushy black hair was gathered into two thick bunches, but there were a few strands that had a way of escaping all forms of imprisonment. At first glance, the book was nothing remarkable. Then again, most books hid their true power within their pages, revealing their secrets only to those who searched, and so Maya flipped open the cover.

All the pages shot out of the binding, circling through the air as the leaves of paper formed an arched doorway. Felix's arms fell limply to his sides. "What kind of book did you pick up in there?"

"A pop-up book," Maya said sarcastically. Felix simply glared at her. As the last page fell into place, the paper door burst open. Wide-eyed, Felix and Maya scurried behind a nearby desk as a stampede of creatures, large and small, rushed out. Winged horses galloped by, making the ground tremble beneath their hooves. Tiny fairies gossiped and giggled. In the far corner, a dragon threatened to be more hazardous to the library than a box of fireworks in a barbecue. On and on, throughout the library, countless creatures galloped, trotted, crawled, flew, and slithered through the bookshelves.

As an enormous ball of water whirled through the mystical portal, misting the room as sirens sang their song, Maya gulped. "I think we just released a horde of magical creatures into the library."

Felix beat back a bird that was trying to make a nest in his short cropped hair. "You think?"

At one end of the library, a winged horse was eating pages from the dictionary. In the cooking section, several fire-breathing chickens were roasting *Mama Betsy's All Chicken Cookbook*, while a unicorn tried to remove the picture book, *The*

Pony I Got for Christmas, from its steely horn after accidentally goring the book. Three dozen snails slowly oozed their way along the desks, corroding everything their slime touched, filling the air with an acrid scent, and a giant smashed the desks underfoot as he tried to avoid hitting his head on the light fixtures, high up above.

Felix jumped, barely escaping a baby dragon's fiery sneeze. In an instant, the entire desk next to him shot up in flames and crumbled into ashes. Stomping out the remaining embers, Felix asked, his voice cracking, "What do we do?"

A frog jumped into Maya's arms. He was slimy to the touch and smelled distinctly like bog. "Kiss me, kiss me," the frog crooned, puckering his lumpy green lips.

"Er, no?" Maya said, holding the frog an entire arm's length away.

The frog snapped his sticky fingers and, a moment later, Maya found she was holding a man with wavy blonde hair, purple tights, and a crown. "Kiss me now?" he said seductively in a deep voice that only betrayed a hint of a croak.

"Definitely not," Maya replied, tossing the prince to the side. He landed with a ribbet. Blowing a raspberry in Maya's direction, the frog bounced away.

In response to Felix's former question, Maya suggested, "We could try ignoring the problem until it goes away?"

"I don't think that's an option," Felix said, his eyes wide with horror.

Maya turned around to see a pillar of flames consuming a bookshelf in the far corner.

The bookshelf collapsed, and a brown-eyed girl emerged from the other side in a glow of light amidst the smoke and shadow, eyes sparkling like stars, skin as dark as the midnight sky, springy curls framing her face like a halo. Knitting needles clicked between nimble fingers as the colorful yarn draped across her bare arms, forming a dynamic tapestry that changed and bloomed and grew more beautiful with every movement. Though she looked bewildered, she walked with the grace of a gentle breeze, every motion light and unencumbered, unburdened by the weight of this world, a princess from another universe.

"Whoops, didn't mean to step on you little friend," Zizi picked up a hedgehog she had nearly squashed underfoot and stroked its spiny back. The hedgehog quivered and rolled up into a sleepy ball in her hand. At that moment, an entourage of adorable woodland animals surrounded her. Bluejays tied ribbons through her hair, bunnies hopped around her feet, and squirrels scurried along her arms with a measuring tape.

"Who's that?" Felix asked, unable to pull his gaze away.

"New girl," Maya shrugged. She carted a neon tortoise back to the paper door and tossed it through, but for every one creature Maya lobbed inside, another two scurried out.

Zizi turned an inquisitive gaze towards the siblings and asked, "Say, you don't suppose I've lost my mind, do you?"

Maya laughed, "Welcome to Ambrose High, the school where you never quite know. Now, how does everyone feel about simply running away?"

As she said it, the principal's voice boomed from the hall outside the library, "Prepare to explain."

The siblings froze. "What do we do?" Felix hissed at Maya.

Maya gulped and looked around at the chaos surrounding her, the centaurs and the unicorns and the dragons. "He'll understand?" A poisonous porcupine started nibbling on Maya's toe. With an exasperated harrumph, Maya kicked the porcupine aside and exclaimed, "For goodness sakes, just go back to wherever you came from."

What power such words held in the midst of chaos and confusion! Instantly, every single one of the mythical creatures charged right back at the door, a stampede of epic proportions leaving a wake of smashed desks, of over-turned bookshelves, of fire, and of some sort of glittery poop that exploded spontaneously. The magical door disintegrated into a flurry of pages, and when the pages had ordered themselves back into the book, the cover snapped shut in Maya's hands. In short, the creatures left no trace of themselves except the destruction of the library.

Felix crossed his arms and raised a brow at Maya. "Still think he'll understand?"

Maya searched for an escape. After all, a man like Mr. Elegans would never believe that chickens had set the school on fire, and Felix would never lie about it. The door handle rattled. Maya scrambled across the debris to one of the tall windows. The lock was jammed. She looked out and her stomach lurched. A beast flew overhead, a lion cub with wings like an eagle. Maya gulped, panic rushing through her veins. Some of the creatures must have escaped. She tried the next window, but too late. The principal burst onto the scene.

Zizi gasped. Mr. Elegans was the greyest man she had ever laid eyes on. Grey hair, grey eyes, grey suit—even his skin seemed to have an ashen tint to it. Paralyzed with horror, he fixed his steely eyes on Maya and the leather-bound volume in her hands, and his skin lost even the slight color that remained. With a voice as monotone and unremarkable as the rest of him, he stated, "Oh heavens. The fate of the world lies in the hands of criminally insane high school students."

"I'm not a criminal," Maya protested.

Sirens wailed up to the school. A deluge of water doused the library as firefighters turned their hoses on the flames. Then, Maya added, "Wait, did you just say *fate of the world*?"

Two
There was a girl

A team of firefighters rushed into the smoldering library. Smoke and rubble clouded the four from view. Maya's eyes watered, her throat itched, but she stayed put, straining to hear Mr. Elegans over the sound of boots stomping and water rushing and fire cackling and sirens howling.

The grey principal, his grey suit fading more and more into the swirls of ash, explained, "The Library of Souls holds books of every life that has ever been lived, but the guardians of the Library, the protectors of humanity, the Librarians—"

"Hold up, Librarians?" Maya scoffed. "Protectors of humanity, and the best you can come up with is Librarians?"

Mr. Elegans readjusted his glasses with a twitch of his nose, "The Librarians sealed the Library of Souls shut to protect it, yet in doing so they brought a curse upon the Library. A dark magic now corrodes and corrupts every book—in truth, every soul—it touches. Only the champion—" he cleared his throat and glanced nervously at the book in Maya's hands, "—the one who laid claim to the First Book of the Library of Souls and thus accepted the challenge—" He ended with a grimace, as though he were hoping someone else would step forward to refute his suspicions. Felix and Zizi both looked to Maya at once, and his face fell. Maya wanted to appear confident or nonchalant or amiable or literally anything that might suggest competence, but unfortunately she was too busy hacking up a lung amidst all the smoke. Asphyxiation did nothing to help her charm, which was already severely lacking. Firefighters shouted at them to evacuate. Mr. Elegans sighed and finished, "Only the champion can hope to rescue the Library."

"And my father?" Maya rasped.

"Your father is trapped inside the Library, in a twilight zone of existence outside of time."

"How do I save him?" she pressed.

"Find the seven books, defeat the seven challenges to unlock the Library and break the curse, and you will save your father," Mr. Elegans answered, fixing his steely gaze on Maya as the smoke enveloped him completely. Then, he was gone.

~ ~ ~

Yellow yarn streamed behind Zizi as she ran along the path behind Felix, the football stands rising up before them, sparkling in the last golden rays of sunset. Yellow and black banners fluttered in the wind, and the crowd roared in anticipation for the match. The pungent smell of roses sweetened the hot September air as they dashed between towering rosebushes, spotted with red, yellow, pink, and lilac blossoms. She wished she could stop to look at them more closely, they were so beautiful, but alas Felix was already so late for his football game, and she did not want to slow him down. They did not even have time to clean themselves up though soot sprinkled from her blouse and hair with every footfall. Zizi glanced back, but Maya was nowhere in sight. Without a word of explanation, the small, fiery girl with messy black pigtails had run off the moment they had slipped out of the burning library.

Maya was in several of Zizi's classes, which was an interesting experience to say the least. Maya always sat at the back of the classroom, sprawled out like she was trying to claim as much territory as possible despite being a relatively short person, especially when compared with her brother. Indeed, Maya was small, but Zizi would never consider calling her dainty or petite or delicate. No, Maya carried herself like her body was simply a covering for something far bigger and stronger inside. Her glare challenged anyone who dared approach her, and so most people never ventured a conversation with her. Even in class, Maya seemed to defy teachers to make her learn, and just when the teachers thought she had stopped paying attention, she whipped out questions that both stunned and baffled them. It was obvious she did not want to be there, and yet her presence filled the room. The girl was a mystery to Zizi, who always sat in the front row, took diligent notes, and asked questions only when they did not disrupt the class, and the mystery continued to grow after the events of the library.

Zizi jerked to a halt as a yard of yarn coiled itself around a particularly wild growth of white roses, weaving between branches, catching on thorns, interlacing as though the yarn had a distorted will of its own. Unfortunately, the fate of the yarn was intimately tied to that of Zizi's half-finished mittens. Not that anyone needed mittens in Los Angeles, especially not on a day like this one, but it would be a shame to lose the progress. Zizi reached through a gap, into the carnivorous mouth of the rosebush and yelped as she pricked her finger on one of the thorns.

"Zizi?" Felix rushed back towards her, which was a little terrifying since he was huge and slightly rough looking, but Zizi had come to realize that he pretty much always looked like that. Though he spoke softly, his voice was steady and strong, a little gruff but kind, like a mountain unaware of its magnitude as it stood unmoved by storm or wind or time itself.

Zizi shook the sharp pain out of her fingertips. When Felix saw what had happened, he knelt down next to her and helped untangle the web of yarn. Her usually nimble fingers fumbled in haste. She knew she was making him late for his game. Still, Felix's coarse hands moved with a patience and gentleness she would not have expected from a football player. If he felt rushed, he hid it well.

Knot by knot, thorn by thorn, Felix and Zizi freed the yarn from the rosebush until, at long last, it came loose. Zizi breathed a sigh of relief and clutched the yarn close, but as she turned to thank Felix, he was already plodding down the path, a hulking mass of muscle disappearing in the distance. As she gathered herself together, Zizi bounced after him with a charming smile. "Thank you. It was very nice of you to help me with that."

"Well, I wasn't going to leave you there, now was I?" Felix said as blood rushed to his face. He quickly turned his eyes away and quickened his pace.

"It was still nice, though," Zizi pressed. Felix eyed her suspiciously from behind thick, caterpillar eyebrows before hunching his massive shoulders and marching on. Zizi watched him for a moment and shook her head. What a hard place this must be if even kind people did not believe kind words.

~ ~ ~

Mr. Elegans rubbed his temples and sighed before he finally dialed. All these students, all these bright young minds, all these powerful athletes, all these diligent leaders, the kind that made him hopeful for the future, and of all of them Maya had become the champion. Maya, the girl who was in his office every week for disrupting some class or other. Even her brother would have been a better choice, but no. All of his hopes rested on this insolent force of nature. Once again, fate had conspired against him.

The principal tapped the table impatiently as the phone rang and rang and rang. He passed the time by watching the comings and goings in the atrium below. His office was on the second floor, and windows filled the walls on both his left and his right. The window to his left looked out at the outdoor courtyard and the pale red sky. Through the opposite window, he could look down on the main entrance hall of the school. Firefighters were still bustling in and out of the library, trailing soot across the marble floors of the atrium. The rest of the principal's office was as unremarkable as its owner, containing little more than a desk, some chairs, and two half-empty bookshelves against the far wall where one would have easily sufficed. Behind the desk hung a mirror with a plaque, which read, "For Charles Elegans – The man who inspired us to always look beyond the surface. Here's to you." The principal shivered. The mirror always made him feel like someone was watching him, and the sword dangling on the wall above it conjured up an element of symbolism he would have rather relegated to English classrooms. Unfortunately, that mirror was rather permanently attached to the wall.

At long last, a woman picked up on the other end, "Charles, this had better be important."

"There is a new champion."

For a moment, all he could hear was the static in the line. Then, she asked, "Who?"

The principal hesitated, "I'm not sure." It was a lie but a necessary one. Her son he could keep from talking with only a simple command, but regardless rumor would reach her soon enough that there was a new champion. All Mr. Elegans hoped to do was to stem the flow of information. He sacrificed a pawn, a piece of intelligence that would be hers soon enough anyways, in order to gain her faith, to hide a more dangerous truth without raising suspicions. After all, why would a man who had trusted her with this knowledge not trust her with the rest? Miyuki Mori was a dangerous ally at best, and if she discovered the identity of the champion—he shuddered—it could end in disaster.

"Then figure it out," she commanded. "We have to find the champion before the Wizard does. If we don't—"

"I remember," Mr. Elegans said.

"Find the champion before it is too late." She hung up the phone. The dial tone rang in the principal's ear as he placed his phone back on the receiver. He rose from his high-backed desk chair and strode to the place where his two bookshelves met. He ran a finger along the spotless mahogany surface. With the slightest touch, the two bookshelves sprang apart. A dark chamber opened before him, filled with stacks upon stacks of gold-tipped books like treasure hidden away in a secret vault. Sadly, like most treasures, this one was limited, and the stores would run out one day, one day that was always too soon. Rubbing his hands together, the grey principal stepped inside. Mr. Elegans stroked the leather covers of the books stacked in that secret room. He breathed the ancient smell, let it fill him, consume him. This was life itself. His grey eyes glinted in the pale light, and he closed the bookshelves behind him.

~ ~ ~

With a whoosh, Maya slammed the empty garbage bin down over the griffin. Wings beat against the walls of the bin, but the cub could not escape his prison. Maya threw a fist in the air. The trash bin teetered, and she clamped it down again. Finally. She caught the winged lion cub. She only had to chase it around the school, beat off a walking birch tree that may or may not have been Canadian, and steal a dozen cans of tuna from the school kitchen with which to ensnare the beast. Maya hopped to a seat on top of the trash can and pulled the leather-bound book out of her backpack. All she had to do now was open that book again and send the griffin back into that magical door through which all the other creatures had vanished. For a moment, she considered not doing it. After all, not everyone could say they had a griffin as a pet. It could be pretty cool. Then again, Maya could not even keep cacti alive. A mythical creature was out of the question.

Before she opened the cover again, she glanced through the rosebush at the path. The roses shielded her from view fairly well, but she was not going to take any risks, not with a word like "arson" flying around the school. According to the firefighters, the library looked like someone had taken a flamethrower to a pillow factory.

The cub rammed into the plastic, and Maya almost lost her seat. Holding her breath, Maya flipped open the cover of the First Book of the Library of Souls. Nothing happened. Thud—the bin trembled. She tried it again, but the pages remained fixed to the spine. Why wasn't it working? Bam—the trash bin toppled and Maya with it. Scrambling back to her feet, Maya searched the sky and gulped. The winged lion cub had escaped. The cub had escaped, and he was flying directly towards the football field.

~ ~ ~

The timer buzzed as the third quarter drew to a close, the zeros on the timer flashing across a scoreboard that rose above the glimmering stands. Tied at 21 points apiece, the Ambrose High Knights were neck-and-neck with their archrivals, the Lancaster High Fighting Gophers.

Tugging at his chinstrap, Felix rushed to the sidelines and drained cool water down his parched throat. His jersey was soaked through with sweat, and he could not tell if the roar in his ears was from the cheers or from the rush of blood racing to deliver oxygen to his tired limbs.

"Come on, kid," Coach Frank shouted at Felix. The football coach stood five foot flat, but his muscles threatened to tear through his skin tight shirt every time he moved. "Where's your head?"

"Coach, we're doing our best," Felix huffed. Two minutes. Two minutes to rest before he returned to the field.

"That is no excuse for mediocrity," the coach yelled. Felix glanced up at the stands. As always, his stepmother was standing, front and center, waiving a poster through the air: "Go Knights! #88 for the Win!" Felix couldn't help but smile. She meant well, even if it was a little embarrassing. Felix quickly turned his attention back to the coach as Coach Frank jerked his shoulder pads, exclaiming, "You're a warrior, a gladiator—"

"A knight?" Felix finished for him. His gaze flitted back to the stands for just a flash and fell upon Zizi – who was scribbling something in her notebook with as much diligence as she had in their physics class. Felix felt himself flush with embarrassment again. Zizi had tried thanking him for helping her untangle her yarn, and he had completely forgotten how to talk. Combine that with his natural resting face, which always ended up being stonier than Felix meant, and Zizi probably thought he was a total caveman.

"Exactly," Coach Frank slapped Felix's shoulder pads. "You're a knight, fighting for glory and all that whoopla. Now, go out there and act like one."

The referee blew his whistle. Felix fixed his chinstrap and hustled out into the huddle, back into the fray.

~ ~ ~

Maya stomped through the trees towards the stands. Three times, she had chased that griffin around the stadium. Three times, and she still could not catch that stupid beast again. And she had missed most of Felix's game to boot. At this rate, she would be lucky to catch the last few minutes. She wasn't even sure why she bothered chasing the beast in the first place anymore. She couldn't send it back into the book, and she couldn't bring it home, as much as she wanted to. There was no space in the apartment to keep it, let alone hide it from the stepmother. Plus, Felix would flip. Sometimes, Maya wondered why everyone else thought Felix was so "cool under fire." Whenever Maya dragged him on one of her adventures, he was anything but. Then again, most people probably used "fire" figuratively.

A root intruded into the winding path, and Maya skipped over it into a pile of yellow leaves on the other side. They crackled underfoot with a satisfying crunch. Through the branches of the trees, Maya could see the yellow and black banners streaming over the hushed stands. The breeze knocked a few new leaves to the ground. Orange and red and yellow leaves littered the forest floor, dampening the air with the musty smell of decay, but many more still filled the canopy overhead. This was the least direct route to the stands, but Maya had chosen it intentionally. By coming this way, she was most likely to avoid her stepmother, Tania.

The end of the path came into view. And then the view was blocked. A lanky boy dressed in black dropped into Maya's way from a tree branch, his feet barely making a sound as they touched the dirt, and suddenly Maya wished she had gone the other way.

"The woods are a dangerous place to be wandering alone. Where are you off to?" he smirked. The boy had hair as black as coal, skin as white as snow, and lips as red as—okay, his lips were not very red, but they were no less noticeable for all his sneering, grinning like a predator who had cornered his prey. His amber eyes narrowed like a cat's, like he knew exactly how the world was going to end. Most likely because he would be the one ending it.

Maya skidded to a stop and rolled her eyes, "Wolf, what are you doing here?"

Wolf sauntered closer, the shadows dancing across his sharp, pale features, "What were you doing in the library? Heard you caused quite the scene."

Blood rushed to Maya's face. Clenching her fists, she tried to walk past him, "No one got hurt."

"Ah, the phrase that absolves us of all sin," Wolf chortled as he skipped a few steps to stay in front of her.

"It's a shame, you being the devil incarnate. You could really use some absolution," Maya spat.

"If I'm the devil, I guess I'll be seeing you later at my place," Wolf winked with a sly grin.

Maya brushed past him, "Trust me. Another minute with you is hell enough."

Wolf ran his fingers through his inky black hair, the corner of his lip turned up in a playful smirk. Maya scoffed. He must have had a gallon worth of product in his hair to achieve that disheveled-but-in-a-cool-way-like-I'm-just-too-cool-to-care look. Wolfgang Mori had already inherited much in the ways of looks and charm, and he was to inherit much more in the future as the sole heir to a vast fortune. He was the envy of nearly everyone, and he knew it. Which only got on Maya's nerves even more. He sneered, "Say, can you still get burned if you're as hot as I am?"

"How badly do you want to know?" Maya turned back towards him with a snarl, a fire blazing in her eyes. She had to crane her neck to keep eye contact, but she refused to be the first to yield.

"Not as badly as I want to know if you found something...something interesting in the library," he prowled nearer, "Like a book?"

Maya gripped the straps of her backpack and stepped back, wondering how he could have known. Then, she guffawed, "It's a library. What else would I find?"

"It would be a very specific book," Wolf scrutinized every twitch of Maya's face, every blink, every subconscious tick.

Setting her jaw and furrowing her brow, Maya turned on her heel and walked away to the end of the path. The staircase into the bleachers was directly in front of her. Cheers filled the air once more. She could practically taste hotdogs and burnt hamburgers in the smoke wafting over from the squat, concrete concession stand to her right. And Wolf was only a distant, unpleasant memory.

A memory that kept rearing its ugly head.

"You know, it's rude to walk away from people like that. Then again, I guess you would know all about that. Have you heard from your father recently?" Wolf jeered after her. Maya halted, her blood boiling, her fist trembling with fury. She took a deep breath, focused on the stairs, but Wolf kept coming closer, kept talking. "No, I guess you wouldn't have. Most people are saying he ran off with some tramp. Can't say I'm surprised. I mean, he did marry your stepmother."

Maya grabbed Wolf by his shirt collar and slammed him against the concrete wall of the concession stand, her blood vessels ready to burst, her teeth clenched so tight she could do barely more than growl. And Wolf kept smirking. That stupid, spiteful smirk. That smirk that said, no matter how hard she tried, he always won. He always got under her skin. He always got what he wanted. And he was having fun. Maya's grip tightened.

The metal stairs squeaked and clanged as Zizi hurried down them, going as fast as she could without breaking into a run, her skirt bobbing with every hoppity step. At the base of the stairs, a baby lion cub with wings was chewing on a notebook. As concerned as Maya was about the loose griffin cub, she could not help but wonder what on earth Zizi was doing with a notebook at a football game. She knew the girl was enthusiastic about learning, but had Zizi really been taking notes during a game?

Yes. Being part of the crowd at a football game had offered tremendous insights into the nature and anthropology of group identity formation, the rhetoric of rivalries, and the role of physical displays of dominance in the construct of "school pride." It was exhilarating. And crowded. Lots of people. Very strange. Oh, look! Griffin! Wait, that was strange too.

As Zizi dusted off her fallen notebook and scratched the adorable cub's belly, oblivious to the girl in the red hoodie and the boy in black at each other's throats, Maya saw her chance. Shooting Wolf one last dirty look before she went, Maya let go and crept up on the unsuspecting beast. Zizi cooed and giggled, muffling the sound of Maya's footsteps. Then, Maya pounced. Too late. Once again, the griffin was gone.

Zizi looked up startled and smiled when she saw Maya. "Oh, good. You're here. I was getting worried. Do you want to watch the game with me? I think I have almost figured out the rules." With a broad grin, Zizi hooked Maya's elbow in her own and dragged her towards the stairs.

Maya gaped, "You figured out all the rules of football? Already?"

"No, no. The rules of when to cheer and when not to. When the people in silver and blue cross the last line on the field, that's bad," she beamed.

"Zizi, wait," Maya unhooked her arm and scratched the back of her head nervously. She glanced over her shoulder one more time. The smirk had fallen from Wolf's face, and from here he was little more than a lanky silhouette kicking an empty can through the tree line, his hands buried in his pockets. For a moment, Maya almost felt pity for the lone figure in the woods. Then she remembered his stupid face and the stupid things he'd said and the stupid things he'd done, and she hoped that empty can popped up and gave him a good kick in the shins in return. With a deep breath, she explained, "Er, I'm not exactly—people don't—see, it's your first day, and you can still be friends with anyone you want, but if we're seen together, well..."

A gold and white blur dove at them. Maya tackled Zizi out of the way. They tumbled to the ground just as the cub careened past them. Maya jumped to her feet, ready to battle the ferocious beast, but the winged lion cub was already distracted by the ball of yarn that had fallen out of Zizi's purse.

One last attempt to catch him before someone saw, Maya lunged for the cub. Evading Maya's grasp one more time, the winged lion took off again, flapping his brilliant white and brown wings faster and faster and faster until he rounded the bleachers and flew out—out onto the field.

~ ~ ~

All eyes were glued to the five-yard line. A strange hush had fallen over the crowd, an electric buzz, the sound of hearts beating, pounding, hammering with adrenaline, of teeth chomping at nails and of whispered prayers drowning out the loudest cheers. The last play of the game. The Fighting Gophers were up by six points. The Knights needed a touchdown to win.

Black and gold lined up against silver and blue.

"And, with no time left on the clock, the quarterback throws the ball. Looks like it's headed for number eighty-eight, Rodriguez," the announcer said. The ball soared through the air. Felix reached out towards it. His hands nearly closed around it when—*Bam!* The ball hurtled out of the stadium, and a fluffy, golden lion cub with eagle's wings fell into Felix's hands instead. The stands fell silent. Felix froze. "Did he just catch an eagle?"

A whistle blew. "Flag!" The referee tossed a yellow towel onto the field before revising, "I think?"

One thing was sure, though. The game was over. The game was over, and the Gophers had won.

Felix broke into a cold sweat as he stared at the cub trying to roar in his hands. He could feel a thousand eyes glued to him. If he waited much longer, someone would see. He had to do something now.

So he ran off the field yelling for help. "MAYAAAAAAA!" She peaked out around the bleachers. "What do I do with it?" He held the cub out towards her. His voice was muffled by his mouth guard and his chinstrap, but he didn't dare take off the helmet. Never underestimate the importance of personal safety equipment when handling mythical creatures.

"You caught him," Maya delighted. "And he actually seems to like you." She scratched the cub's golden scalp, "Isn't that right?" The winged lion panted and kicked his back leg happily. Then, the cub yawned and snuggled up against Felix.

Felix cradled the cub in his wide palm. His biceps were almost as thick as the little lion's body. Doing his best not to wake the cub, he whispered, "Maya, what do we do?"

"We can't send him back, so..." Maya looked up at Felix with a playful grin.

"No. No," Felix objected. "We are not adopting a ferocious—" Felix took one look at the sleepy, amber eyes smiling up at him and lost his train of thought. A tiny giggle erupted from his manly throat. Grinning from ear to ear, Felix scratched the griffin's belly with his free hand.

And that is how Felix adopted a griffin named Oscar.

THREE
Who loved her family

There was once a queen who was as wise as she was kind, as cunning as she was beautiful, and in her hands the kingdom flourished, the golden city gleaming in the sunlight. But a cloud of envy fell upon the queen's most trusted advisor, a wizard who declared his undying loyalty by day and stole the kingdom's treasures by night. The wizard had all the comforts he could desire, but he was not satisfied, for he was denied the one thing he wanted most of all: the love of the queen. And so he vowed to himself that all the land and all its treasures and all its people would be his before the end.

That very night, the wizard called on the darkest magic he knew and raised an army from the shadows, and with that army he marched on the golden city. When the first morning light crested over the castle towers, the king and all the knights of the kingdom rode out to meet the enemy at the gates, but alas the enemy was already within.

The wizard slipped into the throne room to claim the crown and with it the kingdom, but the treasure had not been left undefended. The queen in all her royal majesty stood guard. She pleaded with the wizard in the name of the oath he had sworn to serve the kingdom, to protect the innocent and the defenseless, the oath he had sworn to her.

The wizard remembered his oaths. And, with a dagger, he pierced the queen's heart.

~ ~ ~

Maya jumped out of the way as Felix slammed the tray of hot cookies on the kitchen counter. Crumbs already littered the well-worn table, but he appeared to have no intention of slowing his baking. Rather, the ferocity of his baking only increased with his frustrations. Cheeks bulging with cookies, he grumbled, "An hour! He made us run for an hour after a game—which we should have won, by the way—because someone keeps stealing protein powder out of the team room. It's not our fault he never locks up!"

He shoved the next batch into the oven. The oven door closed with a *BANG*. Though the kitchen was one of the many places on campus that a sane person would reasonably avoid, what with the dim lights, the clutter, and the suspiciously large cauldron, it also had an impressive block of ovens in the exposed brick walls, and so, after every football game, Maya and Felix stole into the kitchen to talk and eat cookies (Felix did the baking—it was stress-relieving and Maya was incapable of using the oven without setting the kitchen on fire).

"And what's worse, he's going to keep making us run for every additional tub that goes missing," Felix leaned against the oven, brooding with his thick arms crossed over his chest, his brow furrowed, cutting an imposing figure in his bulky letterman jacket.

A sweet, innocent voice piped up from behind what would surely be the biggest scarf ever made, "Maybe it's the gnomes." Felix and Maya both looked at Zizi at once. She smiled and paused her knitting just long enough to pet the winged lion cub purring on her lap, "I could have sworn I saw one move earlier. In the rose garden."

Maya turned to Felix, "Under what rock did we find her?"

Zizi giggled, "My parents do say they found me during one of their archeological digs." She giggled with her whole body, like her happiness simply would not be contained. Oscar pawed at her to keep petting him and eventually settled with playing with a ball of yarn instead.

"I think she was homeschooled," Felix told Maya.

"Isn't school one grand adventure?" Zizi had stars in her eyes, like a girl in love or an explorer taking the first steps of a quest. Maya wondered how long it would take for that light to fade. She hoped, for the girl's sake, it never did. Felix sat down at the table next to Zizi, and Maya joined on the other side. Oscar fluttered onto Felix's lap and licked the sugar from his cheek. He scowled but started petting the beast anyways, and soon enough he was scratching the griffin behind the ears, cooing something about Oscar being the best little beastie out there. Zizi continued, "It—it's like a fairytale."

"Or a nightmare," Maya countered.

"But the people are so nice and helpful. Like your mother," Zizi chattered, oblivious to the storm clouds that such words brought. Maya's gaze snapped up at Zizi as though to check if she had heard correctly. Felix stiffened. "I met her in the stands. She was lovely."

The change that followed was unmistakable.

Maya's jaw clenched. Her eyes blazed. Steam rose from her bright red ears. No one moved or spoke, but the heat of Maya's rage filled the room with a tension so thick that sparks were starting to crackle through the air. Felix glanced over at his sister and braced for the volcanic eruption by stuffing a handful of cookies into his mouth.

Maya kept her eyes fixed on Zizi and growled, "Tania is not our mother."

"Maya—" Felix interjected.

"TANIA IS NOT OUR MOTHER," Maya shouted, slamming a fist on the table so hard cookies skittered off. Oscar jumped after them, and as he knocked Zizi's knitting out of her hands, Maya caught a glimpse of Zizi's glassy eyes trembling, her lip quivering, her shoulders hunched up protectively, and Maya turned away, still seething, before the sight could make her regret her outburst.

Felix turned on Maya with a glare that dripped condemnation, "Maya!"

"What? I'm just telling the truth."

"Yeah, but you don't have to act like you're going to eat her for dinner," Felix argued.

A phone rang. Zizi picked up. Casting an ashamed look about, Zizi rose and scurried out of the kitchen, her voice half a whisper as she said, "Hi, Mama. No, no, I'm not in trouble."

The kitchen door swung shut behind her. Maya jumped up from her seat and threw her hands up, "Excuse me for actually caring." She slammed her chair back into place. A *BOOM* echoed through the kitchen. Maya froze. Felix heard it too, the hollow sound the wooden floor made. The siblings glanced at each other. From Maya, there was curiosity, anticipation, and a hint of mischief. From Felix, dread.

Maya immediately crawled under the table and began to run her fingers along the floor. Her fingers wrapped around a small handle, hidden in the grain of the wood. Felix looked on with the horror of someone watching a train crash in motion. "Maya, the last time you did this sort of thing—HOLY BANANAS!"

Felix and Maya both tumbled down a hole as the floor opened up beneath them.

~ ~ ~

Mr. Elegans looked up from his desk with a start. He felt that familiar tremor in the depths of his spirit. There was trouble afoot.

~ ~ ~

Maya landed first on the hard dirt floor, Felix next, and the table came crashing down on top of both of them. Nice to know at least one of the three had a soft landing. Maya's head swam as she propped herself back up against the cool stone wall of the small cellar. There were some empty wine barrels lined up along the edges of the room, but otherwise nothing. How anticlimactic.

Felix brushed dust and splinters off the golden sleeves of his letterman and grumbled, "Great. We've seen it. Can we go now?" He glanced up at the trapdoor above them. "And...we don't have a ladder."

With a grunt, Maya rolled an oak barrel towards the trapdoor and set it upright. "Help me stack these."

"You have got to be kidding."

Maya rolled another cask next to the first. Felix sighed and began stacking the casks into a pyramid, a makeshift staircase. The casks may have been empty, but they were still heavy, and the coarse wood left splinters with every touch. Maya rolled the barrels over to Felix, and he hoisted them up on top of each other. The system worked until Maya suddenly stopped delivering the casks. Felix wiped the sweat from his forehead and looked down from the top of the pyramid. Standing a full foot taller than Maya, Felix could probably have pulled himself out at this height, but he wanted to add one more barrel just to be safe. "Maya?" She lingered by the last barrel, examining a crevice in the wall. Felix climbed down the pyramid to join her. "What's wrong?"

Maya pulled a thick, leather-bound book out of the crevice. "The Second Book of the Library of Souls."

Felix immediately stood on guard. He glanced at the casks, the clammy stone walls, the trapdoor high above, and then back at Maya with his classic this-is-a-terrible-idea-and-you-know-it-and-I-don't-have-time-to-die-right-now look. It was a look with which Maya was far more intimately familiar than she probably should have been. Maya rolled her eyes and said, "If we have another influx of magical creatures, I'd rather they be down here, wouldn't you?" Felix nodded his reluctant agreement.

Holding her breath, her heart pounding with anticipation, Maya opened the book. The cover ripped out of her hands, and the pages flew out of the binding, swirling through the air in a cloud of paper and shadow. The leaves fused together, forming hoofs that pawed the ground impatiently, a tail that swatted wildly at a thick torso, and horns as sharp as knives. A raging bull. For the first time ever, Maya regretted wearing her red hoodie. The giant beast tore at the soft dirt with firm hoofs, paper nostrils flaring, and charged directly at Maya.

Maya rolled the barrel at the bull and sprinted away as quickly as her legs could carry her. Felix scurried up the tower and pulled himself back into the kitchen. The bull trampled the oak cask to splinters and bellowed with rage. Maya jumped out of the bull's path just in time, but the bull rounded on its side and hit her with the full force of its body. Maya flew against the wall so hard the dust shook out of the ceiling. She recuperated and lunged at the bull's mid-section.

"I got him," she shouted as her arms wrapped around the paper frame. She crashed through the paper form onto the ground. "Oh, come on! That's totally unfai—AHHHH!" The bull turned his horns on Maya and charged again. Maya dodged the initial attack, but then she was trapped in the corner with the bull drawing ever closer.

"I have an idea," Felix called down. He ran off and reappeared in the square hole above seconds later with a crumpled piece of paper and a lit match. As soon as the paper caught fire, he tossed it directly at the bull. Time slowed. The flaming paper ball soared through the air. The bull's every footfall resounded like an elephant's heartbeat. The bull lowered its horns for the kill. The ball of fire passed into its torso. Mere moments before the horns would have impaled Maya, a stream of flames rushed through the pages. The leaves of paper crumbled to ashes.

Maya's jaw dropped. "You just set fire to an irreplaceable book."

"I just saved your life!"

"But the book—"

"Is reforming!"

No sooner had the fire gone out than the ashes gathered themselves up and reformed pages. Which formed an even scarier, angrier, and deadlier bull. Maya took that as her cue to run for the makeshift pyramid. Just as Maya gripped the edge of the trapdoor, the bull crashed through the tower of barrels, and her footing fell out beneath her feet. Maya dangled by her fingertips, millimeters away from the bloody death that awaited her below. Felix reached down and pulled her up.

When fighting evil and mystical forces, it is always wise to bring a football player.

Maya breathed a sigh of relief. "Thanks."

"Of course," Felix grinned. But the relief was not to last. No sooner was Maya on her feet than the pages were swirling through the trapdoor.

Maya gaped, "Good grief, what does it take to beat that thing?"

The bull pawed the ground and charged at Felix.

~ ~ ~

Zizi wandered along the hallway outside the kitchen, speaking on the phone with her mother as she passed back and forth before the same six classroom doors. The hall was long, so long she could barely see the sharp turn at the far end where the corridor branched off to the main atrium. The main school building, which held all the classrooms and offices, was an L-shaped structure with the kitchen and teacher's lounge at one extreme of the L and the library at the other. The L-shaped building and the school gymnasium bordered three sides of a central courtyard, which opened up to the rose garden and other grounds beyond. Zizi had frequently wondered throughout the day how a building that looked so unimposing from the outside could be so impossibly, unwalkably huge on the inside.

The red-brick and limestone building had the old-fashioned feel of a university, and in truth it had been intended for such a fate until the money ran out and the late Mr. Ambrose had to settle instead for the most pompously dignified-looking high school in the nation. The clock tower just off the main atrium was his pride and joy, the intended centerpiece of his institute of higher learning. Mr. Ambrose had imported the whole tower block-by-block from a village in northern Italy, which might account for his fiscal troubles later on, and rumor had it that parts of the tower dated back to the Roman Empire. It was a magnificent structure. Nonetheless, Zizi wondered if the clock tower came with a ghost in the walls. Despite its noble façade, the building had a will of its own. Doors closed unexpectedly, blinds opened of their own accord, and Zizi was convinced that there was a closet that kept switching places with the classrooms around it. Still, she felt a little proud as she strode across that pearl-white marble floor under the wide arches and the high-vaulted ceilings painted with mythical scenes that seemed far less fantastical now than they had even that morning.

"This place is wonderful and a little odd and—oh, I wish I could describe it all to you. And the people," her voice faltered. That part was complicated. *They* were complicated. A few minutes ago, she thought she understood them all. She knew how they fit in the story. But then...perhaps it was just a brief inconsistency. "The people are—" The fire alarm in the kitchen went off. Smoke seeped through the door. Zizi glanced at her watch. "Burning!"

"The people are burning?"

"No, the cookies are," Zizi hung up and sprinted back to the kitchen, her skirt bobbing with every step. Then, she opened the door.

Maya and Felix ran past, screaming at the top of their lungs, a flaming bull close on their heels.

"Felix, stop setting the bull on fire," Maya shouted. "And Zizi, shut the door." Zizi slammed the door shut behind her. "With you out—oh, never mind."

The bull crumbled to ash and then came back to life. Zizi caught a page as it fluttered off the bull. "Is that paper?" The page tore itself out of Zizi's hand and rejoined the rest of the beast. She jumped out of the way as the bull thundered towards Felix. Felix dashed to the edge of the kitchen and clambered up the brick wall to reach the rafters. Pots clattered off the trembling walls.

Yelping, Felix pulled his knees to his chest, toes dangling barely out of reach of the bull as he hung from the rafters. "Better yet, how do we get rid of it?"

"How should I know?" Maya said. Meanwhile, Zizi was bravely rescuing the cookies from the oven. They really were very tasty. If only one thing could survive this adventure, those cookies would be at the top of the list.

The bull charged at the wall behind Felix. Felix yelped again. "I don't know. You're the one who keeps getting us into these messes."

"I know books are powerful, but that one is downright threatening," Zizi said as she put the cookies on the counter to cool. The table was lying in splinters.

Maya said, "It wouldn't be so bad if there was something solid to hold onto, but..." She paused. "Has anyone seen the cover?"

"No. I'm a little busy trying not to get gored by a paper bull," Felix shouted, kicking at the bull's head.

Maya scrutinized the bull's papery frame. "Felix, distract the bull, but try to keep him steady, okay?"

"Oh, great! Now I'm bull bate!" Felix cried.

With an enormous lunge, Maya dove into the middle of the bull again. The bull stamped, crying out as pages whisked around, trying to push themselves back into place, but Maya stayed firmly planted within the bull's torso. She swam through the pages, digging, searching. Once or twice, she brushed up against leather, but the moment she made contact, the cover dashed out of reach again, as wild in spirit as the distressed bull. With a bellow, the bull finally bucked Maya against the far wall. Dazed as she was, Maya pushed herself up, her head spinning as the bull snorted and trotted and bellowed and pawed at the ground and—did the bull just stop to sniff that bunch of roses hanging to dry on the wall? For a moment, the bull seemed almost calm as it inhaled the scent.

And then Felix jumped onto it from the rafters.

"Felix, no!" Maya cried out as Felix wrestled through the pages only to be thrown across the room. He skidded to a stop next to the giant cauldron in the corner. The bull pawed the ground and thundered towards Felix, hate and anger blazing in its eyes. Maya threw a pot through the bull's hind side. "Hey, bull, over here," she taunted as she wrapped her fingers around the bunch of fresh cut roses. The bull took the bait, and Maya hoped against hope that her totally crazy plan would work.

Trapped against the wall, Maya turned her face away and thrust the flowers before her, her last weapon, her last hope no more than a peace offering. A fool's hope. She held her breath, each millisecond feeling like an eternity in the face of her inevitable demise. Actually, this was starting to feel a lot longer than a few milliseconds. In real time. Maya dared open her eyes and saw why it felt so long. The bull had skidded to a stop. As the bull sniffed the roses, a new sense of serenity fell over it, and the brown leather cover plopped right out of the beast's gut onto the floor.

Maya breathed a sigh of relief. She gently laid the flowers on the ground in front of the bull. When she had the cover firmly in hand, Maya held it open high above her head. The pages fluttered back into the book, smelling somehow sweeter, until only the head remained.

Then, the bull spoke, voice raspy and thin, a breeze blowing through paper sails, and it said, "The Wizard is coming."

Maya's stomach lurched, and the blood drained from her face. She'd heard the name before. As the head disintegrated, the cover slammed shut. An electric silence remained, shattered only by the creak of the door. Mr. Elegans stood in the frame.

Maya turned her gaze on the man in grey, "Who is the Wizard?"

The principal inhaled sharply, "The Wizard is the enemy."

~ ~ ~

Maya glanced back at Felix as she plugged the old VHS player into the TV and white static filled the room. He was still soundly asleep. In fact, he had barely stirred at all since they had gotten home. The moment they had walked into the apartment, he had collapsed onto the burnt-orange couch in the living room, and that had been the end of it. The game and the bull fiasco had really taken it out of him. And so he slept, blissfully unaware of the coming storm, a winged lion cub curled up on his massive chest.

Maya, on the other hand, could not have fallen asleep if she had wanted to.

The Wizard was the reason Maya's father was trapped inside the Library of Souls, and the Wizard was the one who had cursed it. It was his ultimatum. Open the Library again, or it gets slowly destroyed from the inside out. And yet, the moment the champion unsealed the door to the Library, the Wizard would be right there, trying to take it for himself once more. And if he succeeded—Maya shuddered to think. That was the true risk, the true burden the champion bore. The Library was not truly free of the curse until the Wizard was no more. Okay, no problem. The champion just had to unlock the Library and then defeat the Wizard in an epic battle for the fate of the world. No biggie. Of course, the only flaw in that brilliant plan was...Maya, this supposed mighty, courageous, honorable, heroic savior of the world who was exactly none of those things. Perhaps destiny had gotten confused.

Maya pushed the tape into the machine. A shaky, blurry image filled the screen, as only homemade videos could. Settling in against the base of the couch, Maya pulled her knees close to her chest and ran her fingers through that tangled mane of hair that flowed over her shoulders. The camera panned to the picnic blanket spread out in a clearing in the rose garden, an orange, dusky sky casting long afternoon shadows across the fountain.

An eight-year old girl with messy pigtails and a missing tooth rushed up to the camera, a broad smile lighting up her entire face as she held up a cardboard box towards the lens. "Mommy, when are we doing the fireworks? Can I light them?"

Her mother's voice was gentle and soft when she answered, "After dinner, when it's dark out."

The picture blurred as the camera shifted towards Maya's father at the grill as a stout little boy watched the flames with a mix of terror and wonder. Her father, a great bear of a man, smiled at the camera, his happiness complete as flames sprang up from the grill and filled the air with smoke.

Maya started to laugh, even before her younger self just up and chucked the whole box of fireworks into the grill, and she laughed all the way through until her father tossed the whole flaming mess—grill, fireworks, food, everything—into the fountain. Maya had watched this video a thousand times, and she still cracked up when the fountain exploded and everyone stood around staring with smoking eyebrows. Well, everyone except little Maya, who was giggling and clapping her hands and asking to do it again. Not much had changed in that regard.

With her knees clutched against her chest, Maya pulled the worn, folded the piece of paper out of her pocket and flattened it against her leg. She skimmed the familiar words, the last words her father had left behind, in the light of a single, warm lamp on the coffee table.

She was a Librarian, one of the last guardians of the Library of Souls, and so she held her post before the door, the last line of defense, the only one who had not fallen for his ploy. She stood alone and unarmed, too late to call for help, too late to prepare, when the Wizard approached. He came in his true form, no more tricks, no magic, no flowing robes hiding his face. She shook her head, sorrow filling the very essence of her being. "Why?"

The Wizard answered, "You know the reason."

The video continued to play in the background. The camera paused on her mother's face as she laughed, sunset sparkling in her eyes, the wind playing through her thick curls. She was so beautiful when she smiled, though she did not do it nearly often enough. She cleared a place for her husband to sit next to her and leaned her head on his shoulder, looking off to the sunset sky in the distance. "It's beautiful."

The guardian planted her feet. "I cannot let you pass."

"You cannot stop me," the Wizard said, drawing nearer.

She moved not, though her heart cried out for her to run, run to her children, to her family, to let the world crumble around her as she held tight and never let go, and yet she remained firmly rooted before the door. She reminded him, "When you became a Librarian, you swore an oath to defend innocent souls."

The camera focused on the little girl as she fell asleep in her mother's lap, a little girl who was almost a stranger to Maya now. As the girl's mind slipped into the land of dreams and wishes and starlight, wrapped in the safety of her mother's arms, she mumbled her deepest confession, a confession that rang true through the ages, "I wish every day could be like this."

The Wizard brushed a teardrop from the guardian's cheek. His eyes were kind and sincere, his touch gentle, and she allowed herself to hope for just a moment. "Have no fear. I would never harm the innocent. I promise."

He lied.

The page trembled in Maya's hand as she buried her face in her sleeves, hot tears soaking through the fabric. Her whole body shook like an engine about to fall apart. Her lungs constricted. She wanted to cry out, to tear through the silence, to rip the darkness to shreds, but all she could manage was a muffled sob. Somehow, she had always known deep in her heart how the story ended, that the guardian and her mother were one and the same and that they shared the same fate. She had just never believed it could be true.

FOUR

With a fiery passion

The chime of the clock reverberated through the tower. Dust shook into Maya's eyes as she traced the line of the rickety wooden staircase winding up the inside of the belfry, all the way to the top. Twelve chimes and the tower fell silent. It seemed like the steps went on forever, a ghostly tower of Babel reaching to the heavens.

Maya set her backpack on the ground and, as she unzipped it, a fluffy golden head poked out. She grinned. The winged lion barely fit in her backpack anymore. He had grown so much over the past month that it was getting hard to hide him from Tania. Plus, it didn't help that the griffin had grown so strong it could pick up the beds under which they hid him and fly around the apartment, toting a mattress like it was nothing. It was a wonder the griffin did not try to break out of the backpack. As she scratched the cub's golden forehead, she slipped out the two Books of the Library of Souls and placed them into a box. She gazed up at the stairs again. Once she had found the remaining five books, then she would make the climb again, but not yet. No point trudging up all those stairs to the clock face if the Library of Souls wasn't even unlocked yet.

The entrance to the Library of Souls had not always been linked to that particular clock, but it always attached itself to some time-keeping device. After all, time was the medium through which humans experienced life. For some reason or another, the Library had chosen to remain in place despite the danger posed by the Wizard, and now, as long as it was sealed shut, it was locked to that position.

Maya lifted a floorboard from the bottom step and hid the books away. She would need them when the time came. If the time came. She furrowed her brow. A month had passed, and still she had made no progress. Slamming the floorboard back into place, she turned for the exit and shut the door behind her.

~ ~ ~

Gold, purple, red—fountains upon fountains of fabric flowed across the vista of the library floor, cascading down the walls, streaming through the air, running from table to table. Amidst hammering, grunting, pulling, and sweating, the painted castle rose in the center of the hustle and bustle, the four wooden walls looming over the festive activity, a metamorphosis in action, the transformation of a half-restored library into a kingdom of fairytales. The Homecoming dance usually took place in the courtyard, but the big donor fundraising gala was going to be held there later that week, and everyone knows that, in school, the students come second. Which might explain why the school had managed to stay open so long despite the high number of "incidents" in its history.

In the midst of all the activity, Felix was standing at the top of a twenty-foot ladder for which he almost definitely exceeded the weight limit, trying to hang up the last corner of a giant tapestry of lights on the ceiling. Zizi's creation, of course. She had found some spare wires and light bulbs and, with her crafty magic, had created a canvas of stars. And, for reasons of which Felix was not completely sure now that he was toting a hundred pound weight to the top of a very tall ladder, Felix had agreed to spend his lunch hour helping Zizi install the light fixture on the ceiling of the library, just in time for the Homecoming dance.

Felix glanced across the long library hall. From up here, he could see nearly everything: the unfinished bookshelves standing empty and forlorn around the edges of the room, tables being arranged to hold refreshments, newly redone oak paneling shimmering gold in the light streaming through the tall windows, people setting up for the Homecoming dance or getting in the way of those trying to do so. Then, he looked down at the base of the ladder.

Big mistake.

No one was holding the ladder. Felix's heart skipped a beat, and it wasn't the nice skipping his heart usually did when he saw Zizi, who was absentmindedly standing by and knitting. His breath caught in his throat. Felix clutched the ladder, and the ladder shook at his sudden motion, at which point every fluid ounce of blood in Felix's body rushed to his feet as he caught a glimpse of that elusive light people were supposed to avoid. Meanwhile, Maya was a few feet away arguing with their stepmother. No surprise there. Like any good business-minded entrepreneur, Tania was at the school to prey on the low self-esteem of teenage girls by promoting her personal "skin-safe" cosmetics line—"Fairest of Them All! #1 Dermatologist Recommended Brand! *Side effects may include heart failure." Of course, she failed to mention that she herself was the "#1 Dermatologist" recommending the brand.

Tania fussed with Maya's hair, which as usual was untidily bound in two bushy bunches. "Honestly, Maya, do you never look in a mirror?" The moment Tania released Maya's hair, Maya tossed her head back with exasperation and shook the loose strands back into place. Or rather, back out of place. Tania raised a perfectly sculpted eyebrow at Maya, "And you wonder why you don't have friends."

"I have friends," Maya argued. "Felix counts, right?"

"Not feeling so friendly right now," Felix huffed as he finally looped the corner of the tapestry onto the hook. The ladder wobbled again, and Felix clung to it for dear life. After the tremor passed, he took ginger steps, stopping every few rungs to hyperventilate before finally reaching the bottom.

Muttering under her breath, Tania straightened Maya's sweater. "If your father were here right now, he would tell you the same thing."

"That I'm friendless and alone?"

"That you should groom yourself occasionally," Tania corrected. "Goodness gracious, Maya, you are turning me grey." In truth, there was hardly a grey hair to be found amongst the dermatologist's luscious mahogany locks, but each one she had discovered had caused such an outcry that the siblings knew almost all of them by heart. Between the hair and the seemingly ageless skin, no one actually knew how old Tania was.

Tania reached for a basket of bright green apples, tucked away under the cosmetics table behind a rosy table-skirt. For the first time that Maya could remember, her stepmother offered her an apple. And it was poison green. "Apple?"

"No, thank you?" Maya stared at the sinister apple in her stepmother's hands like it was a spider that would disappear the moment she looked away, and she leaned back so far she knocked over the ladder. It toppled onto Felix, who had just found his footing again, thus eliciting from him a rather extensive string of threats and curses against all ladders everywhere.

With a harrumph, Tania tossed the apple back in the basket and turned her attention to the next victim in line.

Maya was still staring into the distance like a perturbed statue when Felix crawled out from under the ladder and said, "This morning, she asked me if I could pick up ginger spice while she was heating up the oven. Then she sniffed me and told me I smell good."

"Oh, good. So it's not all in my head," Maya sighed a breath of relief. Her backpack wiggled as she leaned over and sniffed Felix. "Although she's right. You do smell good. Are you wearing cologne?" Felix blushed and tugged at his shirt collar. Rolling her eyes, Maya shot a glance over at Zizi. Her face hardened.

After the first few complaints regarding student safety at Ambrose High, the school had hired a security guard. In no way did this security guard improve safety at the school, except where lawsuits were concerned, and he almost never left his office. For the last week, he had done nothing but sit in front of the security camera monitors and watch "how to knit" tutorials. Dave the security guard was long, rail thin, and lost without his 100% khaki uniform. Combined with the giant, bulging eyes and the way he folded into himself and twitched even while standing straight, he could easily have been mistaken for a gigantic stick insect. A giant stick insect that was stripping Zizi's knitting needles straight from her hands. She had just put the finishing touches on a "scarf" which was really a yellow monstrosity three meters long and two wide, close stitched, thick, fuzzy, complete with a black lancer riding across the golden fields. Even Felix could have literally wrapped himself in school spirit in that thing. However, the yarn was still connected to the knitting needles, so Dave confiscated the blanket too, citing "safety concerns."

Meanwhile, a boy in full armor stomped past, swinging his sword through the air. That was a less pressing safety concern, apparently.

"What are you doing?" Maya shouted at the twig of a man as he wrestled the blanket out of Zizi's hands. Which is when Zizi started to cry. Felix rushed to her side but then he realized that he did not know how to proceed in the department of comforting pretty girls, so he resorted to patting her back until she reassured him that she was doing just fine without getting the air knocked out of her.

"Knitting needles are a security threat."

"A blanket isn't," Maya growled, a low fire smoldering in her eyes as she marched nearer. Dave's mustache quivered. In an effort to reassert his authority in the situation, he met Maya's stare, a threat on the tip of his tongue, but he faltered before he could say anything. Instead, he turned tail and ran all the way back to his office, the blanket streaming behind him.

A cloud of ire settled over Maya's furrowed brow. She pressed her backpack into Felix's chest. "Watch the griffin."

"Should we...stop her?" Felix said as Maya stormed off towards the security office, a tiny bundle of fury in a red hoodie. He and Zizi exchanged a terrified look at the prospect of getting between Maya and her kill and remained put.

Maya sprinted out of the library and into the main entrance. She was gaining on the security guard. Almost there. If she could only catch him before he reached the security office at the other end of the atrium—the door slammed shut with a resounding *CLANG!* And Maya careened right into it with a much less resounding *thud.*

As Maya picked herself up off the marble floors, laughter filled the hall. But not just anyone's laughter. No, this was a laugh she had come to loathe very particularly. Sure enough, Wolf emerged from the shadows in which he so often dwelled. Or, more specifically, from behind the stairwell that led up to the second-floor landing, along which could be found Mr. Elegans's office, the bell tower access point, and a conference room.

Consciously ignoring him, Maya kicked at the door, but it remained sealed shut. She pounded harder. The metallic clang reverberated off the cinderblock walls. No answer. Wolf watched for several minutes before pulling up a chair and settling in for the show, a bag of popcorn in one hand, a copy of the school newspaper in the other. With a harrumph, Maya continued beating on the door until he said, "You do realize I'm the only person to have ever successfully broken into the security office."

"I thought you told Mr. Elegans that was me," Maya countered. "Do you know how many detentions I served? And when they finally figured out you were the one blackmailing all the teachers with the security camera footage, a sudden 'anonymous' donation appeared out of nowhere, and you got off scot free. I wonder how that happened. What a mystery."

"Ah, yes. Gotta love being rich," Wolf chomped down on a handful of popcorn and flipped through the paper. Led by editor-in-chief Franco Frank, a very small, very strange, and very earnest fellow who was in no way related to Coach Frank (the coach would have you know), the newspaper staff referred to the paper fondly by its proper title, the Daily Harold, named after its founder, Sir Edmund Harold III. To everyone else, it was less fondly known as the Daily Horror. Today, it featured an article on a new worm species discovered on campus, but Wolf had flipped to the back page, which had a lengthy discussion about a new IQ test for pigs. The test primarily consisted of determining what building materials the pig gravitated towards.

A voice crackled over the loudspeakers, "Attention, students of Ambrose High!" Franco Frank himself. He panted like he had run quite a ways to deliver this message, "This morning, the Daily Harold, Ambrose High's most reliable news source," and only news source, he failed to mention, "published an article on the discovery of a new worm species on campus. I have an important update: STAY AWAY FROM THE WORMS. Thank you, and please remember to pick up a copy of today's Daily Harold to keep up with the most exciting events happening here at Ambrose High. That is all." As the loudspeaker shut off, Maya suppressed any curiosity she might have had about the back story behind that announcement. She had a sinking feeling the worms had been amongst the escapees from the First Book of the Library of Souls.

Wolf interrupted her musings with a word, "When class starts and you still haven't gotten inside—"

"That's not going to happen." Maya stole a pin out of a passing student's hair. Lock picking was never Maya's forte, but these were desperate times. She wriggled the pin in the lock, to no avail.

"Some teachers might actually be grateful if you skipped."

"I'm not skipping class," Maya barked.

Wolf studied Maya, "I never did understand that part about you. I thought most delinquents get their start by skipping class."

"I am not a delinquent," Maya protested, growing more and more agitated with the lock.

"You blew up a lab bench last year."

"One time. I blow up a lab bench one time, and suddenly I'm a delinquent. It was chemistry. Sometimes that's what happens when you're working with dangerous chemicals."

"The experiment consisted of food coloring and water."

"Food coloring can be dangerous."

"Food coloring doesn't explode."

"Then maybe Dr. Takahashi shouldn't have left the jar of solid sodium on my desk," Maya jammed the hairpin into the lock one more time, but before she got anywhere with it, Dave rushed out of the security office, shouting and chasing Maya with a Super Soaker filled with pepper water.

"And watch out for the pepper water," Wolf advised as he flipped a page in the paper, the bag of popcorn lying empty at his feet.

Maya returned with eyes burning and nose in contortions to keep from sneezing, but she still managed a sarcastic, "Thanks," before pepper erupted through her nostrils. The paper rustled in the wake of the sneeze.

"Anytime."

Maya tried ramming down the door. She tried climbing through the vents (and lost a shoe in the process). She tried charming her way in. In the end, she was just as much outside as she had ever been. Minus a shoe. Finally, Maya took a deep breath and trod over to the chair where Wolf was still lounging.

Wolf smirked as he folded down the paper to see Maya, "So, you finally realized how much you want me."

Maya replied tersely, "How did you break into the security office?"

"What a shock! She wants me for my brains, not my stunning good looks."

Maya rolled her eyes. "Trust me, both of those would only appeal to a zombie."

"At least I have my personality," Wolf shrugged as he leaned back in his chair and put his hands behind his head. His amber eyes flickered with amusement.

"How did you get in?" Maya repeated.

Wolf shook his head. "Sorry, champ, they changed the locks."

"But you know how to get a key?"

"Maybe, but why should I help you?"

"To be a good person?"

"Except you and I both know that I'm not."

"There's always a chance for self-improvement."

"Says the girl who wants to break into a locked room."

Crossing her arms, Maya huffed, "Look, are you going to help me, or are you just going to watch?"

"It is pretty funny," Wolf chuckled. The laugh was met with a glare that could scorch hell itself. Finally, Wolf said, "Why don't you tell me how your search for the books is going?"

Maya scowled. "I already told you, I don't know what you're talking about."

Wolf rose from his chair with a nonchalant shrug and turned away. "That's really too bad. I was so convinced you were the champion, despite your many faults, but since you're so obviously *not*, I see we have nothing to gain from each other. Although, I am amazed that you haven't pursued the conspiracy anyways."

Maya spun Wolf back towards her and poked Wolf in the chest, punctuating each syllable as she steadily drove him back into the wall. "I would, but you keep getting in the way." Wolf grinned the irritating grin that meant, once again, Wolf had gotten the exact information he wanted. Twitching her nose in annoyance, Maya said, "I guess that answers your question. I've found two books, and I'm missing five. Now will you help me?"

As soon as Mr. Elegans saw Maya and Wolf talking, almost amicably, across the hall, he gasped and tore through the crowds to shove Maya and Wolf apart. "They're conspiring, and my worst nightmares are coming true." He grew a shade more ashen at the very idea.

"If you'll excuse me, I have something very important to do," Wolf announced with a wink at Maya. Then, he stripped down to his Batman boxers and sprinted across the hall. Mr. Elegans and Maya's jaws both dropped, although Maya suspected they did so for different reasons. After all, the principal was probably not fixated on Wolf's surprisingly well-sculpted abdominals. Although she wouldn't judge him if he were.

"What in heaven's name has gotten into that boy?" Mr. Elegans muttered.

Wolf hollered as he ran, "Yippee-ki-yay OOF!" The security guard huffed and he puffed and he tackled Wolf to the ground. After struggling for a few minutes, Wolf broke free. He ran back at Maya and slipped something into her hand, "Now we're even."

Then, Wolf dashed off again, yodeling as he went. As soon as Mr. Elegans and the security guard vanished from sight, Maya peaked at the token in her hand. A key. Wolf had stripped to his boxers to get her a key.

~ ~ ~

Felix soared over the table, holding the package under his arm as tightly as a football in a rivalry game. His feet hit the ground and he kept running. He had only to take a step, and the crowds parted before him. Reams of fabric flew through the air as decorators jumped out of his way. One startled student almost crashed into the wooden castle set in the center of the library. Felix never even hesitated. He slowed for no one. He rounded the corner, and there she was. Huffing hard, Felix slid to a stop before a very stunned looking Zizi and shoved the tangled ball of yarn into her hands. She held the bundle uncertainly for a moment, too shocked to react.

"I also found these," he pulled two knitting needles out of his pockets and added them to the pile. Not hers, of course. Hers were still under lock and key. Unless Maya had gotten through.

Zizi started to cry again.

Felix panicked, "I'm sorry. I know it's tangled. Here, let me try." He pulled on the strands of yarn and only made the knots worse. He used to be able to untangle yarn so well. The harder he tried, the more tangled the yarn became. His hands moved frantically, wilder and wilder until Zizi leapt at him and wrapped her arms around his massive chest.

Felix froze. His heart swelled. Surely, she must have heard the pounding. Her ear was pressed right against him. There was also a knitting needle stabbing into his shoulder blade, but that didn't matter right now. She was happy, and he had helped. When she let go, their eyes met for just a moment before the blood rushed to their faces and they both looked down at their shuffling feet. Except their gaze kept intersecting even that way, so Felix decided to look up instead. His jaw dropped.

The lights above flickered. A shower of shooting stars streaked across the tapestry. One minute, the lights went dark, the next they displayed the Milky Way or an enchanted pirate ship soaring through the night sky or the moon's journey from birth to death, waxing and waning from new moon to full moon to new moon again.

"You made that?" Felix gaped. Zizi simply smiled. Of course she had made it. Only someone who understood beauty so deeply could create beauty so brilliant. She had made a perfect replica of the world she saw, and it was wonderful. "It's—it's," Felix wanted to tell her all that and more, but he struggled to find an adjective good enough, and as he was searching his mental Rolodex, another thought crept in, as such thoughts often do, and panic struck the most central chord of his nervous system. "The griffin."

Felix rushed to the corner where he had left the bag. The backpack lay empty, like a popped balloon. With frantic hands, he turned the backpack inside out, but to no avail. Gone. Felix had left for just a minute, and now Oscar was gone. Felix surveyed the mountains of table runners, the bins of fabric, the castle set, the thousand other places the griffin could be hiding, and he broke into a cold sweat. He knew taking in a wild mythical creature was a bad idea. Those blasted puppy eyes. One look and his judgment had flown through the window. This was going to be impossible.

~ ~ ~

The closet-sized security office was lit only by the pale glow of the monitors on the far wall, which perfectly illuminated Maya's missing shoe, lying in the middle of the floor. Maya quickly slipped it back on. She had missed the sneaker's warm embrace. Then, she swept Zizi's blanket off the desk and hoisted the bundle under her arm.

Maya was halfway to the door when she noticed something else lying on the desk. A file, lying open to a hazy picture of a figure robed in a hooded cloak. With a glance out the door to check if the coast was clear, Maya inched back towards the folder. It was filled with picture upon blurry picture of the same figure, shrouded in shadows, a black cloud at his feet, his face always hidden behind his black hood. Even through a picture, the apparition left Maya unsettled, but she could not draw her gaze away from it. This was the Wizard.

Along the left side of the folder was scribbled a list of dates. Maya lingered on the last one, her breath catching in her throat. March 15th. The day her father had disappeared. Her stomach lurched. Her head buzzed. She knew she should leave, but her feet refused to obey.

At least not until Wolf skidded into the room and pressed himself against the wall. "Wolf, what are you doing in—what are you wearing?" Wolf was dressed in a onesie with cotton balls glued on to make it a very sad looking sheep costume.

"Oh, this old thing? Found it in the drama department," Wolf strutted and posed, a playful grin on his face. "I guess you could say this makes me a—"

"Don't you dare say it."

Another silhouette appeared, filling the doorway. "Maya, we lost Oscar," Felix panted. With wide eyes, Maya ran out as fast as she could, Zizi's blanket billowing behind her like a long cape as she went. Felix studied Wolf for a moment before chuckling, "I get it. Wolf in sheep's clothing."

"See! It's funny," Wolf insisted. Felix wavered. "A little?"

~ ~ ~

The stacked rolls of golden fabric formed a barricade in the far corner of the library next to the librarian's desk. Behind this barrier, hidden from view, Zizi sat cross-legged on the floor, grinning to herself like a fool. Zizi wrapped the yarn around her needles, the soft click-click-click calming the thunderclaps in her heart. Where had Felix even found knitting needles at this school? She giggled as she recalled the ridiculous way he had looked while he was sprinting across the library, yarn in hand, a deadly serious look in his eyes, as though the delivery of such a package were a matter of life and death. Heat crept up her cheeks, and she had to remind herself that the knitting needles probably meant nothing. He was just a friend, concerned for another friend.

A shadow fell over her fingers. Zizi looked up. The ashen principal was observing her work. She jumped to her feet and, with one rapid motion, hid the knitting needles behind her back lest he confiscate these as well.

Mr. Elegans chuckled and readjusted his glasses disarmingly, "No fear. I won't take those. And I may have a conversation with our dearest security guard about what he is and is not allowed to confiscate from students." Zizi breathed a sigh of relief and let her arms fall. "Will you be attending the Homecoming dance?" the principal asked.

"Of course," Zizi beamed, and her thoughts drifted back to the boy who had lifted a hundred pound tapestry of lights for her and who had chased down yarn for her and who waited by her locker nearly every day with a fresh batch of cookies. He'd started baking a lot more lately, so much so that Maya had started a surprisingly lucrative cookie smuggling business to sell them to other students. But there was always a little left over. "With a theme like fairytales, how could I not? True love, a handsome prince, a fearsome dragon—it's perfect. Not to mention, it's the night before my sixteenth birthday."

Mr. Elegans wiped his glasses clean, "Yes, but you never can be too careful around dragons." He placed his glasses back on the bridge of his nose and peered at Zizi. "I've noticed that you have been spending quite a bit of time with the Rodriguez family. Our new *champion* in particular."

Hesitating, Zizi took note of the principal's disdainful lisp, his steely grey eyes, his rigid stature, and she stated, "You don't approve."

The frankness took Mr. Elegans aback. He fiddled with his glasses once more and noted, "The girl has quite the temper."

Zizi shrugged and ran her nimble fingers over the first row of her new project to straighten out the kinks, "She's fiercely protective of her treasures." When Zizi's gaze met Mr. Elegans's again, it had none of its usual softness or delicacy. A sunbeam fell on her eyes, and the light transformed her brown irises into brilliant gold. Her eyes shimmered as brightly as the swaths of golden fabric stacked on her left, and those golden eyes defied the dull grey ones to respond. The tension lasted until a shout drew their attention.

"Zizi," Maya hollered as she barreled through the library, the gold and black blanket whipping the air like a tail, fluttering from her outstretched arms like wings in flight. Zizi turned to Mr. Elegans to make one last comment, but when she did, he was gone, vanished like smoke in the wind. Maya skirted around the barricade of fabric and bundled the blanket up for Zizi. "We lost the griffin."

Zizi nearly dropped the bundle in alarm. "How do we find him?"

"He likes dirty laundry. And socks. Don't leave him alone with your socks." Zizi did not see the relevance. Maya gestured towards the piles of fabric scattered about the room, "I'd start there."

Felix dashed up, glitter sparkling on nearly all of his clothes. When he saw Zizi, he tried his best to brush the glitter off, but it only spread, multiplying like a sparkly virus with an incubation time of about two seconds. Glitter infected his clothes, his hair, his face—glitter even sprinkled out of his caterpillar eyebrows. Zizi giggled, and Felix never looked so miserable in his whole life. "Oscar's not in the craft supplies. Any luck here?" he said.

A crash echoed through the library, followed by the sound of a thunderous and magnificent collapse, the fall of a castle. Maya's heart stopped. Felix's jaw dropped. Zizi gasped. The wooden castle set in the center of the library had caved in under the weight of a flailing, chomping, full-grown Great White Shark. The winged lion cub flew in tight circles above, proudly displaying his catch. The room fell silent.

Then, Maya said, "On a positive note, I think he learned how to fish."

Behind the barricade, Zizi and Maya exchanged a glance and burst into laughter. Felix harrumphed and crossed his arms with his you-are-not-taking-this-nearly-seriously-enough-and-I-am-the-only-sensible-person-here-this-is-not-funny-this-is-serious look. Which only made Maya and Zizi laugh harder. For a moment, as her sides ached in the best way possible, Maya had a strange thought. Could Zizi possibly, maybe, perhaps actually be a friend? Like, a real friend? But before she could consider it, screams and thrashing and crashing sounds drew Maya's mind back to the present. First things first, she had a shark to deal with.

~ ~ ~

It was just one of those days—a security office heist, a Great White in the library, a griffin on the lam, and now this. Maya had stolen into the chemistry classroom after school, and as she was stretching to reach the top shelf of the chemical cabinet, which she could barely reach even when she stood on the stepstool, she accidentally bumped a hidden lever. Maya tumbled off the stepstool as the cabinet swung back into the wall. She blinked thrice just to be sure of what she was seeing. Complex equations filled a blackboard. Steam bubbled up from a round-bottomed flask dangling over a Bunsen burner. Glass jars lined a shelf on the other side, filled with such choice ingredients as "Ground Batwing; Best used by third contact of solar eclipse," and "Student Tears; Collected during October exam, Potency: 9.5," and "The Alchemist's Finest Chili Powder." Maya blinked again.

"We're just gonna...leave that there," Maya decided as she gently closed the door again. It locked with a click. She shook her head to clear the fumes. It actually hadn't smelled all that bad. Smelled like chili. Chili that might have been made with ground batwing, newt hearts, and tears of students. Maya's stomach turned.

"Maya?" Felix poked his head into the chemistry classroom. Droplets formed at the end of his nose, and his shirt was soaked through. Was that still sweat from football practice? Or had he forgotten to dry off after his shower? Maya hoped for the latter.

"Ready for the big game tomorrow?" Maya rubbed soap suds out of Felix's ear. He squirmed away and dried his face with the towel around his neck, shifting the carton of eggs under his arm in the process. Maya quirked a brow. "And what's with the eggs?"

Felix wasted no words, his voice earnest, "Mr. Elegans wants to see you."

Maya's face fell. The pit of her stomach dropped. Her lip trembled. Mr. Elegans had never liked her very much, and he had certainly been less than thrilled when Maya had become the "champion," whatever that meant. Whenever she ended up in his office, which was far more frequently than she would have liked, he told her that she was just like her father, as though that were a bad thing. But those visits had resulted from general disruptive behavior and the occasional lab accident. After a day like this one, there was nothing good Mr. Elegans could possibly want to talk about.

Mr. Elegans was cleaning his glasses when Maya stepped into his office. Despite the giant windows on either side, gloom seemed to cling to the room. Whereas brick and stone dominated the exterior of the school and some of the halls, the rooms themselves were all lined with polished wood paneling. The classrooms were light and natural, the library almost golden, but the principal's office was a deep, rich mahogany. The matching furniture intensified the austerity, and wine-colored drapes hung heavy over the windows. If only Mr. Elegans would open those windows from time to time, the room would not always smell like someone had just attacked a nasty stain with every cleaning product in the closet. The creamy carpet muffled Maya's feet as she approached. "You asked to see me?"

If this was about breaking into the security office, Maya feared it would be the last straw, the straw that broke the principal's patience. If it was about the shark—well, the Daily Horror had printed a second edition that day, with the headline, "Something Fishy: Super-Strength Eagle Drops the Shark," and another one, "Animal Testing at Secret Government Facility," which was unrelated to the first and discussed the precautions government facilities took to protect laboratories from PETA extremists. Unfortunately, the title was misleading, and three dozen black SUVs appeared on campus only six minutes after the paper was distributed. That edition was never seen again.

"Please, have a seat," Mr. Elegans said softly as he put his glasses back on. His demeanor was so muted compared to the stern principal Maya usually saw that Maya was beginning to worry something truly horrible had happened. Maya lowered herself into the chair and waited with bated breath. Like the rest of the furniture in the principal's office, the chair was characterized entirely by bold straight lines. However, this meant that the hard, flat seat in no way complimented the shape of a normal human bottom. Maya had often wondered if these chairs were specifically designed to make students as uncomfortable as possible when they got sent to the principal's office. If so, they were a success.

The principal sighed. Grey eyes lowered, he leaned forward and folded his hands, "Defending the Library of Souls is a tremendous burden."

Maya stiffened. So this is what he wanted to discuss. She almost would have rather discussed the shark. Still, she straightened her back, though it made little difference with her short stature and the shorter chair, and she spoke candidly, "Mr. Elegans, I know you don't think I am 'champion' material, but I *will* open the Library. My dad's in there. I don't care what I have to do. I *will* save him."

A slight chuckle passed through upturned lips as Mr. Elegans shook his head, "I know."

"You do?" Even Maya wasn't so sure. She meant what she had said, but there were always complicating factors. Like the Wizard. And the possibility of death.

Mr. Elegans opened a drawer and pulled out a photograph. Maya had only to see the white dress to know what it was as he gave it to her. She cupped it like a sacred artifact, afraid to leave fingerprints on the glossy surface. Her mother's mane of hair burst from under the veil, but she was smiling so broadly her cheeks had to have been sore for a week afterwards. And Maya's father, too—even in the photograph, his eyes, eyes that had been so heavy for so long, his eyes danced for joy. And next to them stood a twenty year younger Mr. Elegans. Maya squinted. Apparently, the principal had never been very good at smiling. Shaking her head, Maya searched Mr. Elegans's grey mask for an explanation.

The man had always had high expectations, expectations that Maya had never quite met. Up to this moment, Maya had been convinced that he had her picture taped over the definition of "disappointment." Though he was a long-term friend of the family, she had anticipated no help from him in her quest for the seven books of the Library of Souls. And yet there he was, making such a gesture as she would never have believed. She almost did not believe it now.

Mr. Elegans cleared his throat and awkwardly said, "I want you to keep that." Maya's confusion only grew, and Mr. Elegans shifted uncomfortably in his chair, despite the fact that his was far more plush than Maya's. "And...I hope you will trust me with another chance to be the guide I should have been all along. I was often your parents' counsel in times of need, and I believe you can succeed just as much as I believed in them." A jolt ran through Maya's body. Had she heard that correctly? Mr. Elegans rose from his desk chair and stepped over to the bookshelves along the wall behind Maya. He ran a finger across the immaculate mahogany, examining the books with lustful eyes, as though he saw in them something beyond paper and ink. "Still, in such uncertain times, there are very few you can trust," Mr. Elegans warned, facing Maya again. "You must not tell anyone who or what you are."

"And what am I?"

"The champion, the only one who can unlock the Library of Souls."

"But I don't even know how to find these seven books. I found the first two by accident, and I haven't been able to find any since."

Mr. Elegans rubbed his glasses clean with a handkerchief and paced, a teacher instructing his pupil, "The champion must be sure, compassionate, and brave, a beacon of truth amidst doubt, a bastion of power, full of grace and wisdom. The books will test for such qualities at the most critical moments, but they will also guide and teach you if you let them."

Maya's eyes grew wider with every attribute he listed, and she gulped, "The world is doomed." As Mr. Elegans chortled and returned to his seat, Maya asked, "Why don't we keep the Library sealed shut all the time?" She looked up to meet Mr. Elegans's befuddled gaze. "I mean, I know we can't right now because, if we don't open the Library, the books will get eaten by the Wizard's evil evilness, but why wasn't the Library sealed in the first place?"

Readjusting the glasses on the bridge of his nose, Mr. Elegans explained, "Because the Library of Souls is the source of life itself. The longer it remains sealed, the more this world will fall into death and despair."

Maya's heart climbed up her throat, throbbing, pushing itself further up with every beat. "But if I fail to break the curse on the Library, if the Library falls into the hands of the Wizard, who looks really creepy, by the way—Dave has a whole file of pictures, and honestly the Wizard looks terrifying." Mr. Elegans looked up at Maya with a start. Such a file was news to him. "If I have to fight that guy—"

"No need to worry about that until after you find the seven books," Mr. Elegans reassured her with a gentle smile. "But, Maya, if anything unusual occurs, please, come to me immediately. I will assist you in any way you need so that you may accomplish your task. I promise."

~ ~ ~

Warm light flooded the living room from a half-dozen lamps scattered about. The room flowed naturally out of the kitchen, only a counter separating the two. The smell of chicken soup wafted towards Maya as her stepmother tended the stove. Tania always insisted on making her own – something about the real thing being better for the heart. Maya curled further into the burnt-orange couch, as though burrowing into the cushions would provide some kind of shelter from the world around her. Nearly everything in the room had been chosen by Tania. Gone was every trace of the style preferred by Maya's mother, the muted colors, the clean lines, the versatility. In the room Maya now occupied, Tania had chosen the color palate: bright colors everywhere, especially oranges and yellows and blues. Tania had chosen the layout: open floorplan with the television tucked away against the wall, right where the glare from the window made it impossible to see anything in the afternoons, and every piece of furniture too bulky to move. And the light fixtures – it felt like every time Maya turned around, Tania had acquired a new lamp of some sort of another.

The tall lamp in the corner often doubled as a coat rack. The identical lamps on either end of the burnt-orange couch took turns flickering. Nothing they did could stop the blinking, and as soon as they fixed one lamp the other started acting up, so Felix had decided that they must have had a very lazy poltergeist living amongst them. More than once, Maya had returned to the apartment to find her textbooks marked up as historically inaccurate, so she did not discredit the theory. Also, someone or something kept moving the stack of books on the coffee table, thus removing the only barrier that prevented the flimsy paper lantern from tumbling to the floor under the weight of the extension cord. Then, there was the lamp over the armchair that looked like one of those hair helmets at the barber shop and acted like a spotlight, there was the string of Christmas lights along the decorative molding, and finally there was the mysterious cat lamp that only turned on when you pinched the chord exactly three inches from the end of the plug while playing the radio at full volume. And that did not count all the lamps Tania had tried and discarded over the years.

Consequently, Maya was well illuminated as she sat curled up on the burnt-orange couch, a math book on her lap, the wedding photo playing between her fingers. Between the picture and her math homework, only one required her undivided attention, but the other held it. No matter how many times she looked at the photograph, that precious gift, she still could not believe her eyes or her ears or her surely faulty memory. But if it was all true, if it was not a surreal dream, then she was not alone in the fight for the Library of Souls. Help had come from the last person she would have expected.

Tania stepped out of the kitchen, and Maya stiffened.

"Soup is done," her stepmother said, her hair slightly frizzy from the humidity, her ageless skin glistening. By some unknown magic, she still looked like Aphrodite herself, but that was another matter. "Would you like some?"

"I'm not hungry," Maya replied as she did her best to focus on her math homework again. She wished Felix were here. Unfortunately, he was working on a "project" at school, though the nature of the project remained a mystery. Still, when he was around, Maya's absence at the dinner table was much less obvious. Sometimes Felix would get frustrated with her and demand why she refused to eat the soup, insist that it was really quite tasty, reprimand her for being rude, but more often he would simply say, "Missed you at dinner tonight. You should try the soup next time." She never did. Her stomach growled loud enough for anyone to hear, and Maya winced.

With narrowed eyes, Tania crossed her arms, "Are you sure you don't want something to eat?"

"I said I'm not hungry." Maya snapped her books shut and marched off to her room. In all the years her stepmother had lived here, Maya had never once eaten the chicken soup, and she never would. She could feel Tania's sigh blow through the living room, a sigh heavy with every previous rejection. Before Maya could dwell on it any longer, before doubt could take seed in her resolve, she slammed the door shut and cut herself off.

Only the cold moon illuminated Maya's room. A gentle breeze wafted through the window. Maya shivered. She could have sworn she had closed that window. After sitting in the living room so long, it took Maya's eyes a minute to adjust to the cool light and the shadows. Compared to Felix's Spartan cleanliness, Maya's room was always messy. Piles of dirty laundry (plus a griffin) congregated vaguely in the corner, and books littered the floor, books that did not fit into her crammed bookshelf, books she was rereading despite the pile of books she still had yet to read, books she meant to read, books she could not stop reading again and again, books that spoke of a world bigger and grander than her own, books that made the complicated things so easy and books that complicated even the simplest of things. Philosophy, history, art, it was all there, scattered across her bedroom floor. But something was different, wrong, out of place.

Then, she saw. On her pillow was lying a plain envelope, sealed, unmarked, and absolutely alien to Maya's room. Holding the envelope away from herself, Maya stepped into the pale rectangle of moonlight coming through the window and turned out the contents. Three crimson rose petals fell like drops of blood, glimmering in the soft light, until they touched the floor and disappeared in a black cloud. Maya's stomach lurched, and the same unsettled, empty feeling settled over her as when she had seen those photographs of the Wizard. Skipping dinner probably wasn't helping. She ran her fingers along the interior of the envelope. It was empty, but the message was clear nonetheless. Danger was coming.

~ ~ ~

When the sun had set and the day was ticking to its end, when shadows had descended and dusk had risen, Dave the security guard returned to his office, his own little enclave in the atrium, yet, to his surprise, he found it occupied for the second time that day.

"Charles?" he said from the door as yellow light poured out from the lamp on his desk. The monitors had all been turned off for the night. No one watched them anyways.

The grey-clad principal stood in the center of the room, casting a long shadow across the floor. "Interesting project," he said as he flipped through pictures of the Wizard. An unusual book was lying on the desk next to him. It was thick with gold-rimmed pages.

The security guard closed the door behind him. The clang reverberated off the walls. Dave twitched. His voice quivered, "I've been following him for a while now. At first, I thought the "Wizard" was just a rumor, but—if you'd seen the things I've seen over the last few weeks, you'd believe too. But here's the strange part." Dave edged around Mr. Elegans and pulled a few pictures from the file, "In a lot of these, you can see someone, barely an outline, through the Wizard's robes. Same shape, same size in all of them. I think—this might sound crazy, and I know I'm still learning about this magic stuff—but what if this robed figure is just some magical illusion? What if it's controlled by someone else entirely?"

"Do you know who might be behind this *Wizard*?" Mr. Elegans asked as he scrutinized the pictures.

Dave stuffed his hands into the pockets of his khaki pants. It was chilly tonight. "Not sure. Need some more time, but I'll figure it out eventually. After all, I just recently installed the additional cameras I need. At first, I was just doing this because that Mori lady was paying big bucks for it, but now," he chuckled like he couldn't believe it either, "I want to know too."

The principal closed the file with calculated precision, "I'm afraid Mrs. Miyuki Mori has made a poor investment." He turned his steely grey eyes on the security guard. Dave stepped back towards the door, a tremor running through his stick limbs at the sight.

With a flick of the principal's wrist, the cover of the book on the desk flipped open. The pages tore out and contorted to his will as the light flickered behind him. As the pages crumbled, darkness spreading from the gold tipped edges, the flurry took shape. A cloaked figure rose from the dust and ashes, from the corrupted pages at the grey man's command, and as the security guard gaped in horror at the Wizard standing before him, the phantom figure swept over him, the black cloak passing over his heart like a shroud.

The light flickered and went out.

Five
But the Wizard came

A deathly silence blanketed the atrium. Like ghosts reaching for the heavens, gold and silver tarps hung over the walls, the translucent sheets wavering in the cool draft from above. A dozen pillars thick as sequoias loomed over the insignificant beings that walked between them. A soft pitter-patter echoed across the marble floors as two shadows drifted towards the metal door to one side of the imposing hall. The day's classes had not yet started, and the school was as lifeless as a graveyard. Felix was the first to break the silence, "Are you sure this is the best idea? Didn't Mr. Elegans call you into his office for this yesterday?"

"Just trust me," Maya said. The door was grey, much greyer than she remembered it. It no longer glimmered in the daylight but rather wallowed in a special form of misery that dulled even the lights around it.

Felix followed, "Maya, is something the matter?"

"Everything is fine," Maya snapped. She had not yet told him about the mysterious envelope on her pillow or the blood-red petals that had turned to smoke or the sense of foreboding that had filled her heart since. She had not told anyone. Shaking her mind clear, Maya explained, "Dave had a file on the Wizard. I just want to see what he knows."

"And you think he'll tell you? After yesterday?" Felix objected.

"No. That's why I brought you." Maya pounded a fist against the grey, grey door, but it offered no resistance. At a single touch, it swung open, and a pale rectangle of light stretched across the floor within. The siblings froze in place, their jaws as wide open as the door.

In a muted voice, Felix said, "I don't think he's going to be talking much to either of us."

~ ~ ~

The police came, the body went, and Felix and Maya remained, planted in two chairs just outside the principal's office with clear instructions from Mr. Elegans himself: "Your bottoms are not to leave those chairs under any circumstances."

So they waited, seated on the second-story landing overlooking the atrium. They waited as the police strung up yellow caution tape over the doors and students crowded around, trying to get a peek inside, though there was nothing to see. Not anymore. And they waited as Mr. Elegans forced the students out and locked the doors around the entrance hall, and as the bell rang and classes began, and as the police finished their investigation. The only thing suspicious was a black powder like ash that sprinkled the floor between the desk and the body. Strange, yes, but not indicative of anything particularly wayward. Still Maya and Felix waited. They waited and waited and waited. Then, they waited some more. When Maya could wait no longer, she huffed with exasperation and began to scoot away across the landing.

"Maya, what are you doing?" Felix whispered urgently.

"Going to class." She thumped down a stair. Thump, thump, thump, she went until she discovered she could go much faster if she simply pinned the chair to her bottom and waddled a little hunched over.

"You're going to get into trouble."

"Hey, my butt's not leaving the chair." She reached the ground floor and scooted off into the distance.

No sooner had the last screeches of her chair died away than Mr. Elegans poked his head out of his office. His steel gaze shot at the empty space next to Felix and then to the boy himself. Felix started to teeter nervously, "Technically she is still in her chair."

"Find her."

Without another word, Mr. Elegans turned on his heel and stomped off after her.

~ ~ ~

All eyes turned to the door of the classroom. All ears perked up. There it was again. That sound. A long scraping sound from the hallway. No one dared to breathe. Dave's ghost had returned, looking for revenge. Or it was the serial-killing axe-murderer who had offed him in the first place, come back for more victims. Or the evil spirit haunting the school. Somehow, even though the rumor had only started that day, everyone had heard about the evil spirit ages ago.

Another scrape, followed by the sound of shuffling feet. Scrape, shuffle, scrape, shuffle, scrape. Nearer and nearer, it came. Thirty souls held their breath, eyes trained on the door, hearts trying to fit in a few more beats before the end.

The door burst open, and Maya scooted inside. "Hi, Ms. Elliot. I miss much?"

At that moment, the bell rang, and class was over. The room exploded with questions and rumors and a general ruckus which no teacher could have silenced, even if they had wanted to. As students crowded around, Zizi slipped away into the hall and to Felix's locker, Maya scooting at her heels. Before opening the locker, Zizi turned a thoughtful eye on Maya and asked, "Why did you come to class?"

"The principle of it," Maya said flatly, casting a furtive glance down the hall to make sure no one was watching. "Clear."

Zizi opened the locker, and the smell of fresh baked cookies immediately filled the hall as heat radiated from the locker. Zizi swiftly pulled a cookie tray out, poured the contents into the paper bag in Maya's hand, and slammed the locker door shut. Maya checked the locker below Felix's. Sure enough, there was already a bag of cookies waiting to be delivered. The bottom locker had been abandoned due to a "high frequency of spontaneous homework combustion events." Zizi later installed better insulation in Felix's makeshift oven to make the space useable again. Actually, Zizi had pretty much built and designed the whole oven when she discovered his first crude attempts at a "locker-oven" after the Cook kicked him out of the kitchen for the last time. Felix had started stress-baking during the first round of exams and then never quite let up, to the point that neither Maya nor Zizi could keep up with the mounds of cookies he was making. Fortunately, other students were more than happy to help with the bake-pocalypse, and so the cookie smuggling business had been born.

Zizi scrutinized Maya longer, and Maya squirmed. For all her gentleness, Zizi would not be appeased until she knew the truth. It was never cruelly intended, but in matters of the mind, of knowledge and fact, Zizi did not compromise. "I don't understand. You don't like class. Why are you so opposed to missing it?"

"Entertainment value."

"Lie."

Maya harrumphed. Zizi certainly did not mince words. But she had a way about her—like she actually wanted to listen, as those who truly love to learn often do—that soon enough

Maya found herself telling the truth. A partial truth, anyways. With a deep sigh, she said, "My dad and I got into an argument about me skipping class the day he left." What she left off was the part where the argument morphed into one about other things. Including Mr. Elegans. She understood *now* why he and the principal were friends, but at the time it could not have been less apparent, and her father would not hear of it. Then, he left and never returned.

After a long pause, Zizi asked, "What did you skip class for?"

Maya turned as red as her hoodie and scratched the back of her head, doing her best to avoid eye contact as she confessed, "Oh, er, there, er, might have been a band. I was trying to be punk rock. I wasn't very good at it."

"You can't try to be punk rock. You either are, or you aren't," Zizi said with the sort of cool confidence that made Maya do a double take. The image of Zizi as a punk fell apart the moment her face lit up with a smile like melted butter on pancakes, "Ready to deliver the cookies?"

Just then, Mr. Elegans appeared at the end of the hall, his grey face stonier than ever, and Maya had seen some of his stoniest faces. She gulped. And the chase began.

~ ~ ~

"Disaster strikes Ambrose High! Franco Frank, investigative journalist and editor-in-chief of the Daily Harold, has been denied access to Ambrose High's most controversial crime scene, despite his long history of—"

"Franco, you're headlining again," Wolf interrupted as he tightened the ropes one last time. They were both standing on the roof of the building, looking down an open hatch into the entrance hall below. Far below. The wind whistled past, cold in the shadow of the clock tower. Although even the strongest gusts could not disturb the gel-soaked style Wolf wore, Franco's mop of carrot-colored hair flopped about in the breeze.

Franco turned off the voice recorder with an air of great importance, "One never knows when inspiration will strike, and as editor-in-chief of a prestigious news outlet, I must be prepared for anything."

"Then I hope you're ready to jump," Wolf said as he joined Franco at the edge of the hatch.

With so much excited energy that he almost lost his glasses, Franco whipped out the recorder again, "Breaking News: Franco Frank has engaged in a dangerous and top secret mission to uncover the truth behind Dave the Security Guard's mysterious death! He will lower himself into the atrium—"

"Franco!"

"Stay tuned for more," Franco slipped the recorder into the pocket of his tweed jacket and exchanged his glasses for a pair of prescription goggles. His harness was so big on him that, even though the two boys had pulled it as tight as possible, it was probably still a safety hazard. Franco checked his pockets.

Recorder, camera, pen and paper, student press badge. He was set. Franco peered through the hatch and took a deep breath. The terracotta tiles creaked underfoot. A draft pulled him towards that gaping hole and the long drop beyond it. All other entrances had been locked. If Franco wanted to find the truth, he'd have to come in from above. This was the only way. Lucky for him, Wolf was bored enough to help.

"Ready?" Wolf asked.

Franco laughed, "I'm an investigative journalist, Wolf. Truth is my mother and courage her milk." And that courage held up very well. Until Wolf pushed him through the hatch. Franco screamed like a yodeler on a roller coaster, and he kept screaming long after the rope jerked to a halt. Meanwhile, Wolf leaned back and filed his nails until he heard Franco fake a breathy laugh and shout up, "Good one, Wolf. You really had me there for a minute. Wolf released another few feet of rope, and Franco screamed again. When he stopped again, even with the bottom end of the sheets decorating the walls, Franco pulled out the voice recorder and said, "Breaking News: Wolf endangers reporter's life with murderous intent."

"Trust me, that would be far more entertaining," Wolf said with a jaded drawl.

Franco continued to record, "In a shocking twist, authorities have still not observed student dangling from roof. Operation to proceed as planned." When Wolf did nothing,

Franco cleared his throat and said a little louder, "Operation to proceed."

Wolf lowered him an inch.

With a huff, Franco recorded, "Is Wolfgang Mori in league with the shadowy government agency haunting Ambrose High? Stay tuned."

Wolf guffawed, "Shadowy government organization? Do they have you writing the entertainment section again?"

"Consider the evidence: first, the school library is destroyed in a surprisingly feather-ful fire. The same day, the number of chickens in the school chicken coup doubles. No suspects identified for arson. Second, a super-strength eagle drops a shark in the gym. When reported, newspaper is confiscated by scary men in suits. Third, security guard dies less than twenty-four hours later. Fourth, the boys' bathroom has been clogged *all week*—"

"At that rate, we might as well include magic and wizards and fire-breathing chickens in our list of possible theories," Wolf said as he let out another length of rope. A yelp echoed through the hatch.

Franco scoffed, "Magic isn't real."

A holler rang through the hall. Maya scurried by, hunched over and holding a chair to her butt. A few moments later, Mr. Elegans burst into the atrium behind her, and only moments after that, Wolf zipped down through the hatch on a separate rope, whooping and laughing as he chased after the pair.

Franco took a moment to register the scene before realizing, "Breaking News: Franco Frank stuck. Assistance required."

~ ~ ~

Maya crossed her arms and harrumphed as Mr. Elegans closed the door to his office behind them. She was still sitting in the chair out of defiance. The office was as somber as ever, and it grew darker still as Mr. Elegans closed the blinds over the window facing the atrium. This was to be a private conversation, then. Through the other window, the morning haze smeared soft, grey light across the sky. Mr. Elegans turned on her, his ashen cheeks flushed with exertion, which made him look a little like a ghost who had recently discovered makeup and was still learning how to make it less splotchy. "Maya, I need you to tell me very honestly," Mr. Elegans said, his grey eyes both gentle and urgent at the same time, "did something happen that I should know about? Because this might just be the beginning."

Maya took a sharp breath and squirmed in her seat. Something had happened, or rather several somethings had happened one after another. Even though Mr. Elegans would know what it all meant, Maya hesitated to tell him. For just a fraction of a second, she had the sense that she shouldn't tell him, but that sense disappeared the moment she looked into those gentle, wise, urgent eyes again. Her parents had trusted him. He had been their best friend. And he had promised to help her. In that moment, she made up her mind, and she chose to trust him, "It's not really much, but I got this envelope yesterday. On my pillow, which was a little creepy. And when I opened it, three rose petals fell out and turned into smoke. But it's probably not that big of a—"

The splotches vanished from the principal's face. "The Wizard's calling card."

"Wait, what?"

"We must remain vigilant, or the Wizard will strike again."

"Again? Wait, did the Wizard kill Dave? It wasn't because I talked to him, was it? Holy bananas, I killed Dave the Security Guard!" Three police officers poked their heads into the office. "Metaphorically, that is." The three officers disappeared into the conference room next door again.

"It was the Wizard, but no fault of yours. I assure you of that," Mr. Elegans said as he sat down at his desk, his demeanor suddenly cold and distant. "Still, he knows who you are. You must be careful."

Maya squared her jaw as she looked Mr. Elegans in the eye, her fist clenched. "Do I have to worry about Felix?"

"I believe, as the champion, you are the Wizard's primary interest."

"Then I'll be fine."

Mr. Elegans shook his head ruefully as he watched the stubbornness play out across Maya's face, "Why is it always the willful ones?"

"Always?" Maya asked, and the tautness in her muscles fell away. "You mean there have been others?"

"Who have tried to defeat the Wizard? Of course." Mr. Elegans began cleaning his glasses. "The last one—a sweet boy, that one—was a particularly obstinate and talented young magician who, like you, refused to listen to my advice."

Maya's concern mounted. "And what happened to him?" The investigators stepped into the office, and Mr. Elegans rose to meet them. "Mr. Elegans, what happened?"

"Just got word from the medical examiner," said the oldest of the officers. "Heart attack. Looks like our work here is done. Hope we haven't caused you too much trouble."

"None at all. Let me show you the way out," Mr. Elegans escorted the police officers to the door. Maya shouted after him, but he left her behind with far more questions than before and far too few answers.

Still dazed from her conversation, Maya wandered out of Mr. Elegans's office. Then, a voice called to her from above. Maya's gaze snapped up to the boy dangling from the ceiling. Her face fell. "Wolf?" Franco nodded. She cracked her knuckles, "I'll find him for you."

But before she got very far, another set of voices caught her attention. She pressed her ear to the library door. That was

Felix. And Zizi. And suddenly the mysterious "project" wasn't so mysterious anymore. Maya burst through the door, "I knew iiii—what are you doing?" An egg splattered at her feet. She looked up. Felix was standing at the top of the ladder, a carton of eggs in one hand and a box in the other.

"Egg drop. For physics," Felix explained.

Zizi nodded, her face lit up with the brightest smile. "We have to come up with something that will keep the egg from cracking."

"We're doing it without a parachute."

"Extra credit."

Maya rolled her eyes, "Nerds." Muttering under her breath, she turned and left them to whatever it was they were doing. Felix dropped the box but, like the last few prototypes, the yolk of responsibility was too much for it. He and Zizi cleaned up the hardwood floor while discussing newer and better plans, such as adding extra padding or weighing down the bottom to control which side it landed on or using Oscar to fly the box to safety. At some point while they were talking, Maya snuck back into the library and absconded with the ladder, but they never noticed. They were too focused on other things.

Felix looked up at the starry canvas above, the one he had helped to install, and he paused to do a double take. The tapestry had transformed itself once more. He traced the lines of the stars, swirling through the deep purples and blues and blacks of the night sky backdrop on the ceiling, and dwelled upon the rays of the moon as a beautiful princess reached through it into the darkness as though to embrace it.

Zizi noticed him staring and explained, “It’s based on a story—one of my favorites—about a princess, the Princess of Light, who falls in love with the Night but can only see him once a month through a magic mirror hung in the sky, and so they wait for each other, month after month after month, hoping for a day when they will finally be reunited indefinitely.”

“How?”

“True love’s kiss, I suppose.”

Zizi and Felix both snuck a glance at each other and quickly looked away again, both hoping against hope the other did not glimpse the vulnerable truth in those searching eyes. After all, only fools wished for happiness. Only fools, and the greatest fools of all wished for it in the form of another. Felix and Zizi had never been such fools. But on a night of fairytales and foolish things, when dreams came true and happiness was always ever after—perhaps on such a night, they could be fools enough to make such foolish wishes.

When it dawned on them that they were staring at each other again, Zizi cleared her throat, “So, er, want to try that egg drop again?”

Meanwhile, in the atrium outside, Maya was standing at the top of the ladder, trying to free Franco from his harness without killing him, which was made infinitely more difficult by him flailing about, taking pictures and shouting about “Breaking

News!" every time something—anything—happened. Just when she was about to give up, a lanky boy with a catlike tread slipped into the security office. It was the first time Maya had ever been glad to see Wolf, even if it was mixed with a healthy dose of frustration. She rushed down the ladder, but by the time she reached the bottom, Wolf was already on his way out of the office. He rubbed soot off his hands into his jeans, and his eyes were narrowed, scanning every surface one last time before he left.

"You forgot something," Maya said, blocking Wolf's path.

Wolf smirked, "How could I ever forget a face like yours? A thousand gallons of bleach could not erase a face as—" Maya pointed up, and Wolf remembered. "Oh. Well, it's really not my fault he trusted me."

Maya's face burned red with fury, her veins bulging, steam rising from her ears until she burst, "TRUST IS A GOOD THING AND SHOULD NOT BE TAKEN ADVANTAGE OF! GO BRING HIM DOWN RIGHT NOW!"

A camera flashed, and Franco called down, "Wolf, any comment on what you saw in the security guard's office?"

"Highly suspicious. Probably the government covering something up."

Franco fist pumped the air and knocked over the ladder with a clatter. At the same time, the shadowy government agents in the Sunnyside Flower Delivery van outside mistook Wolf's statement as evidence that he had discovered their surveillance equipment and, believing their mission to have been compromised, drove off with screeching tires. With a harrumph, Maya set the ladder upright again and began to climb. If Wolf wasn't going to help, she would just have to do it herself. And do it she did. Wolf could not help but watch, in part impressed but mostly curious as to how she was going to get back down with Franco clinging to her back like a baby koala to its mother. The answer was slowly.

When Maya finally reached the bottom again, she pried Franco's death grip off of her arms and said, "Wolf, I swear, if you drag me into any more of your shenanigans..."

Wolf simply laughed and sauntered away, carefree as ever.

SIX

At a dance

A dance—that flickering moment when endless possibilities hang in the balance, in tension between what is and what could be, a question awaiting an answer, a flirtation, a prelude, a culmination, a shining moment that stands alone and echoes into eternity.

Or at least that's what it was supposed to be. In reality, the Homecoming Dance consisted of a whole bunch of awkward teens standing around pretending they were cooler than they actually were, paranoid that others would see through the mask and cursing their very existence for being such an embarrassment. Naturally, everyone was so focused on their own insecurities that they never noticed that everyone else was just as uncomfortable as they. Chief amongst these very insecure and very awkward teens was a hulking, brooding football player who had spent the first hour of the dance lurking in the corner because he was too nervous to actually talk to the girl on whom he *allegedly* had a crush (he denied it, of course, but he had spent the better part of the day laboring over her birthday cake, so you decide). On the other hand, the girl in question was so busy marveling at how beautiful the room and the people and the clothes and the air were that she forgot to worry about how everyone else saw her. If she had thought about if for even a moment, she might have noticed how every head turned to stare whenever she walked past.

With every step, the layers of her gown swelled to reveal blues and purples swirling against a black base, silver pinholes shimmering through the translucent swaths of fabric like stardust lighting up the night sky. The dress captured all the beauty and elegance of the great beyond, and yet there was a playful quality to the cut, like the dark was nothing to be feared. And yes. She made it herself. For once, she was not carrying knitting needles with her. She had brought needlepoint instead. Why she had suddenly switched to a craft with sharp needles at a fairytale themed dance the day before her birthday remained a mystery. She seemed not to have noticed.

Maya dropped herself against the wall next to Felix and looked out across the crowd. Reels of fabric were draped between the tall windows, shimmering beneath Zizi's tapestry of stars. Flickering candles illuminated tables around the room. A wild assortment of fairytale characters jumped and danced as thumping music shook the building. Someone had even brought a llama. Finally, Maya said, "Glad to see you've made progress on the talk-to-the-girl front since I left you," she checked her watch, "an hour ago." Maya was wearing her usual combination of red hoodie, jeans, and sneakers because "it's a modern twist on that weird story about the girl with the red hood and the cannibalistic grandmother." Also, "I can do what I want." Following instructions had never been Maya's strong suit.

Felix blushed and tugged at his shirt collar. Maya had helped him "borrow" a tuxedo from the music department, which was nice because "free," but the downside was that it didn't fit perfectly. Especially around his neck. The collar just kept getting tighter. Then again, it probably did not help that he had dragged a defender across the goal line by his neck to score a touchdown in the game earlier that day. The winning touchdown. The touchdown that had won him a hundred hearts at once, until he scared his new admirers away with his usual grouchiness. He didn't mind. He didn't like people anyways. Zizi crossed his line of sight. He didn't like people, except maybe that one—he felt blood rush to his face again. He crossed his arms and grunted, trying to cast an aura of cool indifference.

Maya laughed at him, "You can't fool me that easily."

Felix let his arms drop limply to his sides as he said, "I think I'm almost ready. Just give me another minute."

"Oh, good," Maya slapped his arm. "Cuz she's on her way over."

"What?" Felix's eyes popped wide open. Sure enough, Zizi was drifting and twirling through the crowds towards them, too focused on her embroidery to notice the impression she left.

Felix gripped Maya by her shoulders frantically, "Quick. Do I look smart?"

Maya hesitated before answering, "Technically, you could argue that most true geniuses look a little like a nervous wreck, so..."

Felix slapped his forehead, "Maya, you are not help—"

"Hi," Zizi interrupted with a smile that shone brighter than the sun, the moon, and all the stars in the heavens. Felix faltered and lost his words. He straightened himself up, but his gaze dipped. In the face of such brilliant light, Felix feared he might go blind if he held eye contact too long. Zizi bit her lip, unsure of what to say next. After all, when she had seen him standing tall, filling out his sharp black coat, and yet so mild-mannered and soft-spoken, she found that her lips could no longer form casual chit-chat, the sort exchanged by simple friends. At least not with him. Not anymore. And Felix—what could he possibly say to a star? To that light which broke through the darkest hours, a miracle traversing billions of light-years only to meet the eye in this fleeting moment? Time slipped by, the music faded away, and still the silence remained.

In the background, Franco announced that the time had come for the annual couples dance competition. Also, Wolfgang Mori needed to report to Mr. Elegans's office. Immediately. For reasons unknown. At that, a light waltz started up, and couples poured onto the dance floor. Felix and Zizi, however, remained still as statues.

With an exasperated sigh, Maya took the embroidery out of Zizi's hand and, before either party could protest, pushed Zizi and Felix onto the dance floor. The pair pulled apart, horror-stricken as they realized they were standing on the dance floor together. Neither one was quite willing to leave the dance floor, though. Finally, Felix took a small step closer and said, "Er, Zizi, I've been meaning to ask, do you, er, do you want to dance? With me?"

He waited for an eternity for her response, his heart pounding all the while. Running from a Grizzly bear through enchanted bookshelves, escaping a burning library, almost getting gored by a raging bull, none of it compared to his terror in that moment. She stuttered, "You—you want to dance? With me?"

"Yes." She stared blankly back at him. Felix turned bright red, "I mean, we don't have to, but if you wanted to—"

Zizi giggled and took his hands, placing one on her hip and holding the other in her palm, "It would be a wish come true."

A broad grin spread across Felix's face. His stomach leapt. He took the lead, and they started to dance, first with small nervous steps, learning each other, finding their rhythm together until they flew across the dance floor with a step, a swirl, a whirling gait.

Maya watched for a few minutes. Felix had not looked so happy in years, and Zizi—Zizi was a princess, born to dazzle.

Leaving them to their bliss, Maya slipped out of the library and wandered off down the lonely halls.

~ ~ ~

Mr. Elegans was sitting at his desk making himself a pot of tea when Wolf sauntered in. The orange glow of the desk lamp made the office feel almost warm, and the tea almost cozy. With the drapes closed, the room looked small, practically intimate. The principal looked up at the intruder through foggy glasses and nodded, "Wolfgang. You made it."

"Got your invitation to the dance," Wolf leaned against the doorframe as he examined the nails on his left hand. In his right, he held his costume: a masquerade-style mask of a wolf. On his black t-shirt, *The Big Bad* was scribbled in white lettering. "I'm flattered, but I'm afraid I'll have to decline."

"This is no dance," Mr. Elegans wiped his glasses clean and pulled out a second tea cup. The clock on the wall ticked—tick-tock, tick-tock, tick-tock—as Wolf sat down across from Mr. Elegans, draping himself over the chair with careless abandon. "Tea?"

With a smirk, Wolf kicked his feet onto the desk, "You know me better than that." The grey principal wrinkled his nose in disgust. With a bark of laughter, Wolf removed his feet from the desk again, "But I won't hold it against you. It's been a while."

"That was your doing, if I recall," Mr. Elegans noted as he poured himself a cup. The clock ticked on—tick-tock, tick-tock, tick-tock.

Wolf slapped his thigh, "Hardly surprising. I'm aptly named, aren't I?"

The principal trained his steely eyes on his pupil. It was always this way with them. Back and forth, push and pull. "The lone wolf may cry its way into song and legend, but it cannot survive alone for long."

"Then it's a good thing I'm a Wolf*gang*," Wolf punned. Mr. Elegans did not look amused. Sulking in his chair, Wolf muttered, "And you wonder why we stopped spending time together."

"And you never learn."

"Glad to see nothing's changed."

"A few things have." Having peeked Wolf's interest, Mr. Elegans leaned back in his chair and took a long, leisurely sip of tea as he examined the stitching on the drapes. The cloth was heavy and thick, but the stitching was fine, so fine that some strands had already frayed. Tick-tock, tick-tock, tick-tock—the clock went on. When he placed his tea cup back in its saucer, Mr. Elegans said, "I had rather hoped the champion would be you. Alas, life is full of disappointments."

Wolf winced but quickly replaced the pained expression with a sly smirk and a biting word, "You should know."

"How's your father?" Mr. Elegans asked with all the air of benevolent curiosity, a well-meaning check-up, but he could hardly fail to notice the way Wolf's smirk fell away and the mask shattered. If Wolf had been caught any less off-guard, he might have noticed the triumphant twinkle in the principal's grey eyes.

With lowered eyes and a small voice, the voice of a child, Wolf said, "He's—uh—he's fine. The same." Mr. Elegans nodded ruefully, and now he took on the mantle of the wise mentor, powerless to lift his pupil's burden but always ready to impart guidance and sympathy. Wolf squirmed in his seat (they were such uncomfortable chairs) and said, "Is there a reason you called me?"

"I care about you," Mr. Elegans said with the deepest sincerity. "I wanted to see how you are."

"I'm fine too."

"Good. I'm glad to hear it." Mr. Elegans rose from his chair and walked about the room, though he did not walk so much as glide, like vapor and shadow. Wolf remained planted in his seat as his conversation partner circled him, in time with the clock. Tick-tock, tick-tock, tick-tock. Finally, the principal slowed to a stop by the bookshelves, "There is, of course, the matter of your mother."

When the grey man turned back, it was to a look of pure terror.

~ ~ ~

The hall stretched before Maya, long and lonesome. Fleeting shadows wafted through the windows to her right, her only company in the pale moonlight. Maya closed her eyes and breathed, breathed the sweet melancholy of solitude. What a gift it was to be alone with uninterrupted thoughts, simple musings, a perfect moment of complete presence. In such a trance, Maya wandered down the hall, her feet making the only tap, tap, tap amongst flitting shades, the ghosts gliding across her mind.

She paused to peer out the window. The full moon hung low over the rose garden, and in the distance she could see the top of the fountain like a pale white tree in winter towering over the hedges below. The smaller trees in the courtyard cast shadows against the opposite wall. When Maya looked hard enough, the shadows were transformed. They came to life, grotesque distortions who lived only in that twilight between desire and denial, between what was and what could have been. They became a face or a family, a key or a thousand pages swirling through the air like autumn leaves, a woman running to her children, a man hoisting a stack of books on his shoulder. Between the two windows, there stretched only darkness, and Maya shuddered to cross it. She took a step. After all, they were only shadows flitting through a dream.

A sudden draft rustled through the windows. Maya wheeled about. A shadow fluttered across the wall. In the silence of that hall, her heart pounded ba-bum, ba-bum, ba-bum. Only shadows flitting through a dream. And then she saw it again.

~ ~ ~

Zizi could not suppress the smile lighting up her face as Felix spun her around and caught her in his arms again. He was strong yet graceful, every fiber moving only when and where he wanted it to. There was a reason he was the pride of the football team. It would take a great force indeed to take him down. Nonetheless, for all his strength, Felix gripped Zizi's hand as gently as he would a hummingbird, and she wondered if he could feel her pulse fluttering through her veins.

"Where did you learn to dance?" Zizi asked as they glided along the dance floor, not noticing how empty the space had become. She heard only the melody lilting in 3/3 time—one two three, one two three, one two three—felt only Felix's hands, her heart beating within her breast, the cool draft brushing over her warm skin, the floor meeting her feet like a cloud.

"Coach Frank makes all the football guys take classes. Says it keeps us light on our feet," Felix dipped Zizi, and she giggled. Once again, a step, a swirl, a whirling gait, round and round.

"I think he was right."

~ ~ ~

Tick-tock, tick-tock, tick-tock.

Wolf cleared his throat, "What about my mother?"

"Keeping the identity of the champion from her forever is impossible," Mr. Elegans drifted back to his seat and rubbed his glasses again. "I cannot imagine she will be pleased."

"Understandably."

Back and forth, push and pull.

Replacing the glasses on the bridge of his nose, Mr. Elegans fixed a pointed look on Wolf, "You know what she is capable of."

"What are you asking me to do?"

"To trust me."

"She'll know." Wolf's languid frame was rigid, tight, tense. Maya had been champion for a month already. Why had Mr. Elegans never before shown the slightest concern about her identity leaking, especially to the woman on whom he wanted Wolf to spy or worse yet to betray? Because something was coming. Wolf felt it in his bones. It was coming.

Tick-tock, tick-tock, tick-tock.

Mr. Elegans chuckled, and when he looked at Wolf again, his eyes were soft and kind, "Wolf, I know exactly what you are. Fully, completely." Wolf glanced at the mirror behind the principal and averted his eyes twice as fast. "She sees only who you're not."

Wolf looked down at his hands, lying idle in his lap. "The only Mori who could have helped you is dead."

~ ~ ~

Ba-bum, ba-bum, ba-bum—her heart beat within her chest like a war drum. A shadow lingered on the closet door. A shadow like a hooded man in a cloak. She turned around.

No one there. Only a sun umbrella in a breeze. The outline was so clear on the door, though. She stepped closer. She had been here before. She knew this place. She had vowed never to return. Fear gripped her throat. She gulped. Only shadows flitting through a dream. She took another step. A shadow couldn't hurt her.

Ba-bum, ba-bum, ba-bum.

~ ~ ~

One two three. One two three. Zizi said, "I told you a story earlier. Now, it's your turn."

"I don't really tell stories."

A step, a spin, a whirling gait.

"But you have to have a favorite."

Hands intertwined, bodies moving as one.

Eyes met, "I think that one's still being written."

A rising melody, a crescendo in motion.

"Does it end happily?"

A pause.

"I hope so. I really, really hope so."

~ ~ ~

Tick-tock, tick-tock, tick-tock.

"You know I've always believed in you as much as I believed in him."

Back and forth, push and pull.

~ ~ ~

Ba-bum, ba-bum, ba-bum.

She reached for the door.

~ ~ ~

A step, a spin, a whirling gait.

~ ~ ~

Tick-tock, tick-tock, tick-tock.

A nod, a handshake. "I'll do it."

A choice.

~ ~ ~

Only shadows flitting through a dream.

~ ~ ~

A dance, a dance, an echo in eternity.

~ ~ ~

Music rising to a climactic end, Felix hoisted Zizi into the air and twirled. Only when the song had ended and they were both standing still again did they notice the ring of students that had formed around them, the only two left on the dance floor. The throng erupted into cheers. Nevertheless, in the midst of the crowd, Felix and Zizi stood alone. For them, the dance floor would only ever hold two.

~ ~ ~

As Wolf left the principal's office, he felt as though a great emptiness had filled him. Or perhaps it had always been there, and he had simply never noticed. Shaking his doubts from his mind, Wolf held his mask to his face and went forth. The dance was done, the choice made, the answer given. Best enjoy the night before darkness truly fell.

~ ~ ~

A crash shook the hall. Maya quickly drew her hand away from the closet door. Water seeped under the door to the men's room, accompanied by the sound of smashing and gushing geysers. With a cautious tread, Maya thrust the door open and froze, her jaw hanging limply as she tried to process the sight. Towering over the far stall, a giant three-headed snake flicked its forked tongues, leering at Maya with pale yellow eyes. "That explains the plumbing problems."

~ ~ ~

Felix stuffed another piece of chocolate cake in his mouth with one hand as he picked up a second—well, technically a sixth—piece with his other hand. When he had stepped off the dance floor with Zizi, he had first felt like his heart was going to explode and like sunshine was running through his veins, then he had felt limp, then jittery, oscillating violently between ecstasy and terror at these new emotions, and now he just felt hungry. Plus, the cake was delicious—melt-in-your-mouth, bittersweet, fluffy, with a dark chocolate glaze. If Zizi or Maya did not return soon, he might accidentally eat the whole thing. Zizi had gone off to do something about the lights, which were now flashing and flickering in rhythm with the music. She had the magic touch. His insides melted again.

As he shoved the sixth piece of cake into his mouth and grabbed a seventh, Felix noticed the short, bespectacled editor-in-chief of the Daily Harold staring at him with arms crossed and an expression so judgmental it would have made a newborn feel guilty. Felix gulped and glanced back down at the tray of cake. When Franco raised his brow, somehow achieving a level of judgment Felix never knew existed, Felix made up his mind. He set his jaw and, grabbing the whole blasted tray, he turned on his heel and stomped off in the direction of the one place he could eat in peace...the bathroom.

Seven

His curse fell

There once was a beautiful princess who burst into the world at a ball on her sixteenth birthday. She had lived her whole life amongst the stars, isolated, hidden from the dangers of this world. Not even a pin had pricked her fingers. After all, a single drop of blood could hold great power in the hands of a magician. Blood is life, and life is magic. But on her sixteenth birthday, she danced and laughed and charmed every lord and lady at the ball. All fell under her spell. Even she felt the magic of the night as a handsome knight swept her off her feet, and for one enchanted evening, the knight and the princess danced under a silver moon. As the evening drew on, the knight plucked a rose for the princess, the most beautiful rose in the garden. Nevertheless, even the most breathtaking of roses had thorns, and midnight was drawing near. On and on the clock ticked in its march to that dark hour, to midnight, the hour of magic and wishes and farewells—the hour when spells are broken and curses begin.

~ ~ ~

Maya had felt this much panic only three times in her life: that time she had failed an exam and needed to tell her parents about it, that time as a child when she had gotten her head caught in the bannister and was convinced she would be stuck there forever, and now, when she was staring straight into three pairs of yellow snake eyes.

With a battle cry that would have made the Vikings proud, Maya rushed at the snake and smashed one of its heads in with a fire extinguisher. The reptile's tail lashed against the mirror, and Maya saw her reflection pass about two inches before her eyes as a giant piece of broken glass hurtled through the air. Why had she gotten herself into this? This was such a terrible idea.

The remaining two heads snapped at Maya at once, blowing fire from their gaping maws. Maya ducked beneath the flames. The reptilian beast turned its heads to face Maya again, mouths open, fire brewing inside, fangs dripping with poison, ready to attack. It lunged, and Maya pulled the plug on the fire extinguisher. As she filled each mouth with white foam, the snake gurgled and choked. Maya breathed a sigh of relief, a relief which only lasted until she was violently reminded that the head was not the only part of the snake that was dangerous. With a swing of its tail, the snake launched Maya across the room. Sliding on her back, Maya squeaked to a stop by the door just as it swung open.

"Maya?" Felix cried out in alarm, nearly dropping a massive platter of chocolate cake onto Maya's face. A wave of water washed over his dress shoes.

"Sorry. It's occupied," Maya said. The snake lunged at her again. She rolled out of the way. "I think there's another bathroom upstairs."

The snake clamped its fangs into the fire extinguisher. Maya's heart was beating so hard she was convinced it was about to spring out of her chest and give itself up as a sacrificial offering to the reptilian harbinger of death. Maya tugged at the fire extinguisher with all her might, locked in a lethal tug-of-war with the snake until—Whoosh! Whoosh!

Felix chopped off the remaining two heads with the cake knife. Maya fell back onto her bottom, the two heads still limply attached to the fire extinguisher by their fangs, poisoned black goop dripping from the wounds. Before their very eyes, four new heads grew from where the two used to sit. Maya gulped, "I don't think that is a regular three-headed snake."

"Nope. That's definitely not a—wait, what's a regular three-headed snake?" Felix asked as he tossed the knife aside. It could only make things worse now. The cake knife clattered against the tile floor until it came to rest beneath a shattered urinal.

Before the new heads had finished growing, Maya leapt back into the action, a newfound terror drowning out all but her most base survival instincts. She slammed the extinguisher down on one of the four skulls with a satisfying crunch. Another head snapped at her calf. She leapt over it and stood on its neck, slowly asphyxiating it, as she beat at the other head that attacked from above.

Felix gripped the neck of the fourth head in his bare hands and squeezed. The scales were coarse and hard under his calloused fingers. Crack! The head fell limply to the floor. With only one head remaining, the snake writhed and struggled. It smashed the toilets, flooding the room with every pipe it burst. Tearing herself free from the reach of the snake's tail, Maya slammed the fire extinguisher down on the last head. The giant snake twitched once and lay motionless.

Felix peered at the snake with narrow eyes, keeping his distance. "Is it dead?"

One of the heads snapped up at him. Maya stomped it flat, leaving no room for doubt. "Yes." Her heart still raced with adrenaline, her mind with the knowledge that she had almost died. Again. This Homecoming dance was turning out to be one of the most frightening ones yet, and Franco had not even hijacked the DJ station yet. There was only so much NPR a dance could take.

She pointed behind her in the general direction of the bathroom, at the water spraying up from the row of smashed sinks, the mirror laying in pieces on the floor, and the forty-foot, many-headed snake lying on top of the splintered stalls. "I think the toilet is safe to use now."

"I'm good," Felix said, glancing over at the half-eaten porcelain bowl.

Felix picked the tray of soggy cake up from a puddle on the floor and was turning to leave when Maya shouted over to him, "Hey, there's a tunnel over here." Felix froze, the blood draining from his face. True enough, behind the last toilet, the tiles had broken off to reveal a rough-hewn tunnel, sloping gently downwards into the earth. Maya climbed through the hole in the wall, consciously ignoring the sign warning, "Beware: Dragon Ahead."

"Dragon? Maya, dragon?" Felix exclaimed as he paused by the sign. "What are we supposed to do against a dragon? We don't even have weapons."

"We have our brains," Maya continued her march down the tunnel. If this place was what she thought it was, there was no turning back, not until she had secured the Third Book of the Library of Souls. She clenched her fist to keep her hands from trembling.

Felix did not look convinced. "I'm using mine. It's telling me that squishy grey matter does not stand much of a chance against a fire-breathing dragon."

"We also have cake," Maya shouted.

"That—that's not much better," Felix said, but he followed all the same, toting the platter of cake along.

The tunnel descended deeper and deeper into the earth, lit only by a hot orange light from below. A draft of warm, dry air blew several loose strands of Maya's hair into her already watery eyes. Maya redid her hair in her usual two bushy bunches, being careful to pull all the loose strands in tight. Felix handed the cake to Maya for a moment to open his dress shirt. His white cotton undershirt dripped with sweat as they trudged deeper and deeper, towards that distant orange glow. At long last, Felix and Maya both skidded to a stop at the edge of a ledge which protruded out, overlooking a giant cavern.

Below, an inferno blazed up, an enormous ring of fire that licked up the hundred foot cliff face at their feet, shadows dancing across the walls like devils, an all-consuming blaze that snapped and cackled and hissed at the two insignificant figures dangling just out of reach, roasting slowly in the heat.

"Well, that explains why it's so hot down here," Maya said with a nervous chuckle as she glanced at Felix's horrorstruck face. To Maya, fire had always meant light and warmth more than death and destruction, but not to Felix. The platter quaked in his hands. The glassy surfaces of his eyes reflected each new burst of yellow light with a wince.

As she watched the flames dance across his eyes, Maya felt true terror for the first time since entering the tunnel. Not apprehension, not dread, but true, bone rattling terror. She had brought her brother, her rock, the only other person she had left, into the wake of a force that could snuff out their lives in a flash. For the first time, Maya understood what he saw in fire, and she was afraid. She should never have brought him along. She should never have put him in danger. "Felix, you should go back."

"No." His voice was hoarse and soft but adamant.

"Felix, there is still—" Maya shuddered as hot air blew against the back of her neck. Slowly, Maya turned around. Her eyes grew three times larger and her voice three times smaller. "Dragon."

The crimson beast stretched its leathery wings and roared a roar that shook the room. The earth trembled before its might. The flames blazed up all the way to the distant ceiling of the cavern, blinding the siblings with a searing light. The flames were close, too close, and now there was no escape from this stone-hewn tomb. None, except...Maya's eyes flashed back to the ground below when the flames died down again. Now that she was looking for it, she could not have missed it. In the center of the ring of fire was a tiny island of land, untouched by flame. If the book was anywhere, it was there.

The dragon roared again, but this time there was something else as well. A rumble, so soft Maya almost missed it. A deep, rolling thunder that came from within the dragon. The blood drained from Maya's face. "Uh-oh."

"What?" Felix asked, panic rising in his voice.

"The dragon's hungry." As she said it, the dragon flapped her wings and trundled at Felix. Felix closed his eyes and turned his face away as he held the platter of cake in front of him, part shield and part tribute. Maya felt herself cry out, but the world around her was silent. The dragon unclenched razor sharp teeth and flames poured out between them.

~ ~ ~

Zizi paused in front of the puddle outside the men's restroom. She had last seen Felix heading off in this direction with a platter of cake, but that was some time ago and she hadn't seen him since. The sound of gushing water echoed across the tile and through the closed door. But it was the boy's bathroom. She really shouldn't go in. But a quick peek couldn't hurt. Unless someone was in there. What if Felix was in there? She was so distracted by horribly embarrassing hypotheticals that she poked her finger with the embroidery needle and almost broke skin.

With a cocky swagger, that lanky boy Maya and Felix both disliked pushed the door open, "Let me help you with th—"

Zizi and Wolf both froze as they saw the water spewing, the shattered mirror, the splintered stalls—oh, and the forty-foot long, five-headed snake floating in the middle of the obliterated bathroom.

Catching sight of the pair, Mr. Elegans approached and nearly fainted when he saw the wreckage. "Oh, heavens. Couldn't this have waited until after we finished the library renovations?"

~ ~ ~

When the smoke cleared, Felix was still standing, slightly singed, as the dragon chomped at the chocolate flavored charcoal on the platter in his hands.

Maya laughed with relief. "See, I told you the cake would be useful."

"Maya, unless you brought several villages and a barn with you, I don't think chocolate cake is going to be enough," Felix said, frozen to the spot.

When the shock and adrenaline finally started wearing off, Maya noticed a chain running from the dragon's hind leg to the wall of the cave. It was rusty and heavy, so heavy it barely clanked as it dragged along the floor, cutting deep grooves in the dirt. She inched closer to get a better look at the loop around the dragon's leg. The dragon's scales were thicker under the chain, scarred from the chafing. The locking mechanism was simple but far too small for the dragon's giant talons, and there were vertical scars through the dragon's flesh where she had tried to tear herself free with those talons nonetheless, pale lines streaked across crimson red like tally marks on a prison wall. A few even looked recent, puffy, inflamed, oozing, like the dragon was still trying after all these years.

When Felix realized what Maya was doing, he took a horrified step back, "Maya, you're not seriously going to release the dragon. IT'S A DRAGON!"

As Maya gripped the chain, the dragon turned on Maya with a wild frenzy, a frantic light in its eyes. Leathery wings raised a storm of dust, and the dragon bellowed, screeched, howled, driving Maya against the wall. Maya pushed through the whirlwind—every step a struggle, every breath sucked out of her lungs by the raging wind, every blink scraping dust across her dry eyes—she pushed through and reached out a gentle hand to the beast's exposed belly. She could not help herself. She understood the dragon, trapped and alone, powerless and afraid, and Maya could not allow it to stay in pain. Not if she could do something about it.

Even through the armor of scales, Maya felt the rapid pounding of the dragon's heart. She stroked the dragon's scales, not knowing if it could even feel the gesture. Slowly but surely, the dragon began to calm. The wind died down and the dragon sank towards the ground, taking haggard, sharp breaths. Maya continued to stroke until she was sure the dragon was pacified. Then, she took several slow, purposeful steps towards the dragon's hind leg. Maya looked to the dragon for approval before touching the chain again. The dragon's eyes were frightened, and Maya could sense the dragon tensing as she reached out, but it did not resist Maya's touch this time. Maya fiddled with the lock, and the chain fell with a resounding clatter.

The dragon immediately beat its wings into a gale force and took to the skies—or the ceiling, in this case—soaring high above the fire, its crimson wings outstretched. It roared and unleashed a terrible stream of fire upon the scorched earth below. It spun and dove, loop-de-looped and rose. The dragon reclaimed the air that had been taken from her and burned the rest to the ground.

Felix and Maya stood back in wonder at the awesome display of power. When the dragon had had her fill of pillage and plunder, the crimson beast glided in for a landing on the small ledge. She nudged Maya with her snout. With a giggle, Maya petted the beast on her scaly head, and the dragon puffed small clouds of smoke from her nostrils. And that is when the idea happened. The very, very bad idea.

"Maya, I don't know what you're planning," Felix grew nervous as he saw a mischievous smile spread across Maya's face, "but I know that look, and it never ends well."

"Oh, please. I'm just thinking about riding the dragon."

"What?"

"To that tiny speck of land in the middle of the ring of fire."

"What!"

"In the small chance that one of the seven books is hidden there."

"WHAT?"

"What could possibly go wrong?" Maya grinned.

Felix nearly fainted. Staring blankly at Maya, he blinked three times before saying, "I don't know what's scarier. The fact that that idea occurred to you in the first place or that you do not see all the horrible, horrible ways it can go awry."

Maya climbed onto the dragon's back. "Come on! It'll be an adventure!"

"That is not an adventure. That is a dragon! A real, fire-breathing, flesh-tearing drag—ahhhh!" Felix screamed as the dragon gripped him up in her claws and, churning the air with her monstrous red wings, took flight. She tossed Felix into the air and swooped down to catch him on her back. Felix clamped himself to the dragon's back and stiffened like a statue that would shatter before opening its grip. The dragon circled through the air about fifteen feet above the dirt patch. The island was barely large enough to fit a motorcycle, let alone a dragon. There would be no getting nearer.

Maya peered over the dragon's muscular shoulders and calculated the distance to the ground. Fifteen feet. She could survive a fifteen-foot fall. Before doubt could deter her, Maya shoved herself off the dragon's back.

Felix cried out after her, but it was too late. With a thud, Maya landed on the small island of safety. She rolled to soften the blow, but the impact jolted through her entire body, reverberating through her bones. With a groan, she skidded to stop and spat a mouthful of soft dirt. The sleeve of her red sweater passed over the flame surrounding the patch. Only a few minutes ago, the sweater had been so soaking wet she could have crossed a desert with it and stayed hydrated. Now, it was on fire. Maya tore off her hoodie and patted out the flames.

Wiping the sweat from her brow, Maya spotted the book lying half buried in the soil only a few feet in front of her. She brushed the ash off of the leather cover. The Third Book of the Library of Souls. Taking a deep breath, Maya flipped it open.

The pages burst forth. They encircled Maya, shrouding her from the flames. With a radiating boom, the pages surged apart. Like a tidal wave, they coursed across the room, extinguishing the fire. The dragon dove and picked Maya up with her claws. As the dragon flew towards the ledge, the pages returned, trailing behind the dragon's massive tail as they gradually found their proper places in the book. The dragon let go of Maya. Maya's heart skipped a beat while all her internal organs scrambled up, up, as far as they could, as far from the ground as possible.

Just as Maya was beginning to have visions of her kidneys and spleen splattered across the floor, the dragon dove under her and caught Maya on her massive, powerful shoulders. Maya whooped with elation as she felt the dragon's wings beating beneath her, the air whistling past her face as the dragon rocketed towards the tunnel. At the last minute, the dragon tucked her wings to her side and sailed torpedo-style through the tight corridor, up to the destroyed bathroom above. Maya braced for the crash landing, and the scaly beast slid to a stop on the wet floor.

The three figures in the doorway gaped. Zizi nearly dropped her embroidery as Maya skated off the dragon's back, looking muddy and singed and windblown and altogether too elated for having nearly died. Several times. Felix toppled off the dragon behind Maya, muttering to himself, "We rode a dragon. I can't believe we rode a dragon. A dragon. We rode a dragon."

"I've got to hand it to the Homecoming decorating crew this year. They really outdid themselves. Have you seen the dragon?" Maya winked at the trio still standing in the doorway, staring slack-jawed. The dragon whistled at Maya. Then, making a call-me sign, the dragon crashed through the wall and flew off into the night sky, the carcass of the giant snake dangling from her claws. Maya did not even question it. The day already held too many mysteries.

"Is that one of the seven books?" Mr. Elegans asked, indicating the book in Maya's hand. Maya nodded and handed it to him as she let her hair down and started chatting with Zizi. Maya could barely draw her gaze from Zizi's fingers as she threaded her needle with such furious vigor it was a minor miracle she could keep track of its position at any given time. When Mr. Elegans had finished looking at the book, he handed it off to Felix.

The clock struck midnight. It was officially Zizi's sixteenth birthday. With a broad smile, Maya shouted, "Happy—" She glanced over at Felix. They had coordinated this beforehand. Why wasn't he joining in? Her face fell. "Felix?" Felix stared blankly at a paper cut on his finger. A single drop of blood fell onto the book.

A black cloud, a living shadow, burst forth and enveloped them in darkness. From the swirling shadows, a cloaked figured emerged before Maya. Her heart stopped. Ice ran through her veins. Her head rang. The Wizard. The Wizard was here. He rushed past. The black clouds disappeared as quickly as they had come. They lifted just in time for Maya to see.

As the twelfth chime sounded, Felix fell.

Eight

And loneliness was born in the night

Ice. The cold shock sent a shiver down Maya's spine.

Felix lying on the ground. Not moving.

She gripped the edges of the sink, gasping for breath.

She dove to his side. Not fast enough. Wolf measuring his pulse. "I've seen this before."

Water dripped from her face.

Forcing her way onto the ambulance. Arms holding her back. She begged, pleaded, "He's all I have left. Please—please don't leave me behind."

The fluorescent lights were harsh and cold against the sterile white tile.

Lights disappearing around the corner. Sirens wailing.

Maya squinted at her reflection in the mirror. The lights were so harsh. She dried her face. The circles under her eyes were so dark. She pulled her hair into a ponytail. She checked that it was straight. Deep breath. She stepped out into the waiting room.

Lights hummed above. The clock ticked. 2 AM. Only two other people there: Zizi asleep on the couch in borrowed scrubs and Wolf in a chair by the window. Headlights streamed past. Cars not even slowing. Maya's lungs constricted. The room blurred before her. How could the world go on when hers had shattered? Deep breath. Focus. Don't cry. Deep breath. Her vision cleared again.

Maya took a step. Another step. Tania was in with the doctors. They wouldn't be able to fix the problem. This ran deeper than science. This was the Wizard's work.

She wanted to sit with Zizi, but it would be cruelty to wake her. There was a chair next to Wolf. It was blue. The seat was hard, plastic. A deep scratch ran across the back. Even the chair was not hard enough to weather this place.

Another step. Maya's feet were so heavy. Black scuff marks streaked the linoleum floor. One more step. She sat. The chair was as stiff as it looked.

Silence buzzed all around. The hospital smelled so sterile, and yet Maya's skin crawled, like the place itself was a disease. She was infected. Even if she left, the bug would remain within her. Until Felix was well, Maya would find no reprieve, no medicine, no cure for herself. Her whole body ached. Her ribs squeezed tighter and tighter around her lungs. She wanted to cry and scream and rage and dissolve, and yet she stayed perched on the edge of her chair, every muscle tensed, trembling, near bursting. She was afraid to move lest she fall apart. This was the curse of caring.

She clenched her fists and set her jaw. "Let me guess," she said, a sharp edge in her voice, as though speaking forced her lips not to part but to shatter, "I have to break the curse on the Library to save him too."

Wolf nodded.

Fury flared within her. Had the Wizard not taken enough? How was she supposed to defeat a phantom who could snuff out her life in the blink of an eye, to break a curse that had bested the greatest Librarians that were, to lift a darkness that seemed to smother her even now? Her clenched fist trembled with rage. Her eyes brimmed with tears. If only the Wizard were here right now. Forget the world. She would tear him apart on the spot, right where he stood. Her fingers instinctively reached for that precious piece of paper tucked in her red sweater, right over her heart, that last trace of her parents. Her mother, her father, her brother—how much more would he take?

Before the silence could consume them again, Maya asked Wolf, "How do you even know this stuff?"

"Don't you know? I'm brilliant," Wolf said flatly. Indeed, everything about him seemed strangely dulled, not just his voice. His hair gel had long given out so that his inky hair lay subdued across his forehead. A slight frown replaced his ever-present smirk. His drooping lids hooded his usually bright eyes. Plus, he was still sitting by Maya when the party had long moved elsewhere. With a sigh, he shifted forward and answered more seriously, "My mother is one of the Librarians."

"Your mother? The world-famous director?" Maya repeated incredulously.

"You can't honestly expect anyone to succeed in Hollywood without a little stardust," Wolf winked. Maya glared at him. As dampened as his mood was, he was still himself enough to frustrate the living daylights out of Maya. Deep down, Maya was almost glad. It was easier to be angry than empty. Wolf continued, "But, to be honest, the one who really explained everything to me was Mr. Elegans. He was there for me when..." Wolf bit his lower lip and stared out the window. "The Wizard is incredibly dangerous, and so long as the curse persists so will the Wizard. He will not rest until the Library is his."

"What is happening to my brother?" Maya asked, the edge back in her voice. She was tired, so, so tired, and yet her whole body was tense, every fiber straining to hold the fractured pieces together.

Wolf hesitated to answer. "He is destroying his spirit," he finally said, looking Maya in the eye. Hearing those words was like swallowing a wrench. "Seven years ago, the Wizard killed a Librarian." The wrench got tangled in Maya's intestines. All he had to do now was mention the disappearance of Maya's father, and the trauma triumvirate would be complete. "But there is magic in blood, and that Librarian's stopped the Wizard. For a time at least. The Wizard won't make the same mistake again.

Not when he has other tools up his sleeve more wholly destructive than death itself."

"How long do I have?" she said. Her voice wavered, despite her greatest efforts to keep it steady, and every hitch laid bare a piece of her heart. She fixed her eyes on the clock on the opposite wall, clenched the armrest, gritted her teeth, kept her face as steady as possible. If she let the hurt show, she would have to deal with it, and she did not have time for that right now.

"It depends," Wolf answered. "For some, their spirit is corrupted in a matter of minutes. I'm pretty sure that's what happened to Dave the security guard. Others can last a week. But no one can hold on forever."

Maya deliberated whether or not to ask. Finally, she prompted, "You said earlier that you've seen this before." Maya looked at Wolf with questioning eyes, not daring to tread further. Wolf's face hardened, his furrowed brow casting jagged shadows across his face.

They sat in silence for one-hundred and two ticks of the clock until Wolf replied, "I had an older brother once."

"Oh." Maya looked down at a scuff mark on the floor. The linoleum squares were pealing at the edges. Her posture grew less rigid, deflating like the air slowly seeping out of a tire, worn from use and finally punctured by the smallest of pins. Her voice barely more than a whisper, she said the only thing she knew to say, the thing people had been saying to her for years, though she knew it was not enough. "I'm sorry."

Tania stepped out into the waiting room again, and Maya jumped to her feet. She stirred Zizi awake, and they gathered around Tania. "He is in a coma," Tania explained with slow, purposeful words, "but they have him stabilized. We can visit him tomorrow." Maya wanted to protest, but her strength left her as Tania put a hand on her shoulder and said, "Let's go home."

~ ~ ~

The key was isolation.

The pages filled the office at the principal's command. With a flick of his wrist, they poured out of the cover, a flurry of paper swirling about the dimly lit room. Darkness spread from the golden tips all the way to the center, and the pages crumbled, corroded, collapsed into black soot. The wind battered the desk, tossed the chairs, but Mr. Elegans stood untouched at the epicenter. A chill settled over the room, enough to send shivers down the spine of anyone less experienced. A sulfuric smell burned the principal's nose hairs as he allowed a wisp of smoke to escape the growing storm clouds. He hated this part most of all—the destruction of love when hate was needed, friendship when loneliness was needed, but purity could not be achieved without the elimination of all unnecessary elements. Gold in its purest state was malleable, but when mixed with other metals, it often became brittle or resistant.

The remaining cloud of ash, the shifting sands of the decomposed book, began to take on form. Mr. Elegans expelled another wisp of smoke, and the edges of the figure sharpened, the cloud tightened, and color began to spread. Isolate the key element, take away its support, leave it alone and powerless with nothing keeping it from destruction but the gentle guiding hand of the magician, and it had no choice but to obey.

The man in grey lowered his hand and inspected his work. It had taken years to perfect this magic, to recreate the impossible, but perfect it he had. Before him stood a beautiful woman, regal as a queen, her lion's mane of hair sweeping over her shoulders majestically, her back straight as an iron rod, posture tall and proud, skin smooth and lustrous, eyes fierce with a special softness reserved only for him. Wondrous to behold, powerful, flawless, and his. He breathed over her, and the statue sprang to life. Oh, how much more lovely she was in life! The stone façade broke, and she smiled—what a smile! Like the gentle rays of the dawn, warm and kind and loving—she smiled at him. At him. At him alone.

She reached up and cupped the principal's cheek, her hand so soft, so gentle against his skin. He placed his own hand over hers and relished the moment, so sweet, so fleeting. They would only have an hour or so before the magic ran out, and he was quickly running out of books. If only it could always be like this. It could have been if only she had gone with him rather than fight him. When the Library of Souls was his, it would be again. They would finally be together, as they were meant to be.

"It is a pleasure to see you again, Charles," she said, the words carrying a melody of their own, light, sweet, but sad, like the first rays of sunrise breaking the magic of a perfect night.

The principal gripped her hand even tighter, "As always, my dear, the pleasure is all mine."

~ ~ ~

Wolf spooned the rice porridge and ladled it, bite by bite, into his father's mouth for him to chew and swallow with the same robotic motion, again and again. The sleek, stainless steel counter stretched for leagues in either direction, cool to the touch and shimmering like blue ice in the pale white light. White tiles and white cupboards, white walls and a white ceiling, white chairs, white tables, white appliances, white, white, white, like snow drifts over a frozen wasteland, unimpeded, unmarred, unstained, an icy perfection best viewed from afar. The wall-length window behind Wolf looked onto the empty limestone courtyard outside, gleaming like Siberian plains in winter, the outer walls towering like glaciers bearing down on all who approached the Beverly Hills mansion, threatening to crush them in the final collapse.

His father scanned the kitchen with unblinking eyes before asking, "Where is Ran?"

Wolf scooped some more porridge onto his spoon. "He's not here."

"Oh." His father's face fell at the revelation. He and Wolf stuck out like spilled paint against the white canvas of the kitchen, Wolf with his black shirt and his black trousers and his inky black hair and his father with his forest green pajama suit. It seemed like every day his wrinkles grew deeper, like cracks in a glass vase, a spreading web, leaking more and more until one day it shattered completely. "You will keep some leftovers warm for him, won't you? He'll be hungry when he comes home."

"Dad, remember, he—" Wolf's voice got caught in his throat, breaking ever so slightly. He looked down at the bowl and sighed. They had had this conversation too many times.

See, there are some people who leave this world with a bang: sudden, dramatic, devastating. Others, their lives flow like a river into the sea, eventually reaching their inevitable end amidst the appropriate amount of turbulence and tears. But there are a few who simply fade out of existence, like the last glow of light along the horizon after sunset. Wolf's father was one of those, slowly fading away as his body withered, wearily wasting away, much the same way as his mind had.

"I will," Wolf finally said. Wolf could pinpoint to the day, even the moment, that his father's sun had set, the day he had started to fade away. What bitter tragedy it was that that day brought not one death but two, the death of a son and that of his father, cursed to continue breathing, to continue existing in that wretched body. In Ran, the magic had acted quickly, snuffing his life out like a candle, but his father was not so lucky. The venom had seeped through his soul, but it refused to let him die.

Wolf jolted as the frosted glass doors to his mother's office opened. Heels sharp as daggers, slim-fitting power suit on a skeletal frame, eyes like a hawk, an eagle, a vulture—she dominated the doorframe. A blizzard raged beneath those wisps of black hair. She turned her hawk eyes on Wolf and the blizzard turned to ice.

The bad thing about having a world-famous director for a mother was that she could always recognize bad acting. Wolf focused on the lumpy porridge in his father's bowl, on the chipped porcelain, on the tarnished spoon, anything to avoid eye contact. She sat at the counter across from him and kept her eyes fixed on him, watching every move. Wolf felt a bead of cold sweat form on his forehead, but he dared not meet her gaze.

Finally, she spoke, "Who is the champion?"

Wolf gulped and shook his head. They said the Wizard had infiltrated the ranks of the Librarians. One wrong word slipped to the wrong person could mean the end of everything. Wolf did not believe that his mother had anything to do with the Wizard, but it never hurt to be safe. Besides, Mr. Elegans was right. The longer they kept her from discovering Maya, the better. No need to open old wounds.

She leaned in and looked Wolf straight in the eye. "Have you ever heard the story about the golden prince?"

"No," Wolf answered nervously. A thin grey cloud passed over the sun, and a fresh chill settled over the stark white kitchen. He rolled his sleeves down and pinned his arms close across his chest. The shivering did not stop.

His mother leaned back in her chair, a dangerous smile on her face, the kind that extended no further than the lips, the kind where the eyes remained trained on their prey, the kind meant to lure trusting fools closer, closer, closer until she devoured them. The true secret to her success.

She began her tale, "There was once a king who had four sons. One day, he went on a long trip and entrusted his lands to the four brothers, dividing his property between them for safe keeping. To the first, he gave storehouses of grain, to the second a river of textiles, cloth, silks, and luxurious fabrics, and to the third he left lumber from which he built great structures, roads, houses, tools, and beautiful things too. But the fourth? To the fourth, he gave gold. Mountains and mountains of gold, a city that glimmered in the sun where music filled the air from dusk till dawn. As he left, the old king mandated that the four sons protect their treasures above all else.

"One day, the first prince came and said to the one with gold, "Brother, my people are under attack. An enemy from far away has come to claim my land and take my grain. Give me some of your gold so that I may buy iron weapons to defend my people." But, in keeping with his father's orders to protect the gold above all else, the golden prince turned his brother away, and in that year, the first brother's castle fell.

"Some time later, the second brother came to the prince of gold and begged, "Brother, an enemy from far away has come to claim my land and take my fabric. Give me some of your gold so that I may buy food for my soldiers." But, again, the golden prince turned his brother away, and in that year, the second brother's castle fell.

"At last, the third brother came to beg of the prince, "Brother, an enemy from far away has come to claim my land and take my lumber. Give me some of your gold so that I may buy fabric to clothe my people as they endure this siege." Once more, the prince turned his brother away, and in that year, the third brother's castle fell.

"One day, the enemy appeared outside the last brother's gate. Months passed. The people starved. Their clothes wore thin. Their swords shattered. Music no longer rang out over the valley as the enemy pounded at the gates. The prince locked himself in his castle with his gold, but even so, the walls crumbled before the enemy. And in that year, his kingdom fell, and the king's gold was lost." Wolf's mother leaned in again, her eyes fixed on Wolf. "Beware of keeping things to yourself, my little Wolf," she warned. "People get hurt."

A slight tremble in Wolf's hand betrayed him.

His mother rose from her chair, the damage done. Before she left the room, she turned back to make one more comment,

"The boy, Felix Rodriguez I think, he has a sister, doesn't he?" Wolf nodded. "She must be devastated right now. What an odd coincidence that so many in her family have fallen victim to the Wizard." With an icy glint in her eye, Wolf's mother strode into the hall.

She knew.

She knew about Maya.

More than that, she knew Wolf had lied to her.

Once his mother was out of sight, Wolf shuddered and allowed himself to breathe. The Librarians wanted only to protect the Library of Souls, but why did it always feel like the opposite was true? Wolf plucked a strand of his mother's hair from the counter, and he was reminded of a promise he had made to another Librarian. With a deep breath, he picked up the phone and dialed. The phone rang and rang. At last, Mr. Elegans picked up. In that moment, Wolf said the words he had promised, "I have what you need."

~ ~ ~

There was once a witch who lived in a palace of ice. She lived alone except for a hunter and two wolf pups, one white as snow and the other black as night, the only living creatures that brought warmth to her cold heart. The pups roamed freely across the frozen tundra and played in the light of the moon, inseparable from the day they were born. But one day, darkness fell over the earth.

Countless envoys implored the witch to use her sorcery to revive the sun, but in all her power she could not lift the darkness. The curse that had befallen the land was old and powerful, darker and more dangerous than any the witch knew. This she did know, however: all magic had a cost, and the cost to break such a curse would be great indeed. And so, the ice witch locked the gates and all she loved inside her frozen palace until the shadow passed.

But the white wolf was not content to wait. Every waking hour, he heard the cries of the forest, the anguish of the skies, the howl of the wind, and the wolf answered the call. He leapt over the palace walls and ran, ran, ran to find the sun again, but the darkness consumed him instead.

On that day, the witch's heart froze within her breast, the last traces of warmth abandoning it forever as the black pup cried out, joining the chorus around him, hoping against hope for a day when the curse would break and the light return. Until then, the wolf would be cursed to wander the icy flats alone, howling into the darkness.

If only there were light.

~ ~ ~

Maya's eyes flashed open, a fire blazing from within. She lifted the covers, careful not to wake the griffin cub nestled against her. She had not been able to sleep until Oscar had burrowed under the covers next to her, but even then the sleep had been restless, in part because the cub kept wandering off in search of his usual bunk buddy. Oscar must have missed Felix almost as much as Maya did.

Maya switched on her desk lamp. In the dim light that the yellow orb shed over the room, she dug into her closet until she emerged with a large roll of paper. The blueprints to the school. She had found three books there already, and she had four more to go, the clock ticking away faster and faster, no time to lose. Too many people had been lost already.

A flame burned deep in Maya's heart. The time had come to fight back.

NINE

So she herself fought

"Campus Ravaged by WAR!" read the Daily Harold that Tuesday morning. "Three days after the eventful Homecoming dance that started it all, the deadly water balloon battle rages on. At 8AM, the Upperclassmen took the courtyard, forcing the opposition to fall back to the gym. The nurse's office has recorded up to 19 minor injuries, with more expected in the coming days if the fighting does not end. Debris litters the campus. Slipping hazards mark the site of every skirmish, and the truancies only continue to rise. In an effort to curtail further destruction of property before the school's annual fundraising gala, scheduled for tomorrow night, Principal Charles Elegans has cut off all water supplies to the school. His efforts have been undermined by a mysterious water balloon dealer driving a golf cart. This dealer, who wishes to remain anonymous, has declared no allegiances but rather has expressed a desire to continue the war simply, "for the fun of it." In a press conference this morning, however, Mr. Elegans declared, "Any student who is found outside of class may be subject to immediate expulsion."

Consequently, it is the opinion of this newspaper that students should probably go back to class."

Maya had barely noticed this "water balloon war," but as she looked at all the full seats in the classroom, it dawned on her just how empty indeed her classes had been over the last few days. She had been consumed with the blueprints of the school, which were laid out in front of her even now. Maya wasn't sure why she'd bothered looking at them anymore. She and Zizi had already scoured every single room in the school, and the blueprints did not show any of the secret passageways that Maya already knew about. It was pointless.

The only other thing Maya had noticed over the last few days was how quickly time was slipping away. It had been three days since Homecoming. For the rest of the school, that meant three days of water balloon battles. For her, it was three days of watching the life drain out of Felix. The circles under her eyes were so dark she could have joined a raccoon colony undetected. Still, dark circles did not prevent her from giving Franco a scorching death glare as he scooted his desk closer to ask for a quote. Again. Since Saturday, he had practically been stalking her to "ask a few questions for the Daily Harold." She'd told him off every time, but he still did not get the hint.

"Psst, Maya," Franco whispered to her. After all, Ms. Elliot did not take kindly to being interrupted, especially not when talking about a subject as dear to her heart as Axel Orlick's Epic Laws. "Maya, how do you explain—"

Maya scooted her desk away, towards Zizi. Zizi, as usual, was diligently taking notes. Her handwriting was neat and legible, always, and her notes comprehensive. Indeed, the words seemed to fly onto the page the moment Ms. Elliot spoke them, "Next, we have the Law of Contrast, the polarization between characters as good and evil, beautiful and ugly, young and old."

If only it were that easy.

"The Law of the Single Strand. This means that there is only one plotline with no extraneous details."

Extraneous details like this class? Like the water balloon battle? Like being forced to sit and listen to a squeaky-voiced English teacher talk about simplistic stories that aren't even true? The tip of Maya's pencil snapped off, but she could not loosen her grip. A thick, black, jagged line cut across the thin blue paper.

The boy sitting behind Maya told Franco, "Dude, I just about died—" Maya's heart skipped a beat. They'd said Felix would last a week if he's lucky. She'd already wasted three days. Three days, and there were still four books to go. "—I was laughing so hard."

Franco scribbled away in his notebook, his story about Felix already forgotten.

"The Law of Logic of the Sage – events and characters cannot be measured by the logic of our world."

Zizi's pen continued to glide across the page.

The boy kept laughing, now with his friends, "And when you slipped and fell just when Mr. Elegans turned the corner—I saw my life flash before my eyes."

Franco scooted closer to Maya again, daring to try his luck once more.

The blueprints crumpled to the floor.

"The Law of Unity of Plot. Events occur in a logical sequence and go towards the main plot."

And that's when Maya lost it.

Maya tossed over her desk and stormed out of the room, slamming the door behind her.

The class sat back in stunned silence, until Franco observed, "Is it just me, or did that come out of nowhere?" Truly, he is a credit to journalists everywhere.

In the hallway, Maya breathed and tried to recollect herself. For goodness knows what reason, there was a golf cart sitting in the middle of the hallway. Maya climbed into the driver's seat and threw her backpack into the back. A squishing, popping sound accompanied its landing. Maya looked down the hall, and her heart buckled. She could barely see through the fog in her eyes. Before her stretched classroom after classroom after classroom after classroom, and that was without counting the maintenance closets and the bathrooms. There must have been a hundred doors yawning down at her like the gaping maws of a hundred hungry beasts. The hinges even shrieked and cackled when Maya opened them, taunting her with the futility of her search.

Maya was about to do something drastic (she had not quite decided what) when Zizi slipped out into the hall behind her, the click of her knitting needles breaking the oppressive silence. "Maya?"

"I just—I don't get it." Maya brushed the hair out of her face—even when she had it in a ponytail, a few strands always escaped. "We have searched every room in this school. Most of them twice. Why is it that when I am actually looking for these stupid books, I find nothing."

"I wouldn't say *nothing*," Zizi countered as she hopped into the passenger's seat. The golf cart rocked merrily. "We did find Dr. Takahashi making Bunsen burner s'mores in the chemistry room. Oh, and the cult that meets in the teacher's lounge on Mondays and Wednesdays. Those were some good brownies."

"It's how they get you," Maya warned, shaking her head. "First it's brownies and lemonade and fun newsletters, and then suddenly it's sacrificing cats to call on the spirits of darkness."

"I suppose you would have to in order to make brownies that good," Zizi said.

Wolf poked his head out of the classroom across the hall, "Did someone say spirits of darkness?"

"Oh, sorry. We didn't mean you," Maya reassured him.

He shrugged. "Leave the keys in the glove compartment when you get back," he pointed at the golf cart and slunk back into class.

Maya's phone rang. "And sometimes the powers of darkness call on you." Maya answered, "Hello, Tania." Zizi paused her knitting.

"Why is there a half-eaten marlin on my couch?" Even through the phone, Maya could sense her stepmother's pursed lips.

"Oh." Maya squeezed her eyes shut and rubbed the bridge of her nose. "Oscar," she muttered under her breath. She sometimes wondered if the cub was strong enough to ride, but he never stayed still long enough for her to try. Regardless, he was certainly strong enough to carry oversized aquatic animals.

"Oscar? Who's Oscar?" Tania demanded from the other end. "Is he the one who's been shedding blond hair all over?" She gasped, "Is Oscar your boyfriend?"

"What? No. Oscar isn't even a human...I hang out with," she finished with a grimace, a poor save but the best she could come up with at the moment.

Tania kept babbling, "Hmm. Well, you don't have to be ashamed to talk about him, just because he eats raw fish in the living room. You should bring him over for dinner. I know some great seafood recipes. And tell him he still owes me for that chicken he ate. I was saving that for chicken noodle soup."

"You're making chicken noodle soup again?"

"Not anymore, it seems."

The doorbell rang on the other end of the line.

"Is that the door? Why is someone at the door while there's a marlin on the couch?"

"It's the newspaper!" Tania exclaimed gleefully and Maya had to pull the phone from her ear to keep from going deaf. "They're here to photograph our record winning marlin. Longest in the county. I'm going to be in the newspaper!"

"With a fish," Maya reminded her.

"Photographer's here. This will be great publicity for my new line of Omega-3 enriched lip balms. Say hello to Oscar! Got to go," Tania hopped off the phone.

"My stepmother thinks I'm dating a muscular blonde with a penchant for fish," Maya stared at the phone, still in a state of disbelief. Shaking her head, Maya tapped her fingers against the steering wheel as she conjured an image of the blueprints before her eyes, as though thinking hard enough would allow Maya to unearth the school's deepest, darkest secrets through sheer willpower.

After several tense minutes, Zizi asked, "Why don't you and Tania get along? You both love the same people, and you have been part of the same family for four years now. And have you really never eaten her chicken noodle soup?" Maya gritted her teeth, her back more rigid, a dark cloud passing over her brow like scales hardening into armor against an attack. Zizi sighed. She should have known it was too blunt a question, but she always seemed to forget that the most honest questions often elicited the most dishonest responses. "I know you don't like talking about this sort of stuff, but," Zizi bit her lip and hesitated, "Tania actually seems...supportive."

"Like I don't know that?" Maya said gruffly. She honked the horn with a slam of her open palm. "I know she's been there through thick and thin, even when everyone else..." Her fist clenched. Everyone else was gone, gone, gone and only Tania remained. "Look, I don't want to talk about it. I mean, how do you—" *How do you break down walls that have been built over years of stubbornness? Let go of those grudges that have divided you? Start again?* Her blood boiled and rose to meet her skin, burning her from the inside out. Maya furrowed her brow. "It is what it is."

Except it wasn't. The measurements of the rooms all matched up perfectly to those listed on the blueprints. There were no suspiciously thick walls. There was no sign, no clue, and yet four more books had to be hidden here somewhere. With a frustrated harrumph, Maya decided it was time to call on her last resort. She slammed on the accelerator.

The doors rushed past. The wind howled. Zizi gripped her seat for dear life. From somewhere in the golf cart, water balloons splattered onto the floor. The turn approached, faster, faster, faster. Maya grinned. She hit the brakes and jerked the steering wheel. Zizi shut her eyes. Tires screeched. The back bumper scraped a locker. Maya's bag catapulted against the back of the driver's seat. Maya zoomed out of the bend, a manic grin playing across her face under wild, windblown hair. The main entrance hall drew nearer and nearer. Tires left black marks across the marble floor as Maya spun to a stop in the middle of the grand atrium, nearly crashing through the library doors in the process. She glanced up at the banister overlooking the main entrance. The light was on in the principal's office. Leaving Zizi to catch her breath, Maya leapt from the vehicle and took the stairs three at a time up to Mr. Elegans's door.

Maya did not even hesitate as she barged in. The principal looked up at her with surprise. "Remember when you offered to guide me on my journey as the champion? Well, here's a start. How the bananas do I find these stupid books?" she said.

"Would you like to sit down?" Mr. Elegans offered the chair across from him. Maya did not budge. Her arms crossed, she tapped her fingers impatiently, raring to go, ready to pounce at a moment's notice, as soon as she knew her target. Mr. Elegans sat back and started cleaning his glasses, the sun bathing his grey handkerchief and grey fingers in a pale rosy glow as he leaned back in his chair, away from the window and away from the light. Behind him, the sword on the wall glistened, drawing the eye. "The true champion does not sow uncertainty. She does not raise her hand in anger. She does not succumb to fear. She does not doubt but rather stands for truth. The champion must be strong, but she must not hold grudges against her friends or foster hatred against her enemies."

His lack of urgency was starting to get on Maya's nerves, and so was this list. She snapped, "Look, I've done at least half of those things. This doesn't help me."

"Reflect on your past experiences. Only you can know why the books appear to you when they do," Mr. Elegans said. Maya groaned and turned for the door. "Say, aren't you supposed to be in class right now?" Mr. Elegans lifted his grey eyes to meet Maya's. She froze in place, heart racing. For a moment, that morning's front page flashed before her eyes, particularly the part where Mr. Elegans had threatened to expel anyone caught outside of class that day. The principal fogged up his glasses and rubbed them clean again. His focus fixed on his glasses, he said, "Might I venture a guess and say that you are worried about Felix and, more importantly, that you are scared you will not be able to save him?" Maya lowered her eyes. Her face fell, her shoulders slouched, her heart sank, like her whole body longed for the ground, to lie down and rest. She had gotten too little sleep to deal with this sort of existential crisis.

The words lingered in the air until Maya shook them off and donned her more typical irreverent attitude, mostly out of self-preservation. She pointed at the sword hanging over the mirror behind Mr. Elegans and said, "What if, instead of dorking around with these ridiculous books, I just attack the Wizard with a sword. How do you think that would work?"

Mr. Elegans chuckled, "It would work against anything."

Maya paused, taken aback, before exclaiming, "So why haven't we used it yet?" She nearly leaped over the desk for it that very instance.

"Because it can only be used once," Mr. Elegans explained. Maya halted mid-leap. "And we're saving it for something that can't be defeated by human hands."

"And the Wizard can be?" Maya shot another glance at the two-handed blade glimmering crimson in the sun.

Mr. Elegans folded his hands across his chest, his lips betraying the slightest amusement at this exchange, "What do you think?"

"Uh, I think the Wizard is terrifying, and I kind of want to know how I got stuck with the task of defeating him."

"Your circumstances allowed you to see that first book when most would have passed it by without a second glance," Mr. Elegans straightened his glasses, "but you became the champion when you chose to pick it up."

"It should have come with a warning sign," Maya mumbled as she slumped into the chair across from the grey principal. "Warning: you will lose everything you love, but it's for a good cause."

"Sometimes sacrifices must be made for the good of the world," Mr. Elegans said, his face placid, unmoving.

Maya's eyes flashed with anger as she glared at Mr. Elegans, her heart pounding like a war drum, each breath sharper than the last. "The Wizard put my brother in a coma, he drove my father away, and he murdered my mother." On the table before Mr. Elegans, Maya slammed the page she usually kept tucked away in her pocket, her most prized possession. The principal eyed it with a mix of interest and suspicion. "That is not a sacrifice. A sacrifice is something willingly given, not something taken."

Mr. Elegans unfolded the page and skimmed it before handing it back to Maya, "Your mother was very brave."

"And now she's very dead, and my brother will be too if I don't break the curse," Maya said, her heart sinking as the little voice in the back of her head reminded her of the magnitude of her burden. A soundless tension hung heavy in the room, a static electricity making every hair stand on edge. It was then that Maya first noticed the plaque at the base of the mirror: "Charles Elegans—The man who inspired us to always look beyond the surface. Here's to you." Maya halted, fixating on one singular phrase. "Look beyond the surface." Her heart leapt in her chest, her eyes growing wide. It was here. Of course.

There was a knock on the door. Zizi cleared her throat, "I hate to interrupt, but a turf war has just broken out over the golf cart."

War cries drew Mr. Elegans out onto the landing, where he started cursing whoever had instigated this blasted water balloon war and particularly the person who dragged the golf cart indoors. Maya waved at Zizi to stay. The moment Mr. Elegans left to deal with the cart situation, Maya made a beeline for the mirror and explained, "I think I know where the next book is hidden." She pushed against the glass, but it did not budge. She ran her fingers along the bottom of the frame. The smooth surface slid along her skin like a skate across ice.

Zizi glanced over her shoulder at the office door, her knitting needles tapping against each other like a woodpecker's knock. A deathly stillness accompanied the lazy afternoon sunlight streaming through the windows of the office. Her voice shaking, Zizi whispered, "I think this might be the craziest thing I have ever done."

Maya raised her brow incredulously at Zizi. "You are helping me hide a dragon on the roof of the gymnasium. You take a pet griffin for walks three times a week. You've battled a magical bull made of paper. And this is the craziest thing you have ever done?"

"None of those things were illegal," Zizi said. "Breaking and entering is a felony." Maya rolled her eyes and turned her attention back to the mirror. After a moment, Zizi said, "Do you think the dragon is vegetarian? She never eats the meat I bring her, but she does eat all the carrots and apples. Or maybe she's a vegan."

Maya laughed, "Don't mention that to Felix. He'll try to hold an intervention as soon as we get ho—" Her face fell when she remembered. It had been three days, and she still found herself looking for him in the passenger's seat of the car or in his spot at the kitchen table or doing homework on the couch, the place where he had sat so often there was a permanent divot in the cushions. Her fingers caught on a hitch along the side of the mirror. A lever clicked at her touch, and the mirror swung forward towards Maya, revealing a dumbwaiter in the wall.

"Coming?" she asked Zizi with an excited glint in her eyes.

Zizi probably should have said no. The elevator was barely large enough to hold one person let alone two, and even then it looked like it was on the brink of falling apart, rusty screws barely holding rotten planks in place. The gears screeched, the rope frayed, and the safety mechanism on the manual pulley system was broken, but Zizi did not hesitate to put her life in Maya's hands. Literally. When they had squeezed themselves into the tiny space, Maya released a length of rope, and the elevator jerked down with a shriek.

The stone walls of the shaft pressed in against them. They scraped and nudged and jerked their way down into the dark. Until they got stuck on one particularly obstructive rock poking out of the wall. They risked hopping on the rotten wooden boards to get the platform free. They shifted their weight. They jerked the elevator back and forth. The result was that, when Maya tried pulling the elevator up again, the dumbwaiter did not even move an inch. They were stuck. Truly stuck. Halfway down a cramped elevator shaft. As they were sitting puzzled and pretzeled together, Zizi looked around at the rough stones and noted with the utmost optimism, "This is cozy."

Maya laughed so hard she shook. And the elevator broke free. The rope slipped through her fingers as they sped down the shaft, their screams echoing off the rocks. Finally, Maya regained control, and they slowed to a stop. As she caught her breath, Maya shook her head with a smile and said, "I swear, one of these days, you're going to get me killed."

"Then it's a good thing laughter supposedly boosts your immune system," Zizi responded, unfazed.

"I'll remind you of that the next time we start falling from a hundred feet up," Maya said as she resumed the slow descent. The shaft opened up in the center of a domed chamber as monumental as a cathedral. Doors covered every surface: ceiling, walls, even a few in the floor. One thousand and one doors, each numbered in long, slanted writing. A warning, written in the same hand, stretched around the circular room: "Pick a door, but note before: One is your friend, the others your end."

Maya gulped as she let the rope sift through her fingers. The elevator came to soft landing in the dirt amidst a cloud of dust. "Those do not sound like good odds."

"Door number one," Zizi chirped as though the answer was as plain as day. When she noticed Maya's confusion, she explained, "The riddle—it's a play on words. 'One is your friend.' Door number one is safe, but the others aren't." With a nod of assent, Maya charged ahead towards the red door in front of her, door number one. "Although, if I'm wrong—"

"That boosted immune system will come in handy." Maya turned the handle on door number one and pushed it open. A blast of cold, damp air blew through the door, sending a shiver down her spine, but no one died, so she took that as a good sign.

The door led to a tunnel with stone floors and stone walls. A drop fell from the ceiling—*kerplop!* A few seconds later, again—*kerplop! Kerplop. Kerplop. Kerplop.* At the end of the tunnel was another thick, red door. Maya scanned the stone enclosure carefully before stepping inside. The hairs on the back of her neck bristled. She wrapped herself tighter in her red sweater to ward off the cool draft. Funny, the last time she had worn the sweater, she was worried about burning to a crisp.

As Maya took another step, she felt something click below her foot. She looked down just in time to see a stone engraved with a crescent shape. Her shrill cry pierced the air as she was yanked into the air by an invisible net. Grunting and pulling, she struggled to break free, but the net tightened around her. She froze as a sharpened stone hurtled past her face, missing her nose by a hair. Another whooshed past her ear, and the next scratched her cheek just under her eye. A shot of adrenaline coursing through her system, Maya scrambled for a way out. She could not see where the stones were coming from, but one of them lodged itself in her sweater, just above her heart. And this was why Maya loved big sweaters. Extra layer of protection. Maya extracted the sharp rock and began sawing at the invisible strands holding her captive above the earth.

The net snapped.

Maya flailed through the air before face planting on the cold, hard rocks below. "Oof." She laid there, half grateful to have solid ground beneath her again and half cursing it for being so hard, when someone or something picked her up and tossed her against the wall. In a daze, Maya picked herself up to face her enemy and found herself facing...a rock?

A twelve-foot tall humanoid shaped creature made completely of rocks stared down at Maya, its stony hands tightening into massive fists, the shadows of craters in its form deepening in the pale, silver glow cutting across the hall from the door. One of the rock's monumental fists swung at Maya. She leapt out of the way just as the rock smashed against the walls of the tunnel, bits of gravel spraying like shrapnel from the collision. Pebbles and rocks pelted her from behind as Maya ran towards the far door, keeping an eye out for unusual stones underfoot. The rock creature knocked Maya's feet out from under her. She hit the floor with a thud, a jolt running through her body from the point of impact. Stones scraped her palms. Her heart raced. Her mouth tasted like sandpaper. She rolled and jumped back up, stepping out of the way just moments before the stone giant barreled past, crashing into the wall. Maya's breath caught in her chest.

Just then, Zizi shouted, "Hey, you! Rock-man." The giant turned to face her. Zizi struggled to come up with a good insult, "Yeah, you, you big rock-head?" The stone giant roared and thundered towards Zizi. Eyes growing wider, fingers flying to finish her knitting, Zizi waited, not moving a muscle.

"Zizi, no," Maya watched in horror as the rock creature threatened to squash her friend. Her heart pounded, the reverberations of the stone giant's every footstep shaking her to the bone. The boulder was only two steps away from Zizi when—*ZING!* The giant flew into the air, caught in its own net. Zizi grinned at Maya, and Maya breathed a huge sigh of relief. Her whole body was aching, scratches, cuts, and bruises stinging, but no one was dead. And no lost limbs either. Zizi bouncing at her side, Maya pushed on to the red door at the end of the hall.

Ignoring that sinking feeling in her stomach, Maya opened the door and stepped into the darkness on the other side. The book lay in the middle of the circular chamber. Maya shivered. It was colder here than it had been in the hall. When she breathed, flimsy clouds floated away into the dark, carrying little bits of warmth away as they disappeared into obscurity. With trembling fingers, Maya picked up the book and flipped open the cover. Like each time before, the pages whirled out of the cover, whirling through the air, until they formed—

Mirrors.

The entire room was covered, floor to ceiling, in a dozen mirrors. Maya spun around and saw her image split into a thousand fractals, everywhere she looked, her face, her frantic face, a dozen panels, and no way out. She was trapped. With herself.

"Zizi, where are you?" Maya called out. The knitter with starlight in her smile was nowhere to be seen.

"Don't worry," a voice behind her said. Maya whipped around to find herself eye to eye with a girl with messy black hair, an old red sweater, and a rusty blood stain smeared across her brown cheek, a mischievous grin on her face. It was as if Maya's reflection had finally stepped out of the mirror, and it was sending all sorts of shivers down her spine that were not even slightly related to the cold. "She's fine. It's just us now."

~ ~ ~

Zizi had only blinked. There had been a thousand pages swirling past her eyes in a whirlwind, and she had blinked, and now she was staring at a silver wall, her wide eyes staring back at her in the matted plate. As Zizi fiddled nervously, a crash shook the knitting needles from her hands. Zizi peaked back into the hallway.

The dust settled, and from a crater in the stone floor rose a pale stone giant, its burly arms bent, lumpy fists closed as it breathed heavily and stared at the open door at the end of the hall. The rock man thundered towards Zizi, each step shaking the floor. He seemed to be in a hurry. Correction, he seemed angry. Very angry. And he was getting closer. And Zizi had no way of stopping him.

~ ~ ~

Maya circled that reflection come to life, scrutinizing every fold, every mark. The girl even had her signature scowl. “Who are you?” Maya demanded.

“I am you,” the duplicate replied.

Maya laughed, “At least I’m still better looking.”

“I know everything about you.”

This doppelganger was starting to irritate Maya. It would be one thing if this thing were a perfect replica, but it wasn’t. There was something slightly off. The girl oozed confidence like it was more than a mask, and her eyes—her eyes lacked the fire Maya had come to claim as her own. An impressive replica, but in the end still a cold mirror at heart. Maya said, “You are a magic trick. Nothing more.”

The doppelganger grinned, her eyes lifeless and cold, and snapped her fingers. The mirrors started to spin around them, faster and faster. “Are you sure?” the girl asked. The panels came to a halt, and they were not mirrors any longer. Figures flitted in and out of the panels, recreating memories, fading into new ones, vanishing, morphing, playing out in plain sight all those moments Maya wished most to forget.

She saw herself standing by helplessly as Felix fell. She saw that look on Zizi’s face again, a look she never wanted to see a second time, after she had snapped at her for mistaking Tania for their mother—such an easy mistake to make, too. She saw herself in a fit of rage slam Wolf against a wall so hard she was surprised he did not have bruises. Or maybe he did, and she just never knew.

She saw that horrible sunrise again, the one that had risen the day after her father had failed to come home. She saw the phone slip out of her hand as she slumped into a restless slumber on the kitchen table. How many times had she called? A dozen? A hundred? How long had she waited, and nothing ever brought him back?

The scene faded, and she saw her nine-year-old self—or was she ten by then? It was hard to tell. She had changed so much in such a short time, in those few months after...after... The only light that night came streaming through the gap under the bathroom door. The girl cracked the door open to find her father slumped on the floor, his eyes blood-shot, a rancid smell lingering in the air. It was the first time she had seen anything but strength in him. She tried to lift him, to carry him back to bed where he belonged, but she was too weak. She was always too weak. So the two of them stayed there on the bathroom floor all night.

She saw Tania coming into their mess two years later, stepping into that dark, grimy apartment, and she saw herself shouting at her that they didn't need her. She saw herself slam the door on Tania over and over again, even as their apartment grew lighter and their world better, and every slammed door sent a pang of regret through Maya.

The mirror panes went black. Through the darkness, a figure appeared, a woman running, running desperately, her black hair—like Maya's—streaming behind her like a lion's mane. The hallway formed around her as the woman gripped her two children in her arms, holding them so tight, like she never wanted to let them go. She led them to a nearby closet. She kissed their foreheads one last time. Though the mirrors remained silent, the words still rang in Maya's ears.

Do not leave this closet until I come to get you, do you understand? Stay here. Maya, watch your brother.

I love you.

She saw the hours pass by, waiting for their mother to return. She saw the nine-year-old sneaking out of the closet and telling Felix to stay inside while she checked what was happening. She saw the girl slip past the police officers standing at the door to the clock tower, saw her climbing, climbing, climbing a hundred and seven rickety wooden stairs, saw her emerge at the top. Her father and Mr. Elegans were there with a pair of detectives. Her father rushed towards her, trying to shield her eyes, but as he did so he moved out of the way just enough for the girl to see—Maya averted her eyes. The image had already burned itself into Maya's memory. She did not want to see it again. She had already seen her greatest failures, her faults played out for her to experience anew. She did not need to relive that one too.

When she opened her eyes again, she was left staring at her reflection in the glassy black walls. Her nine-year-old self was standing in front of her, pigtails as messy as ever, and the girl said, "You are such a child. You have never been strong enough to save anyone. How can you possibly save the world?"

Maya felt her spirit flare up inside her, her heart pumping blood poisoned by anger and regret through her tightening veins. She bit her tongue and clenched her fists. Then, as calmly as she could manage, she said, "You say you are me. Prove it."

The mirrors whirled, and the girl was sixteen again. "Haven't I already? What more do you want?"

"You're magical. Show me the weapon I used to slay the three-headed snake," Maya said with a calculating glare.

The doppelganger guffawed. "That is your test? Easy. It was a—"

"Show me," Maya insisted. "It is the only way I can be sure." The other girl grinned and, with a snap of her fingers, raised a fire extinguisher from thin air and handed it for Maya to examine. Satisfied, Maya nodded and said, "You're right. I've made a lot of mistakes. But you want to know why I know I'm going to save the world?" Maya's eyes flashed as she raised the fire extinguisher, her grip tight, her jaw clenched. "It's because I—" She smashed one of the mirrors with a swing of the fire extinguisher. "Will." Smash. "Never." Crash. "Give up on the people I love." Maya finished bashing in the glassy surfaces, and as she did so the shards transformed into an explosion of paper, pages hurtling in a whirlwind. Maya shoved the fire extinguisher back into the copy's hands. "And that is what makes us different." The reflection burst into pages, and a moment later a leather-bound book lay on the floor and the cover snapped shut. Maya picked up the book and marched out the red door.

She skidded to a stop when she saw Zizi and the rock giant sitting along the wall of the hall knitting a matching pair of mittens together. Maya stared, unable to respond, until she said, "Wasn't he trying to kill us five minutes ago?"

"Yes, but isn't he adorable?" Zizi grinned as the stone giant's face lit up in a smile, a hat placed crookedly on his head. He looked much less threatening now. In fact, he almost looked downright friendly.

The rock man jumped to his feet, shaking the whole hallway and placed his hand against the wall. Maya searched the hallway for their next disaster. A soft rumble echoed through the stone caverns. The rock man picked Zizi up in stone arms and ran towards the elevator. Maya sprinted after him. She took three steps for every one of his. Her legs burned, her heart pounded, but panic lent her feet a special swiftness, like someone had pushed the override button on all her usual checkpoints.

Just as the stone giant started to lift the creaky dumbwaiter, Maya leapt onto the rotting floorboards, her head buzzing with a dangerous combination of adrenaline and oxygen deprivation. All around her, a thousand door handles turn at once. Her eyes grew wide. The stone giant launched them up just as the doors flew open, and he waved at Zizi until the dumbwaiter disappeared into the elevator shaft. An explosion shook the walls, and a blast of smoke and dust and shattered rock thundered up the shaft, rocketing the wooden platform all the way to the top. Wheezing through the soot, the pair collapsed out into Mr. Elegans's office and leaned against the wall, trying to catch their breath.

Finally, Zizi broke the silence, "Amendment: *that* was the craziest thing I have ever done."

The door swung open. Mr. Elegans stopped in his tracks and gawked, completely shocked and appalled by the soot, ash, and gravel littering his office. Pebbles embedded themselves in his mahogany desk. Dust blackened the windows. A chunk of rock had smashed one of his chairs. Finally, Mr. Elegans sputtered out, "What have you done to my office?"

~ ~ ~

The longer Maya waited outside the door, the heavier the weight under her arm became, and yet she could not force herself to move. The plastic bag slipped in her fingers, and she just barely held onto it. The condensation on the outside of the bag made it slick. If she had not been in such a rush to get out of the supermarket, she might have asked for paper instead. She had gotten some very strange looks, what with the pieces of gravel that kept shaking out of her hair and the mud and soot splattered all over her clothes. Maya readjusted the weight and ran her fingers through her loose hair. They quickly got caught in a tangle of mud, rocks, and knots. She had managed to wash the worst of it off of her face and hands, but she was still a sight to be seen.

Maya reached for the door handle and pulled back. In truth, the door had not changed from all the days before. It was a cheerful blue rectangle in a hall that had been whitewashed so often it looked grey, and the bronze number 8 shimmered with yet another reflection Maya had no wish to see. The matching door handle shone, polished with use, and Maya dared not lay her own grubby hand upon it. No, the door had not changed. But something had.

Maya took one last deep breath and plunged through the door.

Tania dropped a plate the moment she saw Maya. "Maya, what happened?"

"I got a chicken," Maya said, holding the package out in front of her for her stepmother.

Tania lifted the offering from Maya's hands gingerly. Grimy fingerprints smeared the plastic. Maya massaged the back of her neck nervously. A pebble hopped out of her hood and scuttled away to the door on tiny stone legs. Glancing between the chicken and the soot-covered girl before her, Tania raised a brow at Maya, "Did you kill the chicken yourself?"

"Oh, no. This is from the explosion," Maya replied, pointing at the stains on her white t-shirt. If anything, Tania's eyebrows only grew more arched. Maya pulled off the soiled sweater and wrung it in her hands. The apartment was warm tonight, and the sweater was the worst offender in terms of grime. Biting her lip, Maya blurted out, "Do you maybe, one day want to, I don't know, make chicken soup together? Sometime? If you have time?"

"Maya, did something happen?" Tania asked, looking more concerned than ever. She took a step closer and traced every line on Maya's face, the dark circles under her eyes, the worry creases in her brow, and it was like Maya's heart, like her troubles and all her fears, like it was all laid out for Tania to see.

Maya's eyes welled up, and she stared at the ground. She could not bear to make eye contact.

"I'm sorry," she croaked out, her throat tightening. "I'm so sorry. You've always been there for me and I—I've ruined everything. I've destroyed this family, and—"

Tania enveloped Maya in a giant bear hug, soot and all, and Maya felt the thud of the chicken on her back. Burrowing her face into Tania's chest, Maya held on as if for dear life, hot streams running from her eyes, soaking through Tania's blouse. Between the tears and the mud, that blouse was done for.

When Maya finally let go, Tania brushed a hardened bunch of hair out of her stepdaughter's face. "I don't blame you for anything. I never did."

"I just—I don't know what I'm doing," Maya confessed, still unable to raise her eyes. The wooden floorboards squeaked under her shuffling feet.

"There is no shame in asking for help," Tania reassured her as she lifted Maya's chin with a gentle hand. The one that wasn't holding a chicken.

"But then people will know I can't do it on my own."

"If you've already tried your best, that's the truth isn't it? And the truth can often alleviate the darkness which causes us to stumble," Tania said, her eyes fixed on Maya, her voice like a caress. Tania had eyes the color of polished mahogany, big beautiful eyes that spoke of deep-rooted kindness and strength, the depths of which Maya could not begin to fathom, and her hair flowed like the branches of the weeping willow, a melancholy safe-haven for those who sought shelter amidst the leaves. She even smelled like October apples, ripe to bursting, the last fruits of the season before winter came.

Tania turned her attention to the chicken and said, "Speaking of truth, we should probably discuss the griffin you are hiding in your room."

The blood drained from Maya's face faster than a planet getting sucked into a black hole. She gulped, "You know about that?"

"It's hard to hide. Especially on laundry day," Tania winked.

Maya palmed her forehead. Technically, it was Felix's turn to do laundry, but since Felix was indisposed, Tania must have done it instead. "I forgot about that."

"I'm not sure who was more surprised: me or the griffin," Tania continued. "Oh, and you're going to have to tell me all about how your quest for the seven books is going. You are the champion, aren't you?"

"You know about Library of Souls, too?"

Tania laughed, "How do you think I met your father? We saved the world and fell in love."

"What? How?"

"Oh, just dealing with a little magician's rebellion. A little scuffle here, a little scuffle there. After your mother passed—I do so wish I had gotten to meet her—some magicians tried to steal the collection from the Library of Souls. We fought. We almost died. We saved the world. What a ride. But first," Tania started to walk off towards the kitchen, chicken in hand, "let's get this chicken into a pot."

A small smile crept across Maya's face as she stood in the hall, relief and joy flooding over her. Just as she was about to follow Tania, though, an envelope slipped under the front door, grating slightly against the wooden floors. Maya's heart crawled into her throat, pounding, pounding, pounding, the moment shattered. Her fingers trembling, Maya picked up the blank envelope and turned it over. Two dark, crimson rose petals slipped out and drifted to the floor, dissolving into black wisps of smoke as they touched the ground. Maya remained frozen in terror.

The Wizard was going to strike again.

TEN

With all her might

For a long time, Maya stood in the hallway, holding that blank envelope, unable to formulate a thought let alone a plan. The sound of a pot clanging snapped her attention back to the moment. Tania was just in the next room over. Maya's first instinct was to hide the envelope from her, to regain that distance between them that had characterized so much of their relationship. And yet, Tania might know something about the Wizard. And Maya did not want to face this terror alone. Not again.

Maya shuffled into the kitchen. Tania was adding water to the pot with the chicken. Maya cleared her throat, "This just arrived." She held up the envelope.

Tania took one glance and said, "I always appreciated that about the Wizard. He at least has the decency to let you know he's coming."

Maya jolted back. Stumbling over her jumble of thoughts, she stuttered, "That's it? The last time I got one of these, the Wizard put Felix in a coma."

"He's trying to get you on your back foot." Tania covered the pot and put it over the burner. Then, she leaned against the counter to face Maya. Though she was wringing the envelope in her hands and shuffling her feet, Maya focused her full attention on her stepmother. She had one eyebrow cocked, anticipating an explanation. Tania provided the explanation forthwith, "The Library of Souls is the source of magic in this world. You can draw magic from anything that has life, but the books contain the most pure magic and therefore the most powerful. However, by using the books for magic, you corrupt them, and this damage can have a detrimental effect even on the books around them. Corrupt enough books, and you endanger the entire Library. The Wizard is doing just that. When your father discovered that the Wizard was stealing books from the Library again, he sealed the doors shut to buy us time to find a champion to defend the Library. The Wizard knows this, and, while he needs the champion to succeed in order to unseal the Library again, he also knows that anyone capable of defeating the seven challenges may also be capable of defeating him. So, you can be assured that he will not harm you personally, but he will do everything in his power to dismay you so that you will not have the will or the courage to fight him when the time comes."

Maya snorted and said sarcastically, "That makes me feel much better."

"It should," Tania said as she peered into the pot again. "I swear, the Wizard has greater faith in your abilities than you do."

"Why does the Library even need a champion?" Maya asked, taking her seat at the kitchen table. The mountain of carrots piled on the table nearly hid Tania from view. Maya pulled the peeler out of a nearby drawer and started work on the heap before her.

Tania joined Maya at the table and started whittling away at her side of the carrot mountain. "Magic is about balance," she said. "The great evil of one must be countered by the great good of another. The cowardice of one must be countered by the courage of another. The greed of one must be countered by the generosity of another. The Wizard must be countered by one hero, the champion."

"Then what the blazes are the guardians for?" Maya exclaimed, tossing a half-peeled carrot out of her hand with exasperation.

Now it was Tania's turn to look confused. "Well, I suppose, as your legal guardian, I am responsible for the well-being of—"

"No, no, the guardians of the Library," Maya corrected.

"Oh! The Librarians, you mean," Tania smiled.

"Yeah, you guys need a better name for that."

"The Librarians regulate who has access to the Library, in theory to prevent disasters like the Wizard, but we also keep an eye on magical activity throughout the world. The cost of magic can be so high sometimes, you don't want just anyone using it to do just anything. I once met a man who nearly eradicated the bees just so that he wouldn't have to get up to get himself a new cup of tea." Proudly, Tania added, "Only those who have performed an extraordinary feat in service of the Library of Souls are honored with the title and responsibility of a Librarian."

Maya surveyed her stepmother across the carrot pile, "So what did you do for the Library?"

With a twinkle in her eye, Tania grinned and said, "That, Maya, is a story for another time."

~ ~ ~

Maya froze the moment she walked into Felix's room. Felix had his own corner room with a window overlooking a small playground, more for the benefit of his visitors than for Felix himself, and a gentle breeze wafted through the drapes. An arctic chill settled over the room. Dark clouds brewed outside, and the fluorescent lights above cast shadows across Felix's features, features that were growing more gaunt by the day. A thousand machines around him beeped and whirred, breathed like a dragon keeping watch over its treasure. Normally, Maya was the only person here at this hour.

But not today.

A pale woman in a sharp power suit towered over Felix's bed, cutting a stark image against the black clouds behind her. The woman scrutinized Maya with ice-cold eyes like a bird of prey. "So. This is our champion."

"How did you know?" Maya took a step closer, her heart pounding like rolling thunder. The woman tossed a newspaper at Felix's feet and examined her talons—er, fingernails—disinterestedly. Accompanied by several incriminating photographs, the headline declared, "Coincidence or Treacherous Plot: Why is student Maya Rodriguez present for every mysterious mishap on campus?" Maya skimmed the article, written by Franco Frank of course. Some of the details were alarmingly accurate. To herself, Maya mumbled, "So that's why he was hounding me for a quote all week."

Mrs. Mori's face fell back into its usual icy glare. "Your lack of restraint, foresight, and subtlety is highly unprofessional and unacceptable for an individual in your position. It is no wonder the Wizard found you so quickly."

"But, to be honest, me becoming the champion was kind of an accident."

The woman swooped around the bed so quickly Maya barely had time to step back before she found those icy eyes about three inches from hers. "You are wildfire. If you are not careful, the fire with either burn out and die, or it will spread, engulfing everything in its path in flames."

"Is this how you greet all the champions?" Maya asked as she leaned back so far she almost fell over, trying to extricate herself from under the woman's gaze. From this angle, with this light, the woman looked almost green.

Mrs. Mori only grew colder, "Do you really believe you are the first to try to break the curse? To defeat the Wizard?"

"No."

"What makes you think you can succeed where others have failed?"

"I have to," Maya answered earnestly as she finally managed to take a step back.

Mrs. Mori softened, if only for a flash. "You remind me of Cyrene." Maya's limbs fell limp, her whole body shrinking in on itself as Maya grew smaller and smaller in that already tiny room with that big name hanging in the air, the name no one had spoken in years. "It may come as a shock to you, but she was my friend, once upon a time. And she was betrayed by someone close to her. Do not make the same mistake." The woman swiped a bony hand over Felix's face, and the color was restored. In the room next door, an alarm sounded, followed by a wail. "You have three more days."

"Did you just kill someone?" Maya exclaimed.

Mrs. Mori scoffed, "Of course not. I killed a plant." She pointed out the window at a tree at the edge of the playground. It wilted before Maya's very eyes, green leaves turning to grey in a flash. Mrs. Mori brushed past Maya towards the door. Outside, nurses and doctors tackled a runaway patient and herded him back into the room next door. "Contrary to popular belief, I am not evil. Of course, I'm not good either. I am simply powerful."

"Then why is everyone so afraid of you?"

"Power unbridled by simple passions is frightening to people for it cannot be easily persuaded. People are afraid because I am powerful, and I am powerful because people are afraid."

"And if they stopped being afraid?"

"You know there is no monster under the bed, and yet when the night is dark and the shadows long, you still scurry as quick as you can back into the safety of the covers." Maya flushed with embarrassment, but Mrs. Mori simply smirked, "Fear never truly leaves us." She put on her sunglasses and stepped into the hall. With an almost casual boredom, as though she were simply commenting on the weather, she said, "The Wizard will be back soon." Maya froze, unable to hide the fear in her dilated eyes. Despite Tania's encouragement, Maya knew there was nothing she could do to stop the Wizard from striking again. Instinctively, she reached for the page hidden above her heart, that reminder of how much she had already lost, but she quickly pulled her hand away. "If you need me, I'll be at the Ambrose High Gala. Try not to come underdressed."

When the woman had gone, Maya sat by Felix's bed, but all too soon that oppressive silence reclaimed the room, that presence, that giant, the true owner of the space. Mrs. Mori was wrong about one thing. There was a monster under the bed: nothing and nothingness, emptiness and oblivion—nothing. And when the monster of nothingness and the giant of silence met, they gave birth to despair.

Just then, Zizi poked her head inside with an optimistic smile, "How's he doing?" One glance at the near lifeless body between those sterile white sheets was enough to know that nothing had changed. Stillness washed over Zizi as she saw and understood. No words were needed.

Zizi placed a warm tray of brownies down on the chair next to Maya as she walked on towards Felix's bedside table. The vase on the small table was nearly bursting with roses. Zizi pulled a pink rose from her purse, tied a yellow string of yarn around the stem, and added it to the other roses. She brought one with her every time she visited. Then, Zizi took her seat next to Maya. She held the tray of brownies in her lap, and for once her hands were idle. Those fingers of hers that used to fly as though of their own accord now lay motionless every time her mind wandered off. It was only with the greatest concentration that she could fumble together a basic cross-stitch these days. Where Maya's grief was like shattered glass underfoot, Zizi's was more like sand sifting through fingers, a melancholy memory half-remembered, a dream fading away in the harsh morning light, an "almost" almost grasped.

Zizi's eyes meandered, searching for solace in that bleak hospital room, and landed on Maya. Maya was watching Felix with such intensity it was as if every fiber in her being was willing, wishing him awake, but the monitors kept beeping, the machines kept breathing, and Felix did not move a muscle. Once, an eyelash fluttered, but it was simply a cruel trick of the wind.

At long last, Maya spoke, her voice wavering like a loose piece of paper lifted in a sudden breeze, "I know it's dumb, but I can't help but feel that if...if I had just left things alone earlier, if I had just given up looking for my dad and never gotten involved in this mess—" Her paper voice crumpled before she could continue.

"Then you would still have Felix?" Zizi finished for her. Maya flinched, the truth etched on her face, and Zizi laughed with the lightness and clarity of birdsong. "Don't you see?" Maya's armor only hardened. "Just because the world resists your demand for right, it doesn't mean you're at fault for demanding it." Zizi's face lit up with such a hopeful enthusiasm that it was obvious she meant every word she said. "It just means we have all that much more reason to fight for it."

"Right. We," Maya snapped, the words as sharp as a razor on her tongue.

"We," Zizi repeated, leaving no room for doubt.

Maya turned on Zizi with a blaze burning in her eyes, "And what are you going to do?"

Zizi offered the tray of brownies to Maya with a grin, "Provide snacks. I got the recipe from the cult."

Maya turned away with an exasperated sigh. Her eyes darted to the hallway, and a thought flirted with fruition. "How does she know that my mother was betrayed by someone close to her?" The chair clattered to the floor behind Maya as she rushed out of the room.

"Where are you going?" Zizi jumped up to follow.

"To find some answers."

~ ~ ~

The living room was pitch black when Wolf walked in. Even with nearly floor-length windows all around the house, it was remarkable how dark a room could be if you closed enough blinds and turned off enough lights. Wolf tripped over some electrical cords on his way to the light switch. His muttered curses masked the sound of his father's rhythmic, shallow breaths. After all, he did not need much breath if he did not intend to do anything. Or say anything. Or think anything.

When Wolf finally did manage to turn on a lamp, the dim glow of the singular light bulb cast cragged shadows across his father's blank face. He had grown a scruffy beard because he would not shave anymore. He had lost weight since he would not eat, at least not much, anyways. But worst of all were the eyes. The eyes that stared unwaveringly at some elusive point in the distance. Wolf opened the blinds to let the afternoon sun stream in. The man in forest green pajamas slouched in his armchair, smelling of body odor and must. Once, this man had been able to fill a whole room with his boisterous laughter. Now, he could barely register the laughter of others.

"Dad, come on. You can't just sit here in the dark. We have to get you out of those pajamas, okay? Come on. Let's go." Wolf tried to help his father out of the chair, but moving a brick wall would have been an easier task. His father offered no resistance, but he offered no help either. He was embedded deep in the leather chair, and his body was so limp Wolf could barely hold on tightly enough to keep his father from slipping through his arms again.

The man slowly trained his eyes on Wolf and crinkled his brow quizzically. "Who—who are you?" he asked.

"Dad," Wolf croaked out, holding back a sob. "Come on. It's me. No more tricks."

"I don't know you. Who are you? What are you doing in my house?" his father insisted. The resistance returned, and the old man pushed himself away.

"I'm Wolf. Wolfgang Mori. Your son," Wolf reminded him, his voice shaking nearly as much as his shoulders.

His father shook his head. "My son is dead. He was the chosen one, but now he's dead."

Wolf's stomach lurched. He feared he might lose his lunch across the tile floors, but his eyes felt suddenly dry. "Yes. Yes, he is. Poor you. All that's left is me." He turned on his heels and slammed the door behind him.

Once in the hallway, his breaths came in heaves, and he leaned against a side table to keep himself steady. When he raised his eyes, he saw his reflection staring back at him with hateful eyes. His hair was disheveled, and not in a good way, his cheeks were hollow and sickly pale, and his thin lips were pulled into a seemingly permanent sneer.

He had heard a story once of a prince, a prince who was a charming young man by day, but by night he transformed into a wolf, a killer without conscience. He was cursed, but the greatest curse of all was that he would know friendship and love—how could he not? He was a handsome prince—but it would be destroyed by his own hand, by his monstrous self every night until love pierced the beast's hide. Yet who could love a monster such as him?

Wolf laughed spitefully and addressed the mirror, "Mirror, mirror on the wall, wouldn't it be better to have no heart at all?"

With a swift punch, the mirror shattered, and Wolf left behind the broken pieces.

~ ~ ~

The double doors opened with a resounding crash. The courtyard fell silent. All eyes turned up the stairs to the girl in the red hoodie. Maya gulped, and the doors swung shut behind her again. Zizi had wisely remained inside. In the courtyard below, guests flitted from one bronze platter of hors-d'oeuvres to another as a string quartet performed a light waltz under strings of lights twinkling against the sky. The men were sweating in tuxedos that used to fit and the women freezing in sleeveless dresses and stilettos that could kill a man, but they looked altogether fabulous, glamorous, frivolous, and completely self-aware of their own collective beauty. And of Maya's lack thereof, her tattered hoodie a stain marring the image of perfection they had labored to maintain.

Coach Frank, the burly football coach, stepped in front of Maya, blocking her progress. He was actually shorter than her, a rare find, but with all the muscles bulging out of his shirt he must have been at least twice her body mass. "Excuse me. This is a private event."

"Yes, I understand. I just need to speak with someone very quickly," Maya tried to push her way past the body-builder, but his arms were so rock hard that Maya nearly knocked herself out by walking into them.

The man picked Maya up as if she was a tub of protein powder and turned her around so that she was facing the door. "Let me show you the way out."

"No, no, wait—" Maya protested as her shoes skidded across the flagstone, trying to break the coach's forward push.

SPLAT! A splotch of paint dripped down the door. A flock of pigeons took flight as small, hard balls arced across the sky and rained down on the gala, spattering paint every time they landed. The donors screamed as they stole the table cloths to protect their own clothes. Coach Frank yelped as a paintball shattered against his back. He loosened his grip for just a moment, and Maya broke free. Only to have an unconscious pigeon fall directly into her hood. Pulling the green paint-splattered bird out of her hood, Maya traced the flight path of the paintballs coursing through the sky and charged into the rose garden.

Sure enough, she found Wolf lounging on the lip of the fountain, shooting a paintball gun at the heavens. The basin gleamed white in the moonlight, the tree statue in the center etching cragged lines across the sky with its bare branches. Water fell from the branches, from the tips and knots and lumps, dripping into the water below with a soft pitter-patter like a drizzle against the window. Before her family's explosive picnic, the fountain had been little more than a glorified, water spewing pillar. Now, it was a hand-crafted work of art. Sometimes, throwing a box of lit fireworks at a fountain has its benefits.

Brandishing the unconscious bird, Maya stomped up to Wolf and shouted, "Wolf, I swear—"

"Hey, I actually hit one," Wolf exclaimed as he sat up to get a better look, setting the paintball gun down on the lip of the fountain. The bird regained consciousness and, with a few wobbly flaps of its wings, took off, brushing through Maya's bushy ponytail as it made its uneven course through the sky. Wolf laughed and slapped his knee, which only made Maya even more furious. "What are the chances? Then again, my aim's been getting better ever since the neighbor kid turned eleven. The estate's been bombarded like you wouldn't believe with these letter-wielding owls squawking and pooping all over the place. He's always been kind of a weird kid, but this is new heights."

"Wolf, don't shoot some eleven year old's bird. That's horrible," Maya said. "And what if the messages were important?"

Wolf scoffed, "They were sent by owl. How important can they possibly be?"

"You're a terrible person, you know that?"

He gasped with a dramatic flair, "I had no idea."

Her brow furrowed, nose twitching with frustration, Maya demanded, "Do you know where your mother is?"

"Ah, yes. Of course," Wolf said bitingly. In a flash, his whole demeanor had changed. His lanky limbs had become more angular, his face hidden in jagged shadows, his fists clenched. He hopped to his feet and began to walk away from Maya along the rim of the basin, "Everyone always wants my mother. The great Miyuki Mori, queen of Hollywood, leader of the magical underground, faithful Librarian, and there was something else in there, wasn't there?" He turned back around and rubbed his chin contemplatively before exclaiming, "Oh, and mother. How could I forget?"

"Wolf, are you okay? What's up with you?" Maya asked, taking a step back.

Wolf's hair flopped as he jumped down from the ledge, "Nothing. Just here to have some fun, isn't that right?" He barked with laughter and kicked the rim of the fountain, "Me and fun. Always fun. Everything is fun. The only thing I care about, right? Fun, fun, fun, fun, fun." With every repetition, he pounded his fist into the stone until red rippled across the water.

"Wolf, stop," Maya tore him away from the fountain.

To her utter surprise, Wolf buckled over and started heaving, strangled wails clawing through a choked up throat. Maya stood paralyzed, watching Wolf's outcry as though from afar, as through a dream, as though she and he were surreal phantoms passing through the endless night. She shook herself back into the moment. This was real. The boy crumpled on the floor, his fists clenched, his face streaked, stained by all the tears Maya had never seen—he was real. Slowly, Maya wrapped her arm over his shoulder.

"Come on. Let me take you home," she said.

Wiping his face dry, Wolf chuckled, "Maya, how forward of you."

She rolled her eyes and groaned, "You know what I mean."

"My house is the last place I want to be," Wolf declared as he stood. "I—It's my dad," he confessed, his entire body decompressing like a sigh. "And that curse. The Wizard let him keep his body, but not his mind—" His voice caught in his throat again, "He doesn't even recognize me anymore."

"But doesn't your mom—"

"My mother stopped caring years ago," he interrupted. "There's always some other crisis more important. As if she doesn't know that magic is rooted in humanity," he scoffed.

The rose bushes rustled, and Mr. Elegans emerged into the clearing, his grey suit splattered in all the colors of the rainbow, a dozen paintballs in his hand. "Wolfgang, I sincerely hope you have a good explanation for this." Wolf hesitated for just a moment and then took off sprinting towards the courtyard. "Wolf!"

"Mr. Elegans, let him go," Maya placed a temperate hand on the principle's raised arm. He lowered his fist and eyed Maya suspiciously with cold, grey eyes. The shadows of the tree statue crisscrossed across his grey suit like a spider web. "I got another envelope from the Wizard." Mr. Elegans's features grew even more withdrawn. Maya shook her head, "You'd think he didn't want me to open the Library for him."

Mr. Elegans sighed, "I don't dare give a reason for anything the Wizard does. But whatever happens," he trained his eyes on Maya again, insistent, urgent, hopeful, "listen to what I have to say. If the Wizard appears again, do not fight. Do not engage."

A cry rose up from the courtyard. Ears pricked, Maya raced towards the source of the commotion. Flames licked the sky. Tables crashed. Mobs raced to get away. And it smelled an awful lot like burnt feathers. Maya's heart skipped a beat. No.

It couldn't be. She ran faster, pushing her way past sooty donors until she skidded to a stop at the edge of the courtyard, her jaw hanging limply as she stared.

It could be.

Wolf had released a horde of angry, fire-breathing chickens on the gala.

The table cloths lit up in flames. Guests collided. A cheese platter whirled through the air over Maya's head. The coach waddled past Maya into the garden, hollering as he went, a platter of teriyaki chicken hoisted above his head as a dozen vengeful chickens clucked behind him to the tune of Vivaldi's *Four Seasons*, performed by the world's most dedicated string quartet.

Perched on a ledge, Wolf took a series of Polaroid pictures and howled with laughter as he tossed popcorn into his mouth. He caught one photo of a woman in a silk evening gown tearing off a chicken's head with her bare hands. And another of two balding men head butting as they crashed into each other. And one of a seventy-year-old man clubbing the birds with a swan ice sculpture. Wolf snorted, "Why have I never thought of this before?"

As smoke enveloped the school and the courtyard emptied, the twinkling lights barely visible through the haze, Maya palmed her forehead, cursed under her breath, and charged into the madness.

Eleven

She struggled against darkness

At first, Zizi tried gathering the chickens and leading them away from the gala, but even her charms were useless against the vengeful fire-breathers, so instead she ended up hiding behind the bar, which was ironically the only part of the courtyard that was not on fire.

"You lost?"

Zizi looked up to see a pale woman in a stark pantsuit sitting at the counter, a very full martini glass in her hand. She had sharp, hawk-like features and an icy stare that sent shivers through Zizi's spine. She shook her head. Without even looking, the woman sprayed a fire extinguisher at a flame that inched dangerously close to the drink cart while simultaneously downing the glass in one gulp.

"This is a disaster," Zizi observed, peeking over the edge of the counter. One particularly gallant gentleman had taken it upon himself to save his personal damsel by brandishing a chair at the chickens. The chair crumbled to ashes, and the man ran away screaming. The damsel managed fine on her own, though.

Mrs. Mori shrugged, "This is life." She filled her glass again and took a sip. "You're that homeschooled girl, aren't you?" Zizi nodded. "Should have stayed at home." Zizi wanted to protest, but she could not find the words. After all, she had never had to run away from fire-breathing chickens while she was homeschooled. Nor had she ever watched the life slip out of someone she cared about. She'd never cared about anyone that way before.

"But my friends—" Zizi started to object.

Mrs. Mori hooted, "Friends? One of them is in a coma, and the other doesn't want you around." Zizi lowered her eyes. The icy woman swirled the olive floating in her glass, "Beware of caring. Only pain and darkness lies down that road."

Zizi shook her head, tears welling as she struggled to contradict those poisonous words. Despite the smoke, she croaked out, "The moon shines even though the night is dark."

"Even the moon goes dark sometimes."

"But then it's reborn, and the light grows again. Some things have to end well, I'm sure of it."

"That's the lie that keeps paying my bills," Mrs. Mori muttered through glassy eyes.

Zizi looked back out across the fire and smoke and ruin. It was a hellish sight. Then, through the haze and dying embers, a book with gold-tipped pages catapulted into the middle of the courtyard and landed open faced—right in front of Maya.

~ ~ ~

It happened as though in slow motion. The book soared through the air. The cover was not imprinted like one of the Seven Books of the Library of Souls, but the pages were lined with gold, like the one her father had left behind. As it careened towards her, everything else faded away. The chickens, the fires, the smoke, the screams, the sirens. It was only Maya and the book. It fell open at Maya's feet.

Pages burst forth, crumbling into a black shroud, a cloud, a poison.

The darkness swirled around Maya like ink, flowing like silk. The only light that played across the surface appeared to come from Maya herself, but when Maya tried to break free, to push through the clouds enveloping her, the wall was as hard as obsidian. When Maya touched the venom, it stung and burned and clawed and bit, an acid to her spirit, a parasite burrowing itself inside her. Wincing, Maya drew her hand away from the mist as quickly as she could, but she could still feel the menace in her throbbing fingers. She made a mental note not to touch mysterious, magical clouds without proper safety gear in the future. Perhaps she was just imagining it, but it seemed the darkness around her grew darker still.

In the corner of her eye, she saw a figure flit through the shadows, and she wheeled to face him. Before her stood a cloaked figure whose flowing robes cascaded right into the swirling black like a polluted waterfall, but when Maya looked under the hood, there was nothing—nothing at all. She stepped back in horror. For a moment, the principal's warning echoed in her mind, but the echoes were overwhelmed by the rage that roared deep within Maya's soul. When she looked at that black nothingness, she saw only her brother dying on a hospital bed. She heard only the wails of anguish that could just as easily have been hers. Setting her jaw and clenching her fists, she charged at the figure.

The Wizard vanished just as Maya launched herself at him, and she crashed headlong into the shadowy perimeter. Typical. Bad guys were so unreliable. As a shock rushed through her body, Maya pulled herself out of the toxic cloud and gasped as though she had just been submerged under freezing water. Her vision started to blur at the edges. She clenched her knees in her hands, trying to hold onto something as the earth wobbled beneath her feet. Is this what Felix had felt before he fell asleep?

Maya felt a slight tug at her sweater. Another tug. One more until at last the page pulled free from her pocket. That page, the last clue her father had left, the last connection Maya had to her mother, that precious page she kept with her always—it slipped out of her possession like soap and floated into the Wizard's. A fire flared within Maya like embers before a fan. She lunged for the page and tightened her grip around it. She would not let go. She would never let go. The Wizard could not take this, too.

But no matter how fiercely she held on, the page crumbled between her fingers. With horror, Maya watched the dark wisps dissipate into nothingness, powerless to stop it. She pleaded, she begged—not this, please not this—but the hooded figure had no mercy. He did not even pause to consider. And then the page was gone. Gone, gone, gone forever. The last trace, gone. Maya fell to her knees, and the impact echoed through her hollow shell. The Wizard looked down on her, no pity in his empty soul. Only power. Then, the darkness vanished as quickly as it had come.

A warm glow washed over Maya from the party lights strung above and from the glowing embers around, but she hardly noticed. The empty, cold darkness clung to her like cobwebs. Mr. Elegans rushed to Maya's side and gripped her shoulders, rocking her motionless body. "Maya, what happened? Are you alright? I told you not to fight back. Maya, speak to me. I can help you."

The voice reached Maya as though through a thick fog. She stayed frozen in place, a four-year-old lost in the supermarket, unable to comprehend the activity surrounding her. Maya could not open her mouth. She could not even look the man in the eye. She knew exactly what had happened: a display of power. She was powerless against the Wizard. So, so unbelievably powerless. She could not even defend a piece of paper, let alone the world. In the end, the Wizard would take everything. There was no use resisting. Powerless. Utterly powerless.

A chicken squawked as Wolf punted it away. "We should get out of here."

Get out. We have to get out. The words rang through Maya's mind. Slowly, she raised her fingers to her lips. She whistled. A moment later, a great leathery beast swooped down and grabbed Maya in her claws. The dragon roared, filling the sky with flames. Even the chickens stopped their clucking to stare. Then, with a flap of her expansive crimson wings, the dragon soared into the sky, each beat of her wings in rhythm with the chiming of the clock. Midnight.

"That...is one way to make an exit," Wolf stated as he watched the dragon fly away with Maya.

Still sitting at the bar, largely forgotten by the others, Mrs. Mori sipped at her drink, her eyes fixed on Mr. Elegans. How quickly he had rushed out of the rose bushes, out of hiding, to run to Maya's aide. How quickly he had done the same for her son until the Wizard claimed his life. How coincidental the Wizard's fatal attack had happened mere days after her son had chosen to ignore the wise principal's "guidance." How coincidental this girl saw the man in the same light her son had. And how comforting to have a wise, fatherly counselor to run to when terror struck, a man who gave wise, fatherly guidance, who told you exactly what you needed to know at exactly the right moment. A man without whom you would be powerless. A man who could turn you into a finely tuned tool with just a few magic tricks.

A blackened piece of paper floated into her open palm. She breathed over it, and the corroded page turned into a silver wisp. Only one thing on earth could create magic like that, but with the Library of Souls sealed, where could such a page come from? She turned her gaze back on Mr. Elegans and narrowed her eyes as she took another sip.

The cool night air streamed through Maya's messy black hair as the dragon circled through the air in the pale light of the full moon. The dragon tossed Maya into the air and caught her on its back. Maya wrapped her legs around the dragon's shoulders. Where the dragon's skin was rough and dry and scaly, Maya's was clammy and vulnerable. The dragon's powerful wings undulated with a steady rhythm like a heartbeat, the muscles in her shoulders rising and falling under Maya in an unending, unstoppable march. Maya breathed. Rise, inhale, fall, exhale. Rise, inhale, fall, exhale. Rise, inhale, fall, exhale. Nothing could get to her up here. She looked down. The school was no larger than a doll's house and the people no larger than specks in the distance. How utterly small it all appeared from up here, from the back of a dragon.

At long last, the dragon floated down into a clearing in the rose garden, where the rosebushes towered like thorny walls and cracked park benches lay forgotten, overgrown, an enclave abandoned by humans and time alike. Maya rolled off the dragon's back and patted her scaly snout. The dragon puffed a small ring of smoke at Maya. Maya's eyes fogged up and her lip began to tremble. As the floodwaters spilled over her cheeks, Maya burrowed her face into the dragon's hard neck, her shoulders racking with each strangled breath. Her heart hurt. Her heart *hurt*. It throbbed, and broke, and bled, and hurt. Maya burrowed deeper into the dragon's scales and sobbed, her cry reaching to the heavens.

Powerless, powerless, powerless.

Her family was lost forever.

When the pain in her chest started to ease and her breaths came more readily, Maya wiped her face dry, curled up against the dragon's side, and let the silence envelop her.

The silence did not last long. At the other end of the clearing, the bushes rustled. Maya's ears perked up. The bushes rustled again, and a dozen muscular gnomes waddled into the clearing with tubs of protein powder conspicuously hidden behind their backs. One of the gnomes shoved a dilapidated stone bench aside. Moments later, the gnomes disappeared into a hole in the ground, and the stone bench moved back into place above them. Maya stared slack-jawed for several minutes before exclaiming, "Holy bananas. The protein-powder gnomes—they exist."

She pushed the stone bench out of the way and looked down the hole, but it was impossible to see where it ended. Maya glanced back at the dragon for reassurance, even though the hole was far too narrow for the mighty beast. A deep breath and she jumped.

Maya fell past layers upon layers of rock, and then the rocks ended and the cave began, and still she fell. Amazing how much she saw in those few seconds. Pyramids of white tubs along the walls. A crowd of gnomes lifting weights, jogging, or jazzercising around a central pillar in the middle of the cavern. A series of banners hanging from the ceiling. In one, a regal looking fellow in a crown held a jug of protein powder to his people with a tagline that said, "Feeding the strength of an Empire." Another said, "Together we are Strong," and another, "Protein Powder = Protein Power!"

Maya crashed.

Tubs of protein powder went flying as the trampoline buckled under Maya's weight. The net brushed against the ground before catapulting Maya and a dozen alarmed gnomes into the air again. Maya and the gnomes flailed, screamed, and crashed back into the net, only to be flung into the sky once more. This process repeated itself several times until, at last, air resistance took its toll and the bouncing came to an end.

Maya rolled off the trampoline onto the dirt floor of the cavern and stared out at the thousand gnomes gathered before her. A thousand gnomes stared back at her with unblinking eyes. Then, the gnomes ran screaming, "Human! She's going to eat us! She's come to destroy us all."

"What? No, I'm not here to destroy anything," Maya objected as she shook herself free from a gaggle of gnomes trying to load her back onto the trampoline. In the chaos, a leather-bound book fell into her hands. "And...the Fifth Book of the Library of Souls. Of course."

~ ~ ~

The moment the dragon landed on the horizon, Mr. Elegans took off running—okay, walking, but he walked so purposefully it might as well have been running—to find Maya. The way he marched off, his brow furrowed, his eye twitching like he was devising some new plan, it was less like a man on a rescue mission and more like a man who had lost a particularly uncooperative gerbil for the third time that week and was plotting new ways to catch it. The mission seemed urgent nonetheless. Wolf, on the other hand, seemed utterly unconcerned, although that might have had something to do with the chickens he was chasing across the courtyard. They had been so effective once, it would be a shame not to use them again, he had argued.

Zizi shivered. The flames had all burned themselves out. Only ashes remained.

The full moon hovered just over the garden. The rosebushes towered over Zizi, branches ensnaring the sky, thorns reaching out like claws, the last remaining flowers rotting slowly as a sickly sweet smell permeated the air. Zizi approached the petal-strewn path and hesitated.

That woman's words replayed in her mind. *You should have stayed at home. Only pain and darkness lies down that road.*

You should have stayed at home.

A cool breeze rustled through the leaves of the rosebushes. She could leave now and not worry about thorns tearing her skin. She could leave and not worry about what she would find if she entered the garden. She could leave, and no one would know the difference. After all, what if Maya really didn't want her around? What if Felix never did wake up? What if the woman had spoken the truth? If she left now, things could go back to the way they had been before, before she knew what it meant to bear the weight of the world.

But her feet did not move. They neither entered the garden nor fled it. They waited on Zizi's command. Taking a deep breath, Zizi made her decision. And she took the first step.

~ ~ ~

The moment Maya opened the cover of the book, all the pages swarmed through the air like bats before clinging to the base of the weight-bearing pillar in the center of the cavern. The gnomes backed away, first from Maya, then from the column. The change came slowly, so slowly Maya hardly noticed at first. The mounds of dirt around the column grew, and the base of the column shrank like it was being hollowed out, like it was a tree trunk in the jaws of a beaver. The earth rumbled. The ceiling cracked. Dust shook down on the gnomes below, and soon rocks began raining down as well. Maya's heart seized up. The book was going to collapse the cave.

Maya rushed through the sea of gnomes, shouting for them to run, to evacuate. They did not need to be told twice. Another lightening crack ran across the ceiling. Maya dove into the hollow at the base of the pillar and pushed her back into it, Atlas with the world on her shoulder. She would hold up the weight of the column as long as it took. As long as it took for the others to escape. The gnomes clambered onto the trampoline twelve at a time. They tightened a winch, released, and the gnomes catapulted through the hole above. But there were so many, so many to go.

The ceiling rumbled again. The weight doubled. Maya gasped and strained. Her legs buckled beneath her. Her arms trembled. Sweat poured from her brow.

The longer she remained, the more pages returned to the cover, but most continued to winnow away at the base. With every passing moment, the weight grew. Spasms ran through Maya's legs. Her lungs tightened. Each breath came more ragged than the one before.

Her vision blurred. Her heart labored. And still there were so many pages, so many gnomes, so many heartbeats to go.

And then the gnomes were running towards her.

"No, go back. Get out," Maya gasped.

The gnomes piled into the hollow all around Maya and formed pyramids three gnomes tall. Though the weight did not become much lighter, it became easier to bear. Only a few more pages. Only the gnomes around Maya left in the cavern. Maya could have cried out of thanks for these silly two-foot tall creatures with their ridiculous red caps and bulging muscles. Only one more page. And then, the task was done. The cover snapped shut, leaving behind nothing more than a trembling stem of a pillar and a few drained bodies to hold the rest.

"I can hold on long enough. You should go," Maya panted as the ceiling continued to rumble above. A hole broke through the earth above. Just as despair began to cement its clutch around Maya's heart, a pile of weights dropped through the hole. And then more. And more until a whole mountain of round plates had risen before them. Gnomes scrambled down on ropes or bounced off the trampoline. Each gnome gathered a few plates at a time and stacked them around the base of the pillar. They wedged a plate on top of the first column so that it was pinned beneath the base of the pillar, and a pyramid of gnomes fell away from Maya's side. The second, and another pyramid dropped away, exhausted from the strain. Another column, another pyramid of gnomes, again and again until Maya fell out, last of all, her whole body aching, too tired to move.

The gnomes erupted in cheers. Maya pushed herself into a sitting position and looked back at the pillar. The ceiling had stopped rumbling, the pillar had stopped collapsing, and the weights at the base—Maya squinted, "Did you guys steal those—oh never mind."

Lifting Maya on their squat shoulders, the gnomes shouted, "All hail the savior of the gnomes!"

"What? Please put me down," Maya said, and the gnomes complied. Even while sitting, Maya was at eye-level with them. "I'm not the savior of the gnomes. I didn't even do it alone."

"Of course not. No one ever does," replied a voice from the crowd, and a gnome in a crown emerged before Maya. The other gnomes gave him a wide berth. "We could not have built this GLORIOUS GNOME EMPIRE—" The crowd cheered muscularly. "If not for the advice of a strong and learned man from above, a man they call *Coach*, who offered us this wisdom: *Drink protein shakes*. And now, in honor of your service to our MAGNIFICENT AND SPLENDID GNOME EMPIRE—" The crowd cheered again. "I award you with this precious artifact." The gnome king handed Maya the Fifth Book of the Library of Souls.

Maya laughed, "How thoughtful."

"Please take it. Very far away," the gnome king said with a shooing motion.

"I'll do my best," Maya grinned as she hopped onto the trampoline. One of the gnomes tightened the winch, and the net pulled down like a sling shot. "Oh, and have you ever considered making your own protein powder instead of stealing it? Would be a good way to make a quick buck."

The trigger released, and Maya only caught a glimpse of the thousand enlightened faces as she hurtled back through the air. It was worth it. The sky opened above her, and she tumbled to a crash landing in the middle of the clearing just as a second figure stumbled through the rose bushes. Maya's face brightened. She scrambled to her feet and tackled Zizi in a hug so tight it knocked the breath out of her.

"You okay?" Zizi croaked as she tried to loosen Maya's death grip.

Maya did not let go, "I'm so glad you're here."

"I won't be much longer if you keep squeezing that hard."

"Oh." Maya released Zizi. As Zizi gasped for air, Maya said, "Thank you. For being here. And for coming with me to the hospital. And for being my friend."

"So is that a yes on the snacks?"

Maya nodded. Then, after a few moments, she added, "The literal embodiment of evil is going to eat my soul."

"Yes, but you have enough spirit for three meals at least," Zizi said with a smile.

Maya laughed and turned the book over in her hands as she slumped against the dragon, who was still purring at the edge of the clearing, filling the air with tiny puffs of smoke. She had two more to go, too many and too few at the same time. Two more before she had a chance at saving Felix, whose condition was rapidly deteriorating. Two more until she had to face the Wizard again, and all would be put to the test. Except it would not be much of a test. How could she possibly lift the curse, that darkness clouding the Library, when the darkness was so overwhelming?

Zizi nestled in against the dragon's belly and turned her gaze to the sky for several minutes until, at last, she interrupted Maya's ruminations, "You can actually see stars here." Maya looked up, noticing the sky for the first time. It was true. Thousands of pinpricks pierced through the darkness. She could even see the vague outline of the Milky Way smeared across the black sky. "Most places in L.A., you can't see any stars. Too much ambient light. But here, they light up the sky."

Maya leapt and gripped Zizi by the shoulders, "Zizi, you're a genius!"

"Thank you."

Maya started pacing back and forth, a spark of hope rekindled within her, "I've been thinking about the problem the wrong way. I've been focused on defeating the Wizard, but you can't fight shadows with force." Maya looked up at the sky with a giddy smile. "Breaking the curse is not about overpowering the darkness. It's about finding the light."

TWELVE

To redeem love

They raced up the stairs and past Mr. Elegans's office, past the door to the clock tower, past the conference room, all the way to the closet at the end of the landing. Maya dragged Wolf in behind her and slammed the door shut, both of them gasping for breath. A grate near the top of the door let in the only light in the tight space, crammed with mops and buckets and an unusually large collection of fire extinguishers. When her heart stopped stomping like a stallion in a stampede, Maya hissed at Wolf, "Why didn't you mention your mother was coming today?"

"Hey, you're the one who insisted on breaking into her office," Wolf mumbled through a mouthful of popcorn. His mother was the president of the board of trustees, and she technically had her own office at the school, but she never used it. Until today, apparently.

"You said she kept her files on the Wizard there," Maya insisted.

Wolf shrugged, "She used to. But—" Maya covered his mouth with a hand and pointed at the door. They both held their breaths as his mother climbed the stairs and stepped onto the walkway, coming towards them, nearer, nearer, nearer. Her look of icy determination was barely visible through the slits yet it sent a shiver down Maya's back. Then, the woman turned off into Mr. Elegans's office, "We have to talk."

Wolf breathed a sigh of relief, but Maya felt her perspiration turn cold with fear. This was not over yet. Maya's ears pricked at the sound of a light *pat-pat-pat*, like tiny feet scurrying over the wooden floorboards. Maya's blood rushed like waterfalls, coursing with the electric hyper-awareness that near-death situations tended to bring. And any scenario involving Wolf's mother was a near-death scenario. A bucket shifted behind her. Without a moment's hesitation, Maya flipped over the bucket and brought a fire extinguisher down with a smash.

Wolf switched on the light. "Behold: Maya, great slayer of small, furry rodents." The grey mouse lay dramatically sprawled out on its back, its tongue hanging out of its mouth, one paw clutching its chest.

"The last time I underestimated a mysterious noise, I ended up fighting a three-headed snake," Maya justified, brandishing her fire extinguisher at Wolf. "Not happening again."

As she said it, several dozen mice crawled out from shadows and corners and buckets and every nook and cranny.

The mice stared at the scene with placid faces until a chestnut colored mouse with skittish brown eyes crawled onto a high perch on the shelf and a team of mice in white coats rushed to the fallen one's side, a stretcher carried between them, as the chestnut one squeaked in—was that a Spanish accent?—"You! You bad human!"

"You talk," Maya lowered the fire extinguisher and stared, open-mouthed.

Wolf shrugged, "We live in a magical world with dragons and griffins. Why wouldn't the mice talk?"

"You killed our prince," the chestnut mouse cried, raising a toothpick at Maya.

The grey mouse sputtered and twitched. He sat fully upright. One of the mice in white coats shouted, as much as a squeaky-voiced mouse can shout, "Wait, I think he's alive." The grey mouse fell back over with a thump. "Nope. He's dead."

The chestnut mouse turned her attention back to Maya, her toothpick sword trembling with her rage. "My name is Indigo Montana. You killed my prince. Prepare to die." The other mice drew toothpicks from the strings tied around their plump waists.

"I am going to die by toothpick," Wolf observed. "Unexpected, but strangely fitting."

Maya palmed her forehead, "I have got to stop disrupting magical societies."

"But aren't they adorable?" Wolf said as the chestnut brown mouse dangled from his fingers.

"I am not adorable!" the mouse squeaked. "I am vengeance! I am death! You will fear me! Attack!"

Hundreds of mice rushed at them at once, toothpicks drawn. Maya grabbed Wolf by the wrist, and they tumbled out of the closet, an army of angry mice hot on their heels, their war cry ringing through the marble hall. The mice flanked around them, blocking off the stairwell. Maya turned and crashed into the conference room. The conference room itself was a mirror image of the principal's office, except where Mr. Elegans had his mirror/secret dumbwaiter, this room had a fireplace. The mice slipped under the closed door, and the pursuit continued. Maya and Wolf sprinted around the oblong conference table, but there was nowhere to run. They backed into the fireplace, Maya wielding her trusty fire extinguisher to face the mouse army, Wolf a bag of popcorn.

Thousands upon thousands of mice poured into the conference room, their massive flanks completely surrounding the pair in the fireplace with archers and flags and drums and—were those trebuchets? The pebble to the forehead was answer enough. Maya rubbed the sore spot and cursed under her breath as they retreated further into the fireplace.

"Every time," Maya muttered. "Every time I am around you, something disastrous happens."

"I don't know," Wolf leaned back against the blackened brick wall as he looked lustfully at the last kernels of popcorn at the bottom of the bag. "I'm having great fun."

Maya glowered, blood bubbling up just beneath the surface as every one of Wolf's grievances flooded through her mind at once, culminating in his utter lack of involvement or sincerity at the present moment. Grinding her teeth, she muttered, "Wolf, this is such bad—" One of the pebbles shattered a brick in the wall behind them, and a book fell open in Maya's hand. "—timing."

Pages stormed around the pair, a tornado spiraling up the chimney. The fireplace rumbled. The wind tugged up on Maya's hair like a vacuum. Her fingers lost their grip on the wall, the brick scraping against her skin as her feet left the ground. The chimney squeezed around her. And then she was flying.

~ ~ ~

Zizi paused mid-throw, the apple still in her hand. A low thunder echoed over the rooftops. A flock of birds took to the skies. And the dragon whined. Turning her attention back to the scaly beast, Zizi grinned, "Always have to be at the center of attention, don't you?" She lobbed the apple into the air.

The dragon burned it to a crisp and swallowed it whole. Licking her lips, the dragon lifted another apple from the pile, carefully holding it between her front teeth, and she nudged Zizi to throw again. Zizi shook her head and took a seat on one of the air conditioning units on the roof of the gym, leaving the dragon to toss the apples herself. Maya had left a mountain of Red Delicious for the dragon, which was nice and all, but it was seriously interfering with Zizi's experiment. Zizi scribbled a note in her logbook.

Dairy – No

Eggs – No

Meat – No (except unicorns—RIP)

Greens – Yes

Cake – Yes

Carrots – Yes

Bananas – Only on Tuesdays

Oranges – No

Apples – Always.

Zizi reached into the burlap sack at her feet. "Alright. Let's find out: vegan, vegetarian, or pescatarian?" She tossed a fish into the air.

~ ~ ~

One minute, Maya was being squeezed through the chimney. The next, she was soaring through the air above a giant, craggily, terrifying chasm. She rolled to break her fall and slammed into a wall. The chasm ran through the middle of an abandoned warehouse with high brick walls, a tin roof, and not much else to speak of. Wolf screamed as he flailed through the air after Maya. He crash-landed on the opposite ledge. Maya cried out in alarm.

With a jolt, the floor shifted, slowly inching towards the wall so that both ledges drifted even further apart than they already were and left just a little bit less space to stand on than there had already been. Five, ten minutes and they would not be able to hold on at all. From the chasm, a burst of flame flashed up, a rush of heat washing over them as the fire licked the tin roof above.

"We have to figure out a way to get out," Maya announced as she searched the room for a way to bridge the gap. The roof was too high to reach, and the few crates still sitting in the corner were too small and much, much too flammable, as Maya quickly discovered.

"Gee, what convinced you?" Wolf snapped as another flame leapt forth from the deep.

Maya laughed, "You scared of fire?"

"That is sort of a normal reaction to things that can kill you in horrible, painful ways," Wolf remarked, keeping himself pressed as close to the wall as possible.

Maya peeked over the ledge and pulled back just in time to avoid being roasted by another burst of fire, "I keep forgetting that."

As much as Maya scrutinized the room, there was nothing, no way out, and the ledges kept receding with no sign as to what the challenge even was, let alone how to beat it. Maya dug her feet into the floor and pushed against the wall, trying with all her might to slow or stop the ledge. Between grunts, Maya shouted at Wolf, "Try your side." Wolf sighed heavily, rolled his eyes, and placed his hand against the wall. "Wolf, do you want us to die?" Wolf glanced between Maya and the chasm and then planted his feet and leaned his back into the wall.

~ ~ ~

From the edge of the table, Indigo could survey the whole land. She and her officers had pitched camp atop the conference table, the napkin tents arranged in straight rows and straight columns around the larger central command pavilion made from copies of the Daily Harold. The front cover featured several of Wolf's pictures from the gala while covering the central dispute: "Are New Hotplates to Blame for Fire?" It was an inflammatory article. The chairs had been rolled into defensive positions surrounding the fireplace, a legion on each seat, manned with a trebuchet. Scout teams occupied the mantle. Reserve forces secured the door. The infantry camped in a wide arc around the fireplace, just in front of the wall of chairs. This time, there would be no escape.

The second in command, a straw-colored mouse with a feathered plume tucked behind his ear, approached his fearless leader, Princess Indigo, commander of the mouse armies. Her purple cloak billowed behind her as she overlooked the mighty force below, the pride of her nation, the responsibility handed down to her by her forbearers. The straw mouse cleared his throat, "Are they still in the chimney?"

Groans and grunts echoed out of the fireplace. "I think it's working," the girl shouted. A few moments later, "Nope. Not working. Not working."

The boy yelped, "Slipping, slipping, FIRE!"

"Push harder," the girl said.

"I'm pushing as hard as I can."

"Leaning seductively against the wall doesn't count as pushing!"

"It appears they are," Indigo Montana said as she twirled her whiskers, her eyebrows arched, her nose twitching, sniffing the air for a trace of deception. "Who knows what nefarious plans they have in store. Their sounds are very cryptic, likely a ruse, a distraction to mislead us. We must be ready for anything."

"So what do you propose we do, your magnificence?" the plumed mouse asked.

"We wait for them to return. And then—" the chestnut one swung her toothpick, "we take our revenge."

~ ~ ~

Maya slid down the wall into a sitting position, completely drenched in sweat. Wolf had already plopped himself down on the other ledge and was struggling to catch his breath. Her sore arms trembling with exhaustion, Maya said, "So, that failed. I don't have any other ideas. And our school is the gateway to hell."

"Yeah, but we already knew that," Wolf said as he laid down on his back, his arms pillowing his head as he stared up at the tin roof above. Rising to her feet again, Maya roved back and forth along the ledge, searching for another solution, another idea, another anything. Even the walls were warm to the touch by now, and her clothes surely reeked of char and ash and fire. The concrete ledge was barely wide enough to fit them, and it kept getting smaller. After another blast threatened to burn off Wolf's elbow, which was peaking over the edge, he glanced at Maya pacing like a caged animal and asked, "Care to explain what's going on exactly?"

"I've got this under control," Maya insisted, but Wolf simply laughed at her. Crossing her arms and harrumphing, Maya continued her march, "Okay, I'm still working out a few details, but I've almost got it."

"Don't you trust me?" Wolf winked at her as he sat up.

Maya scoffed, "No. I barely know you."

Wolf laughed, "You know more about me than anyone else. What more do you need?"

Maya stopped and turned to face Wolf. "What happened to your brother? And to your father?" A burst of flame divided them.

Wolf suddenly grew very quiet, "That has nothing to do with me."

Maya shook her head. "It has everything to do with you."

Wolf sighed and leaned back against the wall, "My brother was a very talented magician, perhaps the most talented magician the world has ever known. He thought he could use the magic of the Library of Souls to defeat the Wizard, and he led the Magician's Rebellion to that end, despite the ultimate cost such magic would bring. But his efforts came to nothing. The Wizard destroyed him, and when my father tried to save him, the Wizard destroyed him too."

Maya dropped to a seat across from Wolf, the concrete floor scraping her jeans as it receded beneath her. "My family fought your family, didn't they. In the Magician's Rebellion."

"Yes."

"And you helped me anyways."

"I helped the Library. At first."

"And now?"

Wolf's lips turned up into a faint smile, "I'm on your side. You know that."

Maya jumped to her feet. The solution clicked. The answer. The way out. "We're on the same side. We're on the same side!" She threw a fist in the air with a manic giggle.

Wolf backed as far against the wall as he could go, "Why do I get the sense I am missing something?"

~ ~ ~

Mr. Elegans turned back towards Mrs. Mori and froze. After greeting her, he had taken his usual turn about the room—he almost always did so when he had visitors. It was pedantic, giving the sense of aged wisdom, but it also reminded guests that this was his space, that they were intruders into his cerebral sanctuary, given leave to stay only out of the benevolence of his heart. But when he turned around, he found the woman sitting in his chair—his chair! And using his teapot!

Mrs. Mori poured herself a cup of tea, the steam rising to obscure her rigid, cold features. "Tea?" She offered a second cup to Mr. Elegans, her eyes piercing straight through him like icicles. Cautiously, Mr. Elegans accepted the cup and took a seat opposite her. These chairs were more uncomfortable than he remembered. No wonder students hated coming to his office. "Sugar?"

"As always," Mr. Elegans replied. Mrs. Mori slid the sugar towards him, and he scooped a generous spoonful.

Mrs. Mori sat back in the plush, high-backed chair and sipped her tea, keeping her gaze fixed on the man in grey. Despite his greatest efforts, Mr. Elegans squirmed like a worm under a magnifying glass. Mrs. Mori's face twitched, betraying the faintest hint of a smirk, and she finally allowed the uncomfortable silence to end, "Why did you hide the champion's identity from me?"

Mr. Elegans sighed and lowered his cup, his composure restored. He had been awaiting this visit ever since Wolf had notified him. With a grave voice, he said, "So. You know."

"I am surprised and, frankly, a little disappointed. Especially after all we have seen together," Mrs. Mori stated, a frigid edge to her voice. The words cut like the north wind on a winter day. A shadow sliced across her face, a slanted line that hid her eyes and divided her face in two. She did not move a muscle. Darkness was no stranger to her. When Mr. Elegans remained silent, she said, "Did you really think I would let personal grievances cloud my judgment?"

No. Of course not. The principal knew she had a mind sharp as ice and no heart to warm it. She did not think in terms of revenge. He shook his head sadly, "I could not risk the Wizard discovering the truth. You must understand." Oh, she would understand. The Wizard had discovered the true identity of her son, and he had paid for it with his life. Or at least that was the story. In truth, the Wizard had been his tutor all along, though Ran did not know it until the end. Until the boy's betrayal. There were few things more dangerous than a powerful tool that started thinking for itself.

With all the affable contriteness of a repentant schoolboy, Mr. Elegans lowered his eyes, "Although, it seems I have failed even there."

"A shame," Mrs. Mori said flatly. She leaned forward into the light, her eyes gleaming, "After all your precautions, one cannot help but wonder how the Wizard always seems to know so much."

"In such troubling times, it is difficult to know whom to trust," Mr. Elegans said, meeting those cold eyes and hoping his own did not betray him.

Mrs. Mori smiled at Mr. Elegans, the same way he smiled at his more delinquent students before pardoning them, leaving them indebted to his grace, and she poured herself another cup of tea, "It is a good thing we have each other, then. The only two true magicians amongst the Librarians."

The principal felt his breath come more easily and smiled in return, "I should never have doubted you."

But his relief came prematurely, for no sooner had he taken a sip of his tea than Mrs. Mori said, "Then again, my son trusted you. And he died."

It took all of his self-control not to spew tea everywhere. Mr. Elegans set the cup back down as carefully as he could, yet despite his best efforts, tea sloshed out into the saucer. He dared not raise his eyes. "I did my best."

"Ah, yes. You saved him from sinking his own soul into darkness, but alas you came too late and it cost him his life. That's the story, is it not?" Her tone was flippant, as though she were simply rattling on about the neighbor's new landscaping, but her body was ridged, and the intensity of her being was pushing in on Mr. Elegans like a thumb pressing into a bruise. Mr. Elegans snuck a glance at his bookshelf. If things got desperate, he could still gain the advantage. She continued, "It was four years ago, was it not? At that banquet. It had been three years to the day since Cyrene's sacrifice had driven the Wizard away. We were such fools to think the spell would last forever, were we not? How we celebrated that night! Until, of course, half of the Librarians dropped dead." Her gaze bored straight through Mr. Elegans, but he was unfazed. His mask was steady as ever.

"I remember. I helped bury them," he whispered with tears in his eyes. The moment he had been able to cross the threshold of the Library again, he had sought out the books of all those Librarians who had opposed him before. Sadly, the Librarian he most despised had had the foresight to hide his own book. In consequence, Leo Rodriguez had been spared from one doom only to watch his friends and co-conspirators fall at the hands of the Wizard. Or of a gas leak, depending on which source you consult.

"And do you remember how that sparked the Magician's Rebellion? How my son rallied the remainder to storm the Library in order to defeat the Wizard at any cost—even if that cost meant the destruction of countless souls? Had Leo and Tania not stood in the way, he might have succeeded and armed himself before facing the Wizard, but alas we will never know if it would have worked for the best. Still, I'm not sure where he even got the idea. He certainly never got it at home, and I always thought that you staunchly opposed the use of the books for magic. Am I not right?"

It took Mr. Elegans a moment to realize that it was not a rhetorical question. As he wiped the sweat from his brow, he stammered, "Yes, yes. Of course. I have no clue where he learned that sort of sorcery."

That was a lie.

Ran had been destined for greatness. Through his veins ran the blood of two families with a long and proud history of serving the Library of Souls, and he was more powerful than any of those who had come before. He was ruthless and strong, he was clever and calculating, and he was as noble as any Mori could hope to be. In short, every Librarian agreed that Ran Mori was their greatest hope of defeating the Wizard once and for all, should the phantom ever pose a threat again. Ran felt that pressure acutely. In his quest to grow more powerful than the Wizard, he sought knowledge of all forms of magic, including those the Wizard himself was using. And who better to teach him than Mr. Elegans. However, there was one caveat Mr. Elegans had overlooked in taking the boy on as a student. When doing magic, a bit of the magician's soul mixes in like a catalyst – the soul is not consumed in the process, but it gives the magic its own unique flavor. The night of the Wizard's attack, Ran had recognized traces of Mr. Elegans's particular brand of magic, and he sought out his tutor for an explanation. Ran was wed to his duty, and no force on earth nor any argument of reason could have convinced him to spare the Wizard let alone join him.

Mrs. Mori leaned further across the desk, "And do you remember how it ended? How could you not? You were there. Do remember how he ran off to confront the Wizard on his own? Do you remember the choice?"

"I remember him making the wrong choice," Mr. Elegans rebutted as he too leaned in across the desk, his face suddenly hardened.

The pair were only inches apart, neither willing to budge. Mrs. Mori hissed, "According to you, that is."

"When he entered the gymnasium, the Wizard was waiting for him. No other living beings were in sight. There were only two books, lying on the floor. One was his own, the other his brother's. The Wizard would give him a chance to defend himself and fight, but he had to choose. And we both know which one he was going to pick. After all, it was only logical."

Mrs. Mori flinched, and Mr. Elegans knew he had struck a nerve. Her lips tightened until only a pale line was visible. Her knuckles grew white. Her posture grew straighter. And Mr. Elegans knew he would not need magic today.

He continued, "If your husband and I had not intervened, at great personal cost, you would have lost two sons that day, not one."

"But the Wizard would have been defeated."

"And Ran would have replaced him. He battled darkness with darkness, and the darkness won. It always does."

In truth, the two books had been two random volumes from Mr. Elegans's collection. The choice had been meant to stall Ran long enough that Mr. Elegans could save himself, either through persuasion or through flight. To his surprise, Ran had made his choice instantly, and it was all Mr. Elegans could do to defend himself from the boy's onslaught. Only when Ran's father burst in unexpectedly was Mr. Elegans saved. The interruption distracted Ran for just a moment, and in that moment Mr. Elegans cursed them both, buying himself freedom and anonymity just a little longer. None of them could possibly understand the nobility of the Wizard's quest – it was love, true love that drove him, and love conquered all. Love was worth any price.

In this way, the man who served love without integrity came face to face with the one who served duty without love.

After a long pause, Mrs. Mori replied, "There is yet hope for the dawn."

~ ~ ~

Maya crouched near the edge, a confident gleam in her eyes, a smirk playing across her lips. The fire flared up between them. The ledge lurched back another inch. The brick wall behind her radiated heat. A sulfuric smell filled the air. Maya breathed and never felt so alive.

On the other side of the chasm, Wolf waved his hands in the air in protest, "Maya, this is not the time for trust exercises."

"Just catch me, okay?" she insisted.

"That's a fifty-foot jump."

"No, it isn't," Maya tensed her muscles. The sinews trembled like strings on a violin, a light tremor that remained as the note lingered and faded into obscurity, swallowed by the silence of the amphitheater. "The room itself is the book. The laws of physics don't apply."

Wolf did not look convinced, "You do realize if you die so do I, and I like living. I want to keep living."

Maya fixed her eyes on the opposite ledge, "We're already on the same side. All we need is a little faith." She launched herself off the ledge just as it was about to vanish completely. The fire flared up from below. Wolf's heart stopped. Then, Maya burst through the flames. She crashed right into him, slamming him against the brick wall, pressed so close they could feel each other's hearts racing. When Maya glanced back, the chasm was gone. She laughed and untangled herself from Wolf, "Not as dumb as I look, huh?"

"That isn't saying much," Wolf teased as he straightened himself up, a playful glint in his amber eyes. Not for long, though. The floor gave way, and his eyes popped. The room disintegrated in a flurry of pages. Holding on to each other for dear life, Maya and Wolf fell, falling, falling, falling, until at last they landed with a small *poof* in a pile of ashes, the book close behind. Maya picked the book up and laughed. The Sixth Book of the Library of Souls. Only one left.

A war cry rose from the mouse army, "Attack!"

Maya and Wolf scrambled to their feet and backed against the fireplace wall. "Right," Maya muttered as the flanks closed in around them and pebbles pelted them from a series of chair-top towers. The mice had really outdone themselves. "Forgot about the mouse problem."

The legions charged at them until a tiny mouse voice cried out above the rest, "Stop! I'm alive."

The mice halted mid-step. All at once, they turned to look. At the edge of the conference table, the grey prince waved down at them, his whiskers a little bent, his nose a little crooked, but alive. Very much alive.

The chestnut mouse squealed with delight, "My prince, you're safe." She scurried across the table and tackled the prince in an embrace before brandishing her toothpick at Maya and threatening, "This has been your last warning. Do not test me again. Ranks, fall back!" The mice picked up camp with the efficiency of a well-oiled machine and marched back to their holes.

When Maya and Wolf were left alone again, Maya stepped out of the fireplace and caught sight of Wolf's bag of popcorn lying on the ground. She picked it up eagerly only to be met with the crushing disappointment of an empty bag of popcorn. With a sly grin, Wolf pulled another bag out of his back pocket and snapped his fingers. The bag expanded with a *BANG!* On the window sill, a leafy plant withered and drooped.

"Why have you never told me you can pop popcorn on demand?" Maya exclaimed as Wolf handed her the bag of popcorn.

He laughed, "I come out of one of history's most legendary magical families, and the only thing I got was the ability to pop popcorn. It's not something you advertise."

Through bulging cheeks, Maya murmured, "Hey, this is amazing." She swallowed another handful of popcorn and looked up at Wolf with an excited sparkle in her eye. "And you're not bad yourself."

She smiled at him, and for a moment—when their eyes met and time sighed, when the soot and the room and the past fell away and only the heart remained, when the moment reached its fulfillment and they were with each other and for each other and undeniably intertwined in one of those fleeting instances in which history was erased, the future forgotten, and the present complete—in that moment, all was well in the world.

Then, a war cry rose through the walls, and Indigo Montana reemerged from her hole, shaking a toothpick at Maya. Dust shook from the ceiling as thousands of mouse feet scampered through the rafters. The chestnut mouse princess cried out, "Traitor! Prepare to taste my vengeance, Maya of the Chimney, murderer of princes!"

Wolf looked alarmed, "But I used the plant. Why did the mouse die too?"

The door to the conference room swung open and, like a pillar of pure ice in a blizzard, a blade that could slice through storm winds and flesh alike, Mrs. Mori entered. "You two have a lot of explaining to do."

A wronged mouse army. A vengeful ice queen. Wolf and Maya united against the world. With just a glance, they agreed on their battle strategy: "RUN!"

THIRTEEN

To overcome the challenges

There once was a kingdom that was cursed to dwell in darkness, its gates sealed, its queen dead, its king lost.

There once was a knight who fell in love with a beautiful princess, but he pricked his finger and fell into a deep and dreamless sleep.

There once was a wolf damned to howl into the night alone, surrounded by a frozen wasteland, until the sun rose once more.

There once was a wizard who tried to steal the light of the sun for himself alone, who drenched his hands in blood and drove the world into night, but the light slipped through his own fingers too, and the darkness was made complete, the curse unbroken. After all, magic had its own price, and curses were broken only when the price was paid. In a barren and desolate land, frozen in despair and drenched in eternal night, even the smallest flame, a flicker of hope, could work wonders if one only had the strength to find it.

~ ~ ~

Oxygen filled Maya's lungs one last time as a gentle drizzle rained down on her from the fountain, the branches of the tree bare above her. The roots opened up below, a gaping threshold to watery depths unknown, ringed by the warning, "Treasures in the deep do lie. Please do try not to die." A crumpled envelope drifted across the ripples. Only one petal this time. Good. Only one book left too, and then it would be the moment of truth.

Maya plunged into the clear water, the sun and sky disappearing above her. What little light broke through the eternal mist above died all too quickly when it struck the surface of the water. She should have known it would be here, here at the fountain where she had spent so many happy days with her family. The family that had been stolen from her by the Wizard. She should have known even before she found that plain envelope waiting for her on the lip of the basin. Before that perfect sanctuary of hers, that place that held so many perfect memories, was tainted by the Wizard's touch. A seething hatred washed over her once more.

Maya's lungs burned, ached, screamed within her chest. She gasped for air, but the ice cold water clawed down her throat. Her heart raced, her head pounded, her fingers tingled like static on a television. It was so dark around her she could not even see the contours of the wide concrete tube around her. All she could see was that tiny stream of light pouring from the book down below. The light. If she could only get to the light. Maya pulled herself through the water, small eddies forming every time she took a stroke. The book looked blurry through her bloodshot eyes, but there was light, precious light streaming from it. Fighting the current that pulled her back towards the surface, Maya wrapped her hand around the book and, as her vision started to fade, she flipped the cover open.

~ ~ ~

Tania's shoes patted against the linoleum floors as she paced back and forth, back and forth outside Felix's hospital room. Her grip tightened around the phone pressed to her ear. Third ring. Fourth ring. Voicemail. She hung up and redialed. The alarms from the life support machines blared across the bustling halls. The doctor shouted at one of the nurses. The nurse readjusted his IVs.

Voicemail again.

At the tone, Tania said, "Maya, come to the hospital as soon as possible. It's Felix."

A new beeping sound joined the chorus.

Zizi barreled between stretchers and nurses and medics, her starry skirt billowing as she went until she reached Tania. "How is he?"

"Have you heard from Maya?" Tania's phone rang. She jumped on it, "Charles?" Oscar poked his head out of Zizi's enormous purse. She pushed his fluffy crown back down so he would not attract attention. "You're sure? Right now?" Tania faced Felix's room again. The cacophony of alarms was near deafening. "Let's hope she completes the challenge quickly. The fact he's made it a week is a miracle in itself. I don't think he can hold on much longer."

~ ~ ~

Pages swirled around Maya, drifting slowly through the water like autumn leaves on a breeze, enveloping her in a pale golden glow. Maya sank gently to sleep, wrapped in light as the current dragged her further and further from the world above. Six challenges she had already completed, and this was where it ended.

The pages burst apart, and so did the waters. Maya plummeted through the air—real air—free from the icy grip at last as she slammed into the floor, hard as marble yet fluid, black and white clouds flowing around each other like cream in coffee. She coughed and gasped and sputtered and breathed. She breathed, each gasp filling her heaving lungs with life, reprieve.

Maya pushed herself into a sitting position. She was at the center of a circular room with walls and ceiling like the floor, a living marble. To Maya's left lay a small cube of solid wood, about three inches tall. Maya picked it up and ran her fingers over the edges. "I'm guessing this has something to do with the book," Maya said to no one in particular.

Messy letters written in black appeared on the wall in front of Maya, "Yes."

The cube fell from Maya's hand as she scrambled away from the wall. Maya gaped, "I am literally talking to a wall. I'm talking to a wall. That's a wall. And it's talking."

The wall scribbled, "That which you seek is within."

"Do I get a hammer?" Maya grunted as she tried to pull the wooden block apart. There were no seams or cracks in the wood, but there had to be a secret way of opening it.

"No," the wall answered.

Beads of sweat formed on Maya's forehead from the strain of tugging, "Any clues?"

"Only one force on earth can open it."

"Is it love?" Maya asked irreverently.

"No."

"Then it must be death."

"No."

"Are you sure? I was really getting a star-crossed lovers feel from this thing," Maya said. "Total enmeshment, co-dependence, kind of bland on the outside but intriguing when you break things and see what's really inside."

"The block does not represent star-crossed lovers."

"And clearly the wall does not understand sarcasm," Maya patted the wall. Her hand passed right through the swirling marble, splashing through cold water as she did so. Shaking her hand dry, she settled down in the middle of the room and scrutinized the block. "So. How do you open?"

~ ~ ~

Wolf stood at the edge of the fountain and called out for Maya again. He could have sworn he had seen her just a minute ago.

Mr. Elegans dashed across the clearing, hollering his lungs out. A moment later, a dozen tiny, twisted trees trundled after him on stumpy little roots. Considering the size of the gnarled little trees, they were incredibly fast. Roots gripped the beleaguered principal by the ankles. He tripped and fell right into the midst of the bonsai trees as they wildly swung their branches at him and butted him with their trunks and even stuck out the occasional woody tongue at him. They made odd grunting noises with a sporadic, high-pitched cry, "HIY-yaya-YAH!" that inevitably preceded a particularly well-executed swing of their clumsy branches.

Wolf was contemplating going to the principal's aid when a lively spruce clubbed him over the head with a branch and blocked his path. Wolf rubbed the back of his skull, "Ow. What was that for?"

The tree started to shake up and down, its leaves rustling like muffled laughter. Wolf took an alarmed step back.

"You're all *bark*, eh?" the tree taunted. "If you're not going to fight, then *leaf*, eh?" the tree giggled, shooing Wolf with its branches.

"Do you only speak in bad tree puns?" Wolf asked.

"That is my *branch* of humor, eh?"

Wolf grinned. His moment had finally arrived. "Sorry. I didn't mean to be *root*." The tree shook with so much laughter it fell over. Wolf stood over the spruce in triumph, "Ironically, uprooted by a root pun. Then again, this isn't your *garden variety* tree. Guess this one liked to *spruce* things up. I can't be-*leaf*—" Wolf only stopped when Mr. Elegans dashed past him again, still not free from the radical green agenda. "I should probably help him with that."

~ ~ ~

"Only one force on earth," Maya twiddled the block in her fingers as she lay on her back, staring up at the cloudy white ceiling. She slammed the block down against the floor, but to no avail. "What is wrong with this stupid block?"

The wall commented, "It is not the block but you who are stupid."

With a groan, Maya threw the block at the wall. Getting insulted by an inanimate object was the height of humiliation. For a moment, the block disappeared, absorbed into the wall like a rock being pulled back in a slingshot. Then, it ricocheted back out, directly into Maya's stomach. She groaned and slumped back to the floor. She hated this stupid test, she hated the wall, and most of all she hated the Wizard. Without him, none of this would be happening right now. "I know I'm not 'champion' material, but honestly, failing on the very last test is just embarrassing."

"But you are the champion," the wall said.

"Yeah, but I shouldn't be. I don't have any of the qualities. I mean, for goodness sake, the champion is supposed to be 'sure,' but when I found the very first book, I was pretty much a mess. 'Slow to anger,' but I'd just blown up at Zizi for no good reason when I found the second book. With the third, I was terrified...hold on." Maya paused, the realization slowly dawning on her, "Why would the books show up every time I was the exact opposite of what the champion should be? Uncertain, angry, afraid, doubtful, weak, resentful..." she took a sharp breath and admitted, "hateful."

The wall was silent.

Maya turned the block over in her hand, "For the first book, I told the creatures very clearly to leave, and the chaos stopped. I gave the bull flowers instead of attacking it, and we made peace. Rather than flee the dragon, I freed her, and she was the key to getting the third book."

"The fourth?"

"Faced some truths about myself I hadn't wanted to."

"The fifth?"

"Worked with the gnomes."

"The sixth?"

"I put my grudges behind me and started to trust Wolf. So what do I do to beat this challenge?" She glanced down at the block, that challenge brought on by hate, and, full of indignation, she exclaimed, "I told you the answer was love."

"No."

"Blast." Maya tossed the block into the wall and waited for it to fling back again. Toss, wait, ricochet. Toss, wait, ricochet. It was a little bit like playing catch with the wall. It was literally playing catch with the wall. The block lobbed back into Maya's hand as the realization struck her, "I could die down here, and my last moments are going to be spent making friends with a wall." She scoffed, "You don't happen to know any depressing stories to make it worse, do you, wall?"

"I know one about a boy. About a boy and a girl."

"Did the boy love the girl?" Maya asked as she tossed the block into the wall again.

"No, but he thought he did."

Maya caught the block and set it down on the floor, giving the wall her undivided attention, "And what happened?"

"The girl became a queen." The letters faded and were replaced, "The queen." Replaced again, "My queen."

"Of the Library, you mean?" she asked.

"Yes."

"And the boy?"

"Became a wizard," the wall wrote. The black clouds billowed into a familiar shape, a hooded figure in a long, black cloak. "By day, he confessed his undying loyalty to the queen. But by night..." The black spread across the whole wall, only the pale outline of the wizard left. The words appeared in whirls of cream, "He stole entire shelves of books with which to do his magic." Ribbons and swirls and explosions of light burst forth from the wizard's palm, encircling a crowned woman in white. "Yet for all his sorcery, he failed to win the heart of the queen. And, one day, she discovered the truth."

"And what did she do?"

Black and white clouds split the wall in half. "The queen and the Library were one. To love her was to love the Library. To misuse the Library was to misuse her. So she left him with a choice: abandon magic or become forever more her enemy."

Maya lowered her eyes, the ending suddenly clear, "And he chose magic."

"Why would he choose reality when he could have a fantasy instead?" the wall replied as darkness overtook the surface.

Maya's heart sank, "And he killed her."

"The delusion comes at a cost," said the wall. The black clouds spread over the ceiling.

"And he's been trying to take the Library of Souls ever since," she finished, the darkness around her complete.

As the wall returned to its marbled state, it wrote, "You know the story?"

"I'm going to finish it. One way or another," Maya said, playing absentmindedly with the block. "But I think you told it wrong. This isn't the Wizard's story. It's my mother's and my brother's and my father's. And it's mine. And in my story, it doesn't matter what happens to the Wizard in the end so long as my family is safe and the Library restored." As the block twirled between her fingers, Maya checked one more time, "You're sure the answer isn't love?"

"Completely."

She began to laugh to herself, "Like a wooden block could ever fall in love."

Across the room, a yellow wooden block emerged through the walls. A green block followed shortly afterwards, the light dancing on the exposed wood, the green G's on its sides glistening in the mist. The yellow 'A' block shouted, "How could you do that to me? I—I trusted you. And you broke my heart. I loved you," the yellow block finished in almost a whimper.

The green block scooted right up to the yellow one so that they were almost touching. "I never meant to hurt you," it said in a sultry, deep voice. "And those things I did in the past, they don't matter. I've changed. I'm not that blockhead anymore."

"Really?" the yellow block scooted closer.

"Yes, baby, and it's all because of you," the green one finished. In a tight embrace, the two blocks fell off the edge of the marble floor and back into the water.

Maya gaped in horror. "How long have I been in here?"

"Too long," the wall noted.

Maya then turned her attention back to the original block. "So the answer definitely isn't love." She paused, "Or maybe it's more nuanced than that." She thought for a moment more, then said, "Hatred is irrational. It is an innate reaction when someone hurts us. In fact, you could say that it is the default reaction." She tossed the block at the wall, and it sprang back into her hand. She got to her feet and approached the wall again, slowly reaching out her hand to touch it. Her fingers passed through the barrier without the slightest resistance. "But to love, to forgive, to move on—that requires a choice. It requires a change." Taking the block firmly in her grasp, she plunged her arms into the wall. At first, the wall stretched and pulled like a balloon, and every push felt like she was tugging at her own heart, a heart that resisted her efforts with all its might. Then, with the full force of her body, she burst through into the water on the other side.

The wall quickly closed up behind her, and she was left shivering in those watery depths. A part of her knew what she had to do, but while she still had breath, the other part of her gripped and pulled at the block, refusing to let go. After all, if she let go, she lost control, and how could she hope to force the block open then? As her lungs started to burn, she glanced back at the glowing paper wall behind her, but her former refuge was closed to her now. She would drown down here unless...unless... She took one last look at the block. She made her choice. She let go.

The block floated away from her until it was out of her reach. Just as she was beginning to worry if she had made the right choice, the block collapsed, it morphed, it changed, and then it was an open-faced leather cover waiting to be filled with pages. The Seventh Book of the Library of Souls. The pages peeled off the walls behind Maya. A wave of paper carried her up, up, up through icy waters, all the way into the glorious sunshine, bursting forth from the fountain like a geyser of enchanted pages. At the top of the arc, the pages spiraled towards the cover. It was done.

And Maya was nearly a hundred feet in the air with a book and nothing to stop her fall. Maya clutched the book close to her chest and gulped as she peered down at the ground below. She made a mental note to buy a parachute should she survive. Then, gravity began its work.

~ ~ ~

When Wolf had finally pulled the last bonsai tree off of Mr. Elegans, the principal straightened his grey suit jacket and harrumphed, "Bonsai Beasts. I hate those buggers. Just because something looks grey, doesn't mean it is associated with the demonic force of bad weather."

"I'm guessing they don't like rain?" Wolf handed Mr. Elegans his glasses.

"They despise it. And anything remotely resembling it as well."

Wolf noted the principal's grey suit and grey hair and grey skin and nodded, "That explains a lot. They might be onto something, though. Since the Wizard showed up, I've never been so scared of dark clouds in my life."

The earth rumbled as a spout of water and paper emerged from the fountain. Maya flailed across the sky. As she started to plummet, her whistle rang through the air. Each Mississippi she fell felt like an eternity. One Mississippi. Still falling. Two Mississippi. Getting awfully close to the stone branches of the tree. Three Mississippi—a red dragon swooped under Maya and roared off into the sky, Maya whooping on its back as leathery wings overshadowed the garden.

Wolf was still gaping, dumbstruck, when Mr. Elegans wheeled around towards the school, "I must go. Do not follow."

~ ~ ~

Maya collapsed against the dragon's back and breathed a sigh of relief. "When we get back, you can have as many apples as you want." The dragon soared high into the sky where the air was clear and a stray kite was making a new home. Until it crumbled into ashes. The dragon could be a little territorial at times. Maya sat up and looked down at the school. Where only moments ago she could see every blade of grass reaching up to ensnare her, now the school looked no bigger than the toy blocks she had seen before. "But first," Maya said, pointing down at the clock tower, "we have to make a stop."

The dragon took a sharp dive and spiraled to a hard landing at the front entrance to the school. Her heart racing, Maya hopped off and patted the dragon's nose, "If—if things go wrong, get Tania. She'll know what to do." The dragon did not even wait for Maya to turn her back before flying off again. Maya harrumphed, "Oh, thanks for the vote of confidence."

Setting her jaw, Maya faced the school and entered.

The rusty hinges creaked when she opened the door to the clock tower. The rickety stairs rose, wrapping around the inside of the tower higher and higher and higher. Maya had not made that climb in seven years. It was time to make it again. She lifted the floorboard from the bottom step, and her heart stopped.

Gone.

The books were gone. All six. All the ones she had found before. Gone. She thumped the wooden boards, frantic, reaching for something that was no longer there.

"Is something wrong?" Mr. Elegans's voice came from behind.

Maya could not even draw her gaze away, as though willing the books back into place would make it so. "The books. They're gone."

A heavy weight struck the floor. Maya wheeled around to see. A cloud of dust billowed about the box at the principal's feet. A box which held six precious books. Maya's diaphragm relaxed, and her breath came easily once more. As he cleaned his glasses, the silhouette in the doorframe said, "You should really be more careful, Maya."

Maya hoisted the box and started to climb. It was a longer way than she remembered it being, but seven years was a long time for memories to change. Her arms strained under the weight. The box slipped, slowly, slowly, inching out of her grip. A drop of sweat darkened the cardboard. At fifty-seven steps, she dumped the box on the stair above and panted as she knelt against the steps, her legs trembling, her arms numb. She looked up. Still so far to go. She looked back. So far she had come. With a tremendous heave, she lifted the weight again and continued the climb. She huffed and puffed and pushed for one more step, one more step, and one more, and another after that. One hundred and seven steps until she crested the top of the stairs.

Maya dropped the box and slid it across the floorboards, dragging herself close behind. The space was smaller than she remembered. The bell took up most of the room. A thin layer of dust covered the gears and wooden planks, and two clock faces pointed out on opposite walls, the opaque glass permitting the only light in the room. As soon as she neared the clock face in front of her, the books began to disintegrate. The golden dust drifted towards the glass, filling the surface with light like sunshine.

"One touch and the Library will be free at last," Mr. Elegans said as he stepped up behind her.

Maya's hand trembled, and her lips felt chapped and dry. As soon as she opened the Library, her fate was sealed—she would face the Wizard. But that of her father and brother might not be. If there was hope for them, there was no other option for Maya. A fire in her heart, a fierce resolve in her eyes, Maya reached out towards the clock face.

Mr. Elegans's voice stopped her, "But first, I think you might want to have this." He reached into his briefcase and reemerged with a two-handed broadsword that was almost as long as Maya was tall.

Maya gaped as she held the sword in her hands. It was lighter than she thought it would be. Finally, she looked back to Mr. Elegans and said, "Are you sure? But if I use it now, what if someone even worse shows up and we're like, 'Oh no!' and they're like, 'Muahaha! Without your special sword, you are powerless to stop me. Muahaha!' And then we're dead." The principal responded with the stoniest of stony glares. "Right. Point taken."

With the sword in one hand, Maya raised the other and placed it against the clock face. The gears began to spin, to groan, to whir, and with a click, the opaque glass swung out. A tremor ran through the earth. The Library of Souls was open.

~ ~ ~

The doctors and nurses all ran and hid as the dragon crashed through the window into Felix's room and bellowed a bellow that shook the frame of the building. At the force of its impact, the floor cracked, and the walls started to crumble. Only Tania rushed forward to meet the dragon before the smoke rising from its nostrils threatened to set off the fire alarm. A web of cracks ran through the walls under the dragon's weight, and the whole building shook as another crack stretched across the foundation. The dragon nudged Tania, a worried look in its eye, and roared again.

"It's Maya, isn't it?" she asked. The dragon nodded. "Did she find the book?" Another nod. "The Wizard," Tania muttered as she glanced back at Felix, divided between staying and going to Maya's aide.

"Go," Zizi said as though she could read her mind. "I'll watch Felix."

Tania nodded and hopped onto the dragon's back. As the dragon pushed off, the floor jolted, like the entire corner of the building was teetering on the edge, ready to fall at any second. A moment later, dragon and rider disappeared into the clouds. The medical professionals peeked out of their hiding places, stiff with fear. Zizi waved and smiled, "Don't worry. That dragon's a vegan. Except when cake or unicorns are involved. But she's very conscious about her health. I think you would get along."

~ ~ ~

Maya's jaw dropped as she stepped through the round doorway. The bookshelves towered so high that Maya could not see the top. They radiated out from a central golden waterfall that rushed down from the sky, and golden streams ran between each of the bookshelves, through vibrant green grass. As the water fell and flowed across the vast expanse, filling the room with dazzling light, droplets broke free from the torrent and fluttered away as new pages, page after page, drop after drop, until it was a wonder any water remained at all. Maya hopped over one of the streams and wandered towards the center, dragging the sword through the flowers and grass behind her.

As a series of pages fluttered above Maya, a dark shadow passed through them, and the golden pages wilted, crumbled, sprinkling the grass with ashes. Some of the ashes fell on one of the other books, and black splotches spread across the pages, infecting them with darkness. Maya's eyes widened with horror as she watched the black poison consume the whole book in a matter of minutes. Everywhere she looked, black clouds hung over the library, and many of the once brilliant books withered away, sad and corroded and damaged. Maya's heart broke as she took a weathered book from the shelf, one of billions. How could anyone wish to destroy something as beautiful as the human spirit?

"Maya?"

Maya dropped the book and spun towards the central clearing around the waterfall, towards that voice from a dream. Her feet moved as of their own accord. She barely noticed the black clouds forming above. She barely noticed the water soaking her shoes. She saw only one thing, and even that she did not believe. It was not possible.

"Mom?"

Her mother smiled at her, looking even more beautiful than Maya remembered her. The sharp cheekbones, the lion's mane of hair, the straight back and proud chin—and that smile. A smile like sunshine. But before Maya could reach her, a black cloud encircled her and the Wizard rose from the darkness.

With one swift swing of her sword, Maya sliced through those empty robes and the Wizard collapsed back into the nothingness from which it was born. The sword crumbled into dust. Maya felt a lightness, an elation she had not known for years. It had been so easy. And then she looked up. Black clouds still shrouded the light, and books still crumbled around her. "I thought defeating the Wizard was supposed to break the curse."

"But you have broken the curse," Mr. Elegans reassured her. "We can leave. Celebrate. You've done a marvelous job as champion, as I always knew you would." But as he spoke, he looked lustfully at the endless books around him, books that would be his to use the moment he was alone, and that without ever arousing suspicion. After all, the Wizard was dead! Vanquished! Defeated! And there was a new champion to guard the Library, one who trusted him completely. Everything he wanted with the minimum damage. All she needed to do was leave.

Maya's mother took a step nearer, "Come. Let's leave this place before it is too late. We can go home. We can have our family back."

Maya reached out towards her but pulled her hand back at the last moment, afraid to know what would happen when she touched this apparition. She wanted it to be real. She wanted it with all her heart. "Mom, I can't believe—how?"

"Maya," her mother brushed her fingers along Maya's cheek. Maya's heart leapt, and her eyes began to water. Those fingers, that caress—she felt it. "We have to be quick. I don't have much time."

Maya placed her hand on her mothers and lingered just a moment longer, joy, disbelief, and wonder rushing through her. Of course she wanted to run away with her mother, her mother back from the dead. It was like a dream come true.

But Maya faltered. Something did not feel right. This woman before her was perfect. Too perfect. And her skin felt papery to Maya's touch. Not to mention, her mother would never have caressed her cheek like that. She would have brushed the hair out of Maya's eyes or wrapped her in a hug or kissed her forehead, but she would never have brushed her cheek. Maya pulled away and scrutinized the figure.

"After all," Mr. Elegans stepped into the clearing next to Maya, his eyes soft, "doesn't every child long to find comfort in her mother's arms?"

Maya's eyes flashed between Mr. Elegans and that distortion of her mother before her. "But I'm not a child anymore," she said. Mr. Elegans flicked his wrist slightly, and the woman reached out towards Maya. Maya stepped away. She studied the apparition, "My, what large eyes you have."

"The better to see you with, my dear," she said. "Oh, how I have longed to see you again."

"And what smooth skin you have," Maya observed. This woman had none of the scars her mother had, the birthmark on her collarbone, the pale line below one ear, the burn mark on her forearm. They were all gone.

"The better to hold you with. Come. Give me a hug."

What if the cloaked figure known as the Wizard were simply an illusion? The Wizard had to be someone who was always near when magic happened, someone who knew the inner workings of the Library and of the Librarians, someone her parents trusted.

Someone who was here right now.

"My, what intricate magic to create such a replica, Mr. Elegans," Maya turned on the man in grey, "or should I say, the Wizard."

FOURTEEN

To restore the light

Wolf threw his weight against the door to the clock tower. The hinges groaned but stayed put. No matter how hard he tried, the sturdy old door simply would not budge. With long strides, Wolf marched to the next door down. Mr. Elegans's office. Surely, he had a spare key in his desk. He burst into the office and skidded to a stop.

"Mother?" His mother was scouring the office, turning over every drawer, emptying every shelf. As he scanned the scene, he noticed the sword still hanging over the mirror. Pointing at the heaps scattered across the floor, he asked, "You didn't happen to find an extra key to the clock tower in all that, did you?"

She pulled up with a shrill laugh, "Even if I did, good luck breaking the spell over the door." She yanked another drawer out of the principal's desk and emptied its contents onto the floor.

"There has to be something we can do," Wolf insisted.

"There is." His mother approached the bookshelves and scoffed at the very idea of such a cliché hiding place. Whatever respect she had left for him vanished the moment she began to pull at the shelves. "If nothing else, perhaps we can save a few of the books." The bookshelves sprang apart to reveal a dark room filled with stacks of books, stolen directly from the Library of Souls. Before their eyes could even adjust, the shadows took on shape. A beast with terrible claws and terrible fangs formed from the gloom. And it charged.

~ ~ ~

"You," Maya spat as she circled Mr. Elegans. The vision of her mother crumbled into ashes and floated away in the golden streams of the Library. The heavens thundered, and the air buzzed with static, with an electric aroma. "It was you the whole time. You're the Wizard."

"No," Mr. Elegans corrected her, remaining still and steady as he cleaned his glasses. Dark clouds gathered above him. "The Wizard was merely a tool."

"But you created...it."

The man in grey placed his glasses on the bridge of his nose and met Maya's fiery gaze. "I created life itself."

Maya quaked with fury, the library rumbling around her, and she shouted, "Look. LOOK at what you have created!" Maya gestured at the ashes falling, the books crumbling, the clouds thickening, the darkness overshadowing the entire Library. "You have brought nothing but death and destruction."

"But I have also rekindled love," he said, unmoved.

"You do not know what love is," Maya stated, her voice barely more than a hush. "Mr. Elegans, if you really loved her, you would help me save the Library."

"You could have her back, too," he said, and Maya realized he was deadly serious. "What are a few books, a few souls already liberated from their earthly tethers, compared with love. I know you feel it. You long for it. Just let me have the magic, and you can have your family back."

His words struck a chord—she did want her family back—but they did not move her. As she looked upon the sniveling grey man before her, she tasted bile, foul upon her tongue. She had trusted him, and he had betrayed her. In the guise of a friend, an advisor, a mentor, he had been her enemy all along. He had taken her family. He had known what she feared most, and he had used it against her. And now, he bargained with her, promising lies for treasures, for in truth he could not restore the love he had destroyed.

Maya shook her head, "You killed your love. With your own hands, you murdered her."

"I had no other choice." He really believed it.

Maya did not. "You could have let her be happy." Soot continued to fall from above. It gathered into black dunes that drifted into distant corners or floated down the golden streams in globs. Inky clouds streaked through the air above, and shadows marred every book they touched, leaving the pages wrinkled like wilted flower petals at best. At worst, the pages crumbled into dust. Every fleck of ash carried a piece of human soul, a speck of life destroyed to create a mere illusion. Rage, disgust, and grief swelled up within Maya as she circled Mr. Elegans, evidence of his treachery all around. Her voice barely a growl, Maya threatened, "Break the curse, or I will."

Mr. Elegans chortled, and the chortle turned into howling laughter. He wiped tears from his eyes as he asked, "Do you truly believe you are capable of breaking this curse? Do you think you are worthy?"

"No," Maya said plainly. "But I'm here."

Mr. Elegans turned his grey eyes on Maya, "Yes. And how I wish you weren't."

Planting his feet, Mr. Elegans raised a fist and gathered a black cloud above him, darker and more concentrated than any before. A whirlwind blew through the library as more and more books emptied their contents and crumbled into darkness, joining the spiraling pillar at the Wizard's command. With an open palm, Mr. Elegans punched the air in Maya's direction.

Maya's heart stopped. The entire column of corrupted souls rushed at her at once. Maya swiped a hand through the golden stream. A wave splashed up into the black cloud. Part of the darkness fizzled away, but more remained, hurtling towards her like a runaway train.

Maya ran. She dove through the waterfall. Another blast of darkness followed and broke itself against the water. The back end of the poisonous mass wrapped around like a scorpion's tail, striking Maya from the side. Maya yelped and swung through the waterfall. Three times, she beat away the shadows. Three times, they returned until the clouds encircled the waterfall completely.

Maya pushed herself into the center of the waterfall. The waters beat down on her, pounding her from above. Her heart raced. Her lungs ached. The darkness squeezed around her. The light faded.

There was no escape.

~ ~ ~

It happened so fast.

The creature, a great wolf-like beast with the strength of a hundred men, struck his mother. She flew against the far wall and crumpled to the ground, her magic nullified. He cried out as horror filled him—this is what the principal had wanted her hair for; this is the fate to which Wolf had betrayed his mother. The beast snarled and turned on Wolf. He ducked a blow to reach his mother. With a tremendous heave, he dragged her into the closet, closing the door just as the beast rammed against it.

Wolf pressed his back against the closet door, his heart rattling against his ribcage, his teeth clenched, his shirt drenched in sweat. Each strike resonated through his very bones. The creature hissed and roared and clawed at the floor. And then it rammed into the door again. Dust shook from the ceiling. Wolf's mother sputtered and coughed, every breath laden with exertion. That flimsy door to Mr. Elegans's coat closet was the only defense they had left. It had to hold. The beast hit the door again, and it began to crack.

And then it stopped. Wolf could feel the monster's every tread reverberate through the floor as it paced back and forth. With a course and raspy laugh, the beast said, "So, the pup has chosen his pack. You could have left her to me and gone free. None of them really loved you anyways." Wolf's grip on the door tightened, as did his throat. He closed his eyes and tried to tune out the words, but they pierced right to his heart, "Even your own brother sold you out before the end."

In barely a whisper, Wolf said, "He was only doing what he thought was best."

"He tried to sacrifice you to save himself. After all, he was the chosen one. His life was valuable. And you?" The wolf chortled, "He saw right through you. Useless. Monster. No one could love a creature like you."

Wolf felt the strength leave his limbs as he sagged against the door. After all, only a monster could love another monster. He knew that. He'd always known that, and—he froze. Only a monster could love a monster. He checked his back pocket. He still had one more bag of popcorn, and everyone knows that true love begins with food. Glancing down at his mother's unconscious body, he braced himself for a decision, and under his breath, he muttered, "But that doesn't mean a creature like me can't love."

He burst out of the door, popcorn in hand, a newfound courage in his heart. He instantly regretted his choice. The wolf snarled at him, its lips turned up in an arrogant smirk. Its hot breath smelled of death. Its claws dug into the rug. And Wolf stood alone, a boy in the shadow of the great beast.

~ ~ ~

The darkness tightened around the waterfall, pressing closer and closer. Every time Maya reached for fresh air, poison greeted her lungs instead, an acrid taste lingering on her tongue. Mr. Elegans's voice boomed through the darkness, "Give up. It's over."

More and more books emptied, joining the other corrupted souls at the Wizard's beck and call, and Maya's heart broke for the Library. It was dying. All around her, the souls of every person who had ever lived—they were disintegrating and disappearing and dying. Unable to hold her breath any longer, Maya closed her eyes and forced her way out of the waterfall, expecting to hit a wall of shadows.

She didn't. In fact, the cloud was nowhere near Maya anymore.

Mr. Elegans was aiming the pillar of venom at the door. Tania stepped through into the Library. Maya's gut twisted and dropped. The cloud hurtled towards Tania. Tearing off her soaked red sweater, Maya sprinted as fast as her legs could carry her. She ran, and she cut through the cloud with the light-drenched jacket. The sweater crumbled to ash in her hands, but the cloud recoiled regardless. (Then again, if that happened with the rest of her clothes, things were going to get very awkward very quickly. Fortunately, that didn't happen.)

Maya turned her furious gaze on Mr. Elegans, her brow furrowed, her fists clenched, and she growled, "No more."

The grey man smirked, accepting the challenge, and launched the full force of the poisoned cloud at Maya.

~ ~ ~

The hospital shook again, and screams echoed through the halls. Zizi held onto Felix's hospital bed. The doctors and nurses had all run off to help other patients, more and more of whom were falling into critical condition, and then to evacuate the hospital. And Felix had been left behind.

The earth thundered and rumbled and quaked – the aftermath of the unsealing of the Library of Souls. The building, already weakened by the dragon, cracked like lightning. An entire corner of the hospital was hanging onto the rest of the building by nothing more than some electrical wires and pipes. Zizi's knitting needles flung into the air as her elbows smacked against the floor. A sharp pain shot up her arm.

Felix's stretcher rolled away, nearly slipping out of the hole the dragon had left in the wall. The entire corner of the hospital was teetering, ready to fall as soon as the next aftershock hit, and the divide ran right through Felix's room. Zizi scrambled to her feet and looked for a way to cross the gulf back into the main building. If she jumped, she could make it, but the gap was too far for Felix's stretcher. They were trapped, the knitter and the boy in the coma, and the building was about to collapse.

Rolling up her sleeves, Zizi weighed down the base of the stretcher with the lead pipes that had come loose in the earthquake and tied them down with bundles of yarn. The bottom had to weigh significantly more than the top if this was going to work. Then, she strapped Felix in as tight as she could get him and tore out all the chords and tubes binding him to the spot. They could worry about those after they survived the fall. They were jumping from the top floor, after all. Another quake shook the building, and the room began to tip.

Pushing the modified stretcher in front of her, Zizi charged at the hole in the wall and shouted to the skies, "Screw it! I still believe in happy endings!"

They left the floor behind them, and Zizi leapt on top of the stretcher bed, next to Felix, hoping she balanced the weights closely enough. She had jumped out through the hole just in time, and they were free-falling through the air. The wind blew through her hair. Dust clouds kicked up as an entire wing of the hospital thundered apart. Zizi pressed her lips to Felix's cheek, a goodbye kiss just in case this really was the end. Then, squeezing her eyes shut, Zizi clutched the sheets, waiting for the moment when their bodies hit the earth and their souls joined the stars.

~ ~ ~

The boy held the bag of popcorn out to the wolf. The beast growled. It flashed its red eyes full of hate and bared its terrible teeth, but it did not attack. Wolf was afraid. He hated this creature. No, he despised it. It disgusted him.

But he forced himself to look the beast in the eye with a bag of popcorn extended as a token of peace, and the longer he looked the more he saw. The wolf was made of paper, placed under a spell it could not understand, abandoned to a terrible task by a master who thought more of his own desires than of the welfare of those for whom he claimed to care. The beast could have been powerful, but it had a fragile spirit, deadly but it had not the heart. And it was alone.

The wolf prowled around Wolfgang, sniffing and snarling at him as though it were trying to detect some deception. And the longer the beast prowled, the softer Wolf's heart grew towards him. He placed the bag on the ground and took a step back. With cautious treads, the wolf approached. It sniffed the bag and licked up a piece. And then another. And another, until his whole muzzle was buried in the bag. Step by step, Wolf neared the beast again and reached out his hand, vulnerable and defenseless. No weapons, no tricks, no backup, no other plans—this would be the end.

~ ~ ~

Maya held her ground and gritted her teeth, the darkness pressing into her, pouring into her, reaching to the furthest extremities and the greatest depths of her heart. It felt like every nerve was being crushed at once, but she would not give up ground. Not anymore. Too long, she had feared the dark. No more.

But how could she hold on when the light was fading this fast? To break the curse, she had to preserve the light in the dark, but there was none to be found.

The clouds circled around Maya. She was completely surrounded, and the poison closed in overhead, stranding her in utter darkness, completely cut off from help. The next strike hit, and Maya gasped, her resolve faltering, her strength failing. The clouds passed not through her but into her, into her very being, a poison that ate her from the inside out. Only a list of names ran through her mind. Felix. Dad. Mom. Tania. Zizi. Wolf. Mr. and Mrs. Mori. Ran. How many more had been affected?

Maya shook her head, trying to clear it of the shadows, and planted her feet for the next attack. She had endured seven years without a mother, seven months without a father, and seven days without a brother. She could endure another seven seconds, seven minutes, seven eternities if it meant the end.

A blast knocked her off her feet. The packed earth met her with a wooden kiss. Maya groaned and pushed herself to her knees, her breaths ragged, her muscles burning, everything within her crying out to give up, to quit, to stop resisting the inevitable. The darkness had already triumphed.

Mr. Elegans's voice boomed through the black clouds, "You cannot win."

A spark flew in Maya's soul. A revelation struck her so suddenly and so certainly, she wondered how she had never seen it before. She was not alone in this fight. All along, she had had an ally, and it was not Mr. Elegans as she had once supposed. No, her ally was the Library of Souls itself. From the beginning, the Library had chosen her, helped her, and empowered her. The Library had instilled strength in Maya that she never realized she possessed, and the Library was with her now. The power was hers if she chose. Through the Library of Souls, Maya had done impossible things already, far greater than shadow and ash. After all, what was shadow without the light that cast it? And ash without the fire that created it? She fought for the Library, the force of life, and so long as it remained, the streams of life held power to wash away all the decay. And Maya was the champion of that force. Shadows could not hurt her. A small smirk cracked on her face. With a final push, Maya forced herself back to her feet. The light was not totally gone. Not yet.

For there once was a dragon born, like all dragons, from chaos and destruction, blood and ash. This dragon guarded a golden treasure more precious than all the jewels in the world, a golden city fed by the golden streams of life. But a wizard cursed the city, and it fell into eternal night. When all hope had been abandoned and the light seemed lost forever, flames stirred to life from deep within the dragon and, into the darkness, the dragon breathed.

Maya's fists clenched as the next bombardment began. She took a step forward. In that moment, Maya understood the cost of breaking the curse. It was a price she would gladly pay for her brother and her father, for her stepmother and her friends, and for all those who had tasted the despair and the pain brought on by the Wizard. She took another step. Surrounded by nothing but darkness, the champion cried out with the very essence of her spirit, with the last vestiges of her strength, with that final hope that flared in the depths of her spirit, growing into a mighty inferno, the cry of one prepared to fall in battle to secure a victory bought by blood, and the cry of one already victorious: "I AM MAYA RODRIGUEZ, CHAMPION OF THE LIBRARY OF SOULS, AND YOU HAVE NO POWER HERE."

Words spoken from the soul with all the might of a dragon. Light burst forth from Maya, yellow and red and platinum and white—blinding white. The darkness shrunk and fell away, for it could not extinguish light any more than silence could muffle a roar. Evil could never triumph where love stood firm.

Empty handed and surrounded by soot and ash, the fallen remains of his magic, Mr. Elegans stared at Maya in shock. Every shelf stood empty, every book consumed. Only the thinnest trickle ran through the streams of the library, one soul that continued to pour out light and life amidst the destruction. One soul of one girl. That trickle remained, and there was life. There was life, and the Wizard was powerless.

~ ~ ~

As Wolf caressed the beast's scalp, it disintegrated into the pages from which it had been born. Paper swirled through the air like confetti. Through the leaves, Wolf saw his reflection in the mirror, and for the first time in far too many years, he saw someone he could perhaps learn to like staring back at him.

His mother groaned, and Wolf rushed to her side. She was alive. A little worse for the wear, but still alive. And so was he. A laugh bubbled up inside him, and he could no longer contain his joy and relief. The room had been shredded, the desk smashed, the bookshelves splintered, but the beast was gone.

"The light," his mother croaked out.

Wolf gripped his mother closer and exclaimed, "No, don't look at the light. Stay far away from the light!"

"No, look," she snapped as she pointed at the secret room beyond the bookshelves. The books glowed like the dawn, and trails of dust gathered themselves into golden swirls.

Wolf stared in wonder. That light could only mean one thing. "She did it. She won. She beat the Wizard."

"The night has ended. At last," his mother smiled. And not just with her lips. Her eyes smiled too. Then, she turned to Wolf with a stern look and said, "Also, what that monster said is the biggest load of horse manure I have ever heard. You are very, very loved."

Wolf squeezed his mother in a tight hug, which was not particularly compatible with her stiff posture but, despite her obvious discomfort, she managed a moderately affectionate pat on the back. As another laugh bubbled up, Wolf said, "I know. I love you, too."

~ ~ ~

Felix sat upright with a bolt, his eyes wide with terror. Zizi tackled him in an excited hug, "Felix, you're awake."

"Then why are we still falling?" he screamed.

Zizi slammed him back down against the stretcher bed. "You're throwing off the balance."

The wind rushed past them, an explosion rang through the air, and a shadow fell over the pair as the hospital wall toppled. The blood drained from Felix's face. "Zizi, what is going on?"

"It's kind of like the egg project. Only we're the eggs."

"Zizi, our egg died!"

"Hold on," she braced for impact. And braced a little longer. And a little longer. And they still had not struck the asphalt. Zizi peaked over the edge of the stretcher bed. They were gliding a few feet above the rubble below. She craned her neck further. "Oscar?"

The griffin's wings extended on either side of the stretcher. In his teeth, he gripped the yarn Zizi had strung around the lead pipes. Just as they passed outside the demolition zone, the yarn tore, and the flight came to a bumpy end.

Oscar bounced into Felix's lap, and Felix rubbed behind the winged lion's ear. "Who's a good boy? Who's a good boy?" The winged lion panted and wagged his tail. "That's right. You are." With an excited nod, the lion took flight and circled through the air like a kid showing off a trophy. Felix chuckled and ran his fingers across his cheek. He paused as he brushed against a thin film of lip gloss. He turned to Zizi with wide eyes, "You didn't kiss me, did you?"

Zizi blushed and fumbled for knitting needles that were not there. Stumbling over her words, she explained, "We were dying and the world was ending and—"

Felix grinned, "Wanna...do it again?"

She did.

In the midst of the rubble and the destruction and the collapse, the princess and the knight found each other at last, and for them, the world began anew.

~ ~ ~

Leo Rodriguez blinked as the fog lifted from him. How long had he been trapped here? How long had he been away from his children, Felix and Maya, from his wife, Tania? His limbs felt heavy, like he had awoken from a long and restless slumber. He blinked again. He could not believe his eyes. The Library was in ruins. The books were gone, the golden streams were nearly dry, and black soot covered every surface.

A drop of water fell on his head. Then, another struck his nose. Big, bright splotches wetted the floor as golden raindrops fell like stars shining through the haze. The waterfall swelled into a torrential downpour. Golden streams overflowed their banks, flooding every corner of the Library, washing away the soot. Pages rose from the waters, slowly at first, then faster and faster, and they filled the air like a swarm of birds taking flight as they returned to their homes on the shelf, every book, every leaf, every line restored. Leo splashed through the waters, staring at the spectacle in awe. His prayers had been heard. Someone had broken the curse once and for all.

He turned the corner into the central clearing of the Library of Souls. The pages parted for just a moment, and his heart stopped. Amidst the torrent, a girl collapsed to the floor, and Tania rushed to her side, wrapping her arms around a body that lay motionless in the pool of gold. Maya.

~ ~ ~

The voices were incoherent at first. Just noise. Familiar noise. Someone calling her name. Golden light wrapped around her like sunshine streaming through the window on a lazy Saturday morning when there was no reason to leave the embrace of the covers. She never wanted it to end. Then again, this brand of sunshine was also kind of wet. And she could feel arms wrapped around her body. Maya's eyes fluttered open. Tania's face hovered just above her own, her eyes glistening. Her lips lit up in a smile.

Maya tried to stand again, but her legs buckled under her, and she gripped Tania for support. She was so tired. So, so tired. The last of the pages returned to their places, the Library gleamed like the sun, and the water receded back into the streams.

Across the clearing, Mr. Elegans still stood, looking down at his hands in horror as his skin turned papery and pale, the full weight of the curse realized upon him. Pages peeled away from his hollow shell, and he looked up at Maya one more time, terror-stricken, before he burst apart—the Wizard nothing more than paper in the wind.

A man sprinted through the flurry of pages, and Maya's spirit leapt. "Dad."

Her father enveloped her in an all-encompassing embrace, his arms wrapping around her like a shield. So long as those arms were around her, nothing bad could ever happen. Maya buried her face in his bear-like chest and breathed in the scent of fire and wool sweaters and dusty books, and she started to cry and laugh at the same time, a rush of emotions flowing over her. She did not know what she was feeling anymore. She just knew she was bursting with it. Just loud enough for him to hear, her voice breaking, she whispered, "You're home."

Her father held her tighter and rested his chin on the crown of her head, "I'm home. I'm finally home."

FIFTEEN

Thus, our tale begins

Maya scrunched up her face as Tania fussed over her hair one more time. She was wearing it up in her usual two bushy bunches for the ceremony, but somehow it had only become more unruly. Tapping her foot impatiently against the library floors, Maya squirmed out of Tania's reach.

"Saving the world is no excuse for poor grooming," her stepmother chastised her as she tucked a strand behind Maya's ear. Maya groaned. "Just for this one day, could you at least try to look presentable?"

"It's just us. Well, us and Franco," Maya complained, but she finally let Tania put on the last touches with only a slight scowl. A couple dozen chairs had been set up in the school library—it was still in the late stages of refurbishment since Maya had almost burned it down at the beginning of the school year, although arguably that was not her fault. Dazzling sunlight poured through the tall windows lining both sides of the long room and danced across the trellises of yellow sunflowers leaned against the unfinished wood paneling on the walls. The whole room was filled with familiar faces. In one corner sat a stone giant wearing a knitted hat and knitting a tiny scarf as baby pebbles and toddler rocks hopped around his massive feet and on his massive shoulders. The gnomes filled a full four rows, all dressed up in suits and ties as they strutted about, flashing sample packs of their best-selling "Strong Gnome" protein powder to anyone within reach. Even the cult had come at Zizi's invitation, bearing suspiciously delicious brownies. Felix immediately swapped recipes.

Franco was hiding in the back corner, wearing a trench coat, a hat, and sunglasses as he snapped photos of various flower arrangements, provided courtesy of Sunnyside Flowers. Somehow, he missed the giants and the gnomes. Maya was surprised to see him since he had been so busy recently with a number of unusual stories. First, the hospital collapsed due to unexplained structural instabilities in Felix's wing—no casualties, but a huge repair bill and much drama. At the same time, a team of medical professionals sought psychological help for their shared hallucination of a dragon. Then, Maya's father returned from the grave to resume his role in the school library. And finally, a new principal was hired, but it didn't last long. He took a liking to the sword hanging behind the desk until one day he used it as a fly swatter. That was the deadest fly that ever flew. The office blew up and the sword was never seen again. The principal quit the next day.

"Done." Tania stepped away from her work and nodded approvingly.

"Not bad," Wolf said as he leaned against the back wall in a black dress shirt and black jeans and black shoes—nothing much had changed there. Tania slipped past him to her seat in the front row. Under her chair, Oscar was curled up, taking a nap in a sunbeam. "I don't think I've ever seen you in a dress before."

"It's harder to run," Maya grumbled as she shifted uncomfortably and shook her uneven bangs loose again. The dress was Tania's idea. It was simple and red and the only one Maya had not fought tooth and nail against.

Wolf glanced down at her Converse, "I'm surprised your stepmother didn't wrestle those shoes straight off your feet, though."

Maya laughed, "She tried. Until she saw me walk in heels. I'm not very good."

"Who says you have to be good to have fun," Wolf smirked as he pushed himself off the wall and sauntered closer. "In my experience, the opposite has always been true."

"I'm sure it has," Maya rolled her eyes and brushed past him towards the center aisle. Her gaze drifted to a man with Wolf's nose jutting out between hollow cheeks. He slumped in his chair in the front row, and his eyes stared off at some unknown point in the distance.

"How is your father?" Maya asked as Wolf joined her.

"He's getting better. Slowly." Wolf sighed. "He's having more moments of lucidity, but I don't think he'll ever be the same. Sometimes the damage can't be undone," he shrugged. They lingered in silence for a few moments. Until Maya nudged Wolf with her elbow, and a hint of a smile broke through his cool façade.

With a clatter, Felix and Zizi tumbled into the library with a tray of cookies and a thousand toothpicks sticking out of their clothes. A shrill war cry echoed through the hall as the library door swung shut behind them. Felix gasped for breath as he turned to Maya, "Did you know there are talking mice at this school?"

"You didn't kill their prince, did you?" Maya asked, wincing a little.

Felix and Zizi exchanged a baffled glance before Zizi said, "How did you know?"

Wolf tossed a handful of popcorn into his mouth as he said, "Are we sure that guy isn't narcoleptic?"

The war cries died down as someone squeaked, "False alarm. Still alive."

Maya's father approached and cleared his throat, "Ready, Maya?" She nodded, and the others scattered to find their seats.

As they waited at the back of the library for the ceremony to begin, Maya set her jaw and fixed her gaze on the podium at the end of the library. Mrs. Mori stood center stage. Finally,

Maya asked, "Now that the Library of Souls is open again, how much danger are the books in?"

Her father chuckled with a deep, throaty laugh and placed a wide palm on Maya's shoulder, "We can worry about that later. For now, let's celebrate." Maya nodded, and they stepped out into the light.

All eyes turned to the pair as they strode side by side to the raised platform at the far end. When they reached the end, Maya's father announced, "I present the candidate for induction into the Order of the Librarians."

Mrs. Mori turned her hawk eyes on Maya and asked, "Do you swear to defend the Library of Souls to the best of your abilities till the end of your days?"

Her voice steady and sure, Maya responded, "I swear it."

"Do you swear to protect the innocent and the defenseless, every soul that looks to you for strength and guidance in the darkest times?"

"I swear it."

"And do you, Maya, swear to serve the world as an ambassador of peace and light, of hope and courage from this day forth, until your tale comes to an end?"

"I swear it."

Her father beamed, a broad smile lighting up his face as he lifted a golden sash from the podium and draped it across Maya's neck. "Ladies and gentlemen, in recognition of her outstanding service, sacrifice, and strength of will in the face of tremendous darkness, I am proud to present to you the first new Librarian in a generation, my daughter and the Champion of the Seven Books of the Library of Souls: Maya Rod—"

A roar shook the room as a red dragon crashed through the windows, raining shards of glass down on the crowd. At the same time, Franco snapped a photo of just the wrong flower arrangement, and a squad of special agents rushed into the library. Once more, the library dissolved into chaos as the people screamed and tripped over each other, running for the exits. The dragon landed in front of Maya, a desperate plea in its eyes, and roared again.

"Trouble?" Felix asked, tossing Maya a fire extinguisher.

Maya hopped onto the dragon's back and grinned, "Let's find out." Of course, they would quickly discover that the dragon's "emergency" consisted of a shortage of apples. Still, in that moment, the world was full of possibilities. With a glint in her eye and adventure in her heart, Maya took to the skies.

CPSIA information can be obtained
at www.ICGtesting.com
Printed in the USA
LVOW04s1602191115
463343LV00018B/1408/P